Praise for *A Wonderful Stroke of Luck*

"Every sentence shines with wit, originality, and sharp observations."
—*The Boston Globe*

"Ms. Beattie captures the exhilarating feeling of being young and gifted and specially selected for stardom, but the bulk of her novel is about the long anticlimax that is real life. . . . This is Ms. Beattie's first novel since 2002, but readers of her short stories will be fully at home with its discursive style. . . . The effect is a radical decentering that comes near to conveying the essential disorientation of experience."
—Sam Sacks, *The Wall Street Journal*

"Even if you're not old enough to remember the thrill of reading Beattie's first-ever story to be published in *The New Yorker*, you'll find that the short fiction master's latest foray into long form is a marvel of wry wit and wisdom."
—*O, The Oprah Magazine*

"Ann Beattie's twenty-first book proves to be her best. *A Wonderful Stroke of Luck* shows a complicated relationship between a brilliant teacher and his boarding school students. His influence on them—and their secrets—continues as they become adults."
—*Good Housekeeping* (Best Books of 2019)

"Given a week on a deserted island with a shelf of boarding-school novels, I'd start off with *A Separate Peace*, plow through *Prep* for the tenth time, and then end with *A Wonderful Stroke of Luck*, Beattie's foray into the #MeToo movement, which asks how deeply we internalize the lessons of charismatic, if vaguely nefarious, teachers. . . . A master class."
—Hillary Kelly, *Vulture*

"Ann Beattie's twenty-first book is the work of a master storyteller at the height of her talents. . . . It's a remarkable novel that feels so utterly real that it defies convention. It works the way life works, which is to say with misdirection and events that feel random but probably aren't. It calls to mind, in different ways, both *Stoner* and *The Secret History*—which are, incidentally, two of my all-time favorite novels."　　　　　—Andrew Ervin, *Los Angeles Review of Books*

"I found [*A Wonderful Stroke of Luck*'s] twists and shadows full of secrets and surprises. . . . What makes Beattie's work so interesting, to me, is its resistance to conventional, formal narrative structure. Its artistry is in its wit and its humanity, its remarkable formal verisimilitude. . . . *A Wonderful Stroke of Luck* left me feeling as if I'd expanded my circle of real life acquaintances. . . . I found myself frequently startled by the accuracy, perceptiveness, specificity, and humor of Beattie's observations."　　　　　—Rachel Lyon, *Electric Literature*

"Beattie's writing with its clever rhythm of observation, reflection, and speculation . . . disorients us even as it seems to be moving us forward. . . . *A Wonderful Stroke of Luck* puts us in its well-meaning but hapless protagonist's position—moving ahead, not necessarily getting anywhere, but graced along the way with moments that occasionally confer their own meaning."　　　　　—*Minneapolis Star Tribune*

"How do our charismatic teachers set the stage for the rest of our lives? That's one of the questions that Ann Beattie tackles in this novel. When a former New England boarding school student named Ben looks back on his childhood, he starts to question the motives of his superstar teacher. Later on, his teacher gets in contact, and Ben has to grapple with his legacy."　　　　　—*The Millions*

"I would read anything by Beattie."　　　　　—Lila Shapiro, *Vulture*

"An intellectually rich book with a razor-sharp sense of irony . . . mesmerizingly elegant . . . beautiful to read."　　　　　—*Vox*

"[Beattie's] elegantly sculpted tale is both wrenchingly sad and ultimately enigmatic: as usual." —*Kirkus Reviews* (starred review)

"Gimlet-eyed Beattie has created a stunningly unnerving and provocative tale spiked with keen cultural allusions and drollery. This jarring dissection of privilege and anxiety, gender expectations, lust, ludicrous predicaments, defensive selfishness, moral confusion, and numbing loneliness projects a matrix of angst somewhat countered by the solace and sustenance found in a quiet life far from the grasping, hurried, hostile world. . . . Beattie's literary reign continues apace, thanks to her stealthily eviscerating insights and disquieting wit." —*Booklist* (starred review)

"Beattie details with precision the ambiguities and self-deceptions of Ben and the other teenagers, and shows compassion as she tracks the missteps of a generation shaped by the 9/11 attack."

—Jane Ciabattari, *BBC Culture*

"A deep and interesting novel." —Cosmo.com

"The novel has the mesmeric quality of remembering late youth, its chaos and loose ends, the sweet taste of being free to make bad decisions, the astringency of their potential consequences." —*Public Books*

"Beattie's latest novel . . . is riven with hope and humor. . . . [A] postmodernist Greek tragedy . . . laugh-out-loud humorous . . . Beattie [has] a keen ear for not only what is said but also what is left unsaid, often with tragic consequences." —*BookPage*

ALSO BY ANN BEATTIE

The Accomplished Guest
The State We're In
Mrs. Nixon: A Novelist Imagines a Life
The New Yorker Stories
Walks with Men
Follies
The Doctor's House
Perfect Recall
Park City
My Life, Starring Dara Falcon
Another You
What Was Mine
Picturing Will
Where You'll Find Me
Love Always
The Burning House
Falling in Place
Secrets and Surprises
Chilly Scenes of Winter
Distortions

A
Wonderful
Stroke
of Luck

{ *a novel* }

ANN BEATTIE

PENGUIN BOOKS

PENGUIN BOOKS
An imprint of Penguin Random House LLC
penguinrandomhouse.com

First published in the United States of America by Viking,
an imprint of Penguin Random House LLC, 2019
Published in Penguin Books 2020

ISBN 9780525557364 (paperback)

THE LIBRARY OF CONGRESS HAS CATALOGED THE HARDCOVER EDITION AS FOLLOWS:
Names: Beattie, Ann, author.
Title: A wonderful stroke of luck : a novel / Ann Beattie.
Description: New York : Viking, [2019] |
Identifiers: LCCN 2018028798 (print) | LCCN 2018030241 (ebook) |
ISBN 9780525557357 (ebook) | ISBN 9780525557340 (hardcover)
Classification: LCC PS3552.E177 (ebook) | LCC PS3552.E177 W66 2019 (print) |
DDC 813/.54—dc23
LC record available at https://lccn.loc.gov/2018028798

Printed in the United States of America
1   3   5   7   9   10   8   6   4   2

Set in Janson
Designed by Gretchen Achilles

For Lincoln

*"Remember that sometimes not getting what you want
is a wonderful stroke of luck."*

—THE DALAI LAMA

A
Wonderful
Stroke
of Luck

One

LaVerdere's Leading Lights, a.k.a. The Honor Society. There were many organizations for overachievers at Bailey Academy, but being selected for LaVerdere's group gave them nicknames and an identity. They belonged to him. And, very important, he was more young than old. At Bailey, some students' studies involved an emphasis on mathematics (the Math Majors Club was their Honor Society; its members were known informally as The Brains). There was little gossip about Dr. Timothy Ha, who was in charge of that particular club. He looked right through you outside of class, hurrying, always hurrying toward his flashy red sports car. Dr. Ha was a teetotaler. The Brains spread the word that LaVerdere gave the Honor Society students wine. He didn't. It was sparkling nonalcoholic cider. LaVerdere had gone to Columbia, then Oxford. The persistent rumor was that he'd had a wife who'd died of pneumonia in England.

An hour or so before, Ben had gone with Jasper (sulking, in the backseat) and Jasper's father, Mr. Cabot, to pick up Jasper's new drug prescription. In math class, as he'd studied the computation on the blackboard, Jasper had "seen something" and stood up to whirl along with the 3-D vision. Jesus. Ben could understand how they could be a pain in the ass. Dr. Ha was certainly not up to even the most exquisitely polite human interaction, let alone a student's going Sufi on him in class. When they'd returned, there'd been a very awkward moment when The Man had second thoughts after dropping them off; he'd pulled on the handbrake, jumped out of the car, and blurted, "Jasper, I'm just so sorry, so really sorry, that your mother and I couldn't work things out. If I'd known about the breast cancer I'd never have left. It's your mother who won't have me back."

Jasper had pushed the bag he was holding toward Ben as if it had suddenly become too heavy. Then he'd stepped forward and awkwardly embraced his father before turning and running onto the campus. Talk about being *left holding the bag*. "It's okay," Ben had said lamely to Jasper's father. "Good to see you, Mr. C. Okay, well, see you again, then. Okay." The Man had said nothing; he'd only pressed his palms to his eyes before jumping through the still-open car door into the driver's seat and racing away. His hat lay on the ground. Jesus, what had The Man been thinking, wearing a beret with a white shirt and sweatpants? Ben had picked it up and stuffed it into his pocket. At some opportune moment—though when could that possibly be?—he'd return it.

When Ben and Jasper walked into the Honor Society meeting, LaVerdere was already holding forth: "Talk's overrated. We see an example of this in our current president, George W. Bush, who cannot articulate a comprehensible thought—though politicians who preceded him, such as the estimable Gerald Ford, who pardoned President Richard M. Nixon, were notorious for *actually* falling on their asses." LaVerdere's hands shot into the air.

Oh, the guy could be excruciating—as could anyone whose in-jokes were primarily with himself. Those fey gestures! The way his chin jutted out parodically. His heart was in the right place, though, and he aimed to please at the "social" (as he was amused to call it), where Tessie Ryall and her daughter, Binnie, who (as Lou-Lou observed) might have been Dickens characters, ferried trays to and fro. No saltines that shattered like glass when rubbery cheese squares were placed atop them; that was the math club's bad luck. As everyone knew, Dr. Ha cared nothing about food.

Today there were also enormous purple seedless grapes—a nod, perhaps, to their recent discussion of Cesar Chavez. LaVerdere gestured. As Tessie and Binnie exited the kitchen carrying trays, LaVerdere lowered his voice and suggested that the coffee they were about to be served was sure to be made from freshly roasted beans from an impeccably run Brazilian organic farm too obscure to have been found even by dengue-carrying mosquitoes. Considering that LaVerdere seemed to like to hang out with them, there were endless things they didn't know about him, and even the boldest hesitated to ask. Who were his friends? What did he do in the summer? No teacher had his or her age listed in the faculty directory, so there was no way to check that. Almost every teacher and staff member used an informal snapshot. Dr. Ha was the only one who'd used a formal photograph. Jasper had discovered that the photograph LaVerdere used was Spalding Gray's. It had crossed Ben's mind, the first day he'd met him, that LaVerdere might be gay, though nothing would easily explain him. Ben had never met anyone who seemed so energetic, yet gave off no sexual vibe. It was LouLou—during one of their late-night talks—who'd been smart enough to add, "except toward himself." They agreed, though: LaVerdere was straight. The only thing Ben had ever seen LaVerdere put the moves on was a box turtle he'd been intent on saving from a riding mower.

A conversation had begun between Aqua and LaVerdere. The subject seemed to be whether things that were enigmatic held more fascination than things transparent—the question being: Might we be impressed by having to figure something out, while sometimes failing to appreciate equally important ideas merely because they seemed so accessible?

"What would be an example?" Ben asked LaVerdere. He didn't want to ask Aqua, because she construed every question as a quiz and talked until she ran out of information. She'd grown up in D.C. Her father had been ambassador to Belgium. The year before, he'd given a talk at Bailey about the Walloons, which had been informative not so much because of the subject, but because it explained the way Aqua could focus your attention on her, rather than her topic. Her real name was Aquinnah, which they knew to call her when her father visited.

"Whether willing, but not rigorously trained civilians should be granted their wish to be launched into space," LaVerdere replied.

It was absolutely impossible to outguess the guy.

"So would that be analogous to really bright kids who've screwed up being sent to a New England boarding school?" Hailey asked.

"Has that happened?" Phillip Collins asked, his voice drowning her out. He stopped plugging grapes into his mouth long enough to speak. He hovered behind Ben.

"Indeed it has. I refer to the situation of the very wealthy, accomplished private citizen Dennis Tito. Surely someone has heard of Mr. Tito?"

No one answered.

"Ah. Well, he recently became the world's first space tourist. This was very exciting to Mr. Tito, if not to you. He was a former NASA employee who followed the money. He left his job there and became an investment manager, I believe. But he wanted to orbit the Earth, not sit behind a desk. While he was no doubt qualified in his areas of expertise, Mr. Tito's wishes caused a howl of objection. A mere businessman, in space? The U.S. wouldn't do it—and we might later discuss whether this was a brave and noble refusal on principle, or yet another ill-considered bureaucratic decision. So he appealed to the Russians. Mr. Tito spent seven days, twenty-two hours, and some minutes in space. He did this because it was his passion, and perhaps with an eye toward how it could improve his business in the future—this was what others hinted at, though not Mr. Tito. Primarily"—(*who* but LaVerdere began any sentence with the word "primarily"?)—"he was able to do this because he was rich. Here's my question: Do you think a lottery should have been held, or do you think the rich are entitled to special privileges? Remember that we live in a democracy, or an ostensible democracy. It's an interesting question, though Mr. Tito has orbited Earth a hundred and twenty-eight times, whatever we decide."

"Rich guys pretty much get to do what they want, don't they?" Aqua said. "Isn't the question more who'd stop them?"

"Perhaps, but let's first consider this from the perspective of Mr. Tito—a man of means who quite simply wants something.

Do we find it important to know if what he wants is for personal benefit or the benefit of others? Would knowing that change our minds about his trip?"

"How do we know a person to be egalitarian?" Akemi Hayashi-Myers asked. Since she always answered her own questions, or tried to, there was a pause. She said, "Because we observe their lifelong actions. We cannot just accept their self-regard."

For a while, LouLou Sils, who was hands down the coolest girl at school, with her fantastic chocolate-brown hair and white skin, had amused them behind Akemi's back with a good imitation of her, but their new classmate (who'd joined them only the year before) had grown on them. The moment Akemi spoke, she became less shy. She'd befriended Darius Beltz, which no one else had made much of an attempt to do, and LouLou's gentle chiding was now directed at Akemi. Akemi was no longer shocked if you linked arms with her as you walked from building to building. She'd learned to come up beside people expectantly.

"You mean, like, in space he's going to discover something that leads to the cure for cancer?" Phillip Collins said.

Ben was glad Jasper hadn't yet wandered over to join in. His mother's breast cancer, stage three, was a topic he didn't want to discuss and one that he couldn't avoid; the mention of cancer would have lit Jasper with worry.

"A good question, Phillip," LaVerdere replied. He always commended Phillip Collins when he spoke, because others so rarely did. "What if he believes this might be helpful in that pursuit, or what if he's simply invoking that attitude in order to add legitimacy to what he wishes to do? We think we understand someone's reason for a particular act, but we also have to rely on what we know of precedent, hmm? You'll all remember making fun of me for my deeply held belief that the world is inherently an individual, subjective experience—though we must nevertheless strive to understand it in objective terms. Mr. Tito might be quite straightforward in what he says, but even then, there's the question of what he tells himself versus what is, more objectively, the case."

"*Crime and Punishment*," Benson Whitacre said. "That book's flypaper. Any idea you toss out sticks to it. The thing we're really always talking about is *Crime and Punishment*."

"I promise not to mention it," LaVerdere said. "Ben—any thoughts?"

"Why haven't any of us heard of him?"

"I knew about it. I just didn't know his name," Aqua said. "There was a story on NPR a while ago. Somebody's making a documentary." She turned to look at Jasper, who had just joined the group.

"Is that right?" LaVerdere said. "I didn't know that, but I suppose it seems inevitable."

"Rich people get news coverage for things that ordinary people—even though there's no such thing as an *ordinary person*—have no access to," Jasper said.

"Notice that we keep circling the issue of wealth," LaVerdere said. "Would we be more interested if the nonexistent *ordinary man*—or woman—was plucked from the street in Manhattan and sent into orbit? Might we think we'd find out something from him or her that would be precluded from the perspective of a man who belongs to the upper class?"

"To be honest, I don't get the feeling any of us care about this guy," Jasper said. "I don't think space travel is all that fascinating. I mean, maybe it—"

"Ah. Then does this become a generational question? If Mr.

Tito had gone into space, say, during the time Henry Ford was developing the automobile, or even thirty years ago—let's make it more recent—might we have been quite interested, then, perhaps even staging a parade upon his return?"

"They didn't even do that for Vietnam vets. It was supposed to freak them out because of their PTSD," Aqua said. "That, or people who didn't fight felt too guilty to beat the drums and throw confetti. So if we don't acknowledge people who fought for our country, or for all of us, supposedly, why get all excited about some millionaire who goes into space?"

If *Crime and Punishment* was LaVerdere's favorite text, Aqua's was *Dispatches,* by Michael Herr. This was apparent not only to Ben, but to everyone. Like information revealed by the depth and configuration of lines in the palm of the hand, knowing a person's favorite book was informative. Akemi Hayashi-Myers liked Dostoyevsky (in particular, *Notes from the Underground*). She'd skipped two grades, but Mr. Myers felt his daughter should spend another year with classmates closer to her own age before accepting early admission to Princeton.

"You don't really care about him, do you, Mr. LaVerdere?" Hailey asked. It was a very Hailey sort of remark; she often perceived a basic flaw in a question. The rest of them tended to try to avoid that quagmire—pointing out the invisible—with LaVerdere, who was excited to the point of distraction by any mention of things unseen.

"Whatever my feelings about him, Mr. Tito is a case in point," LaVerdere said. "Though you're prescient in understanding that, to me, he's just an example of something and someone."

"Not to his mother!" Jasper said. He'd been hovering at the edge of the group and had finally poured himself a glass of seltzer.

He knew he'd gotten off a good one. As he stifled a belch, he nudged Ben's shoulder.

"Remember 'The Lady, or The Tiger?'" LaVerdere asked. "Do you think anything about that pertains?"

"Not unless they're debating whether to put more millionaires into space or a bunch of ladies," Hailey said.

"Have I presented all of you with an insurmountable obstacle in mentioning Mr. Tito's financial situation?"

"In your case? If I can turn it around and ask you to go on record, Mr. LaVerdere? You should probably take the lady. Because like Blake said—make that '*as* Blake said'—the jury's out on fearful symmetry," Aqua said.

Aqua got thinner and thinner and wore baggy clothes to hide the weight loss. Aqua was human Velcro, her words the tiny loops she hoped would attach her to whomever she'd cornered. Ben and Jasper agreed that you could almost see her thinking, her eyes locked on the distance like someone peeing in a pool. She'd been expelled from Simon's Rock for a mysterious offense she found too painful to discuss. That was something you could allude to if you needed to silence her, like a little verbal crack chunk put in an addict's palm, or a bit of Kryptonite presented to Superman. Phillip Collins's uncle was dating a teacher at Aqua's former school, and he'd promised to sniff around and try to find out what Aqua's offense had been, though it had happened before his girlfriend was hired.

LaVerdere, accepting a refill of sparkling cider from Binnie (his nickname for her: Binnie Mouse), mentioned that his twin sister lived in a town where Carlos Leon had just moved and opened a fitness studio that also offered nighttime tap classes. Property values were expected to rise.

"Who's that?" Hailey asked.

"Madonna's former personal trainer and the father of her daughter," LaVerdere answered.

Aqua caught LouLou's eye. Who cared about him? LaVerdere had a twin?

"What are your sister's interests?" Ben said. He'd learned not to ask what people did. In Europe, it was considered gauche, and when did the United States not take its social cues from France (as his stepmother—who was Swedish—had asked, yet again subtly informing him of something he hadn't known).

"Her interests? She has quite a few. She's a photographer. She develops her own black-and-white prints that she sells at a gallery in Hudson. She sings with an a cappella group. She and her husband make their living as organic farmers."

"Cool," Ben said. "So what things does she enjoy farming?"

"What does she grow? The vegetables are pretty much the usual suspects, but she's in the process of getting certified to make goat cheese. She's working with an Amish man and his sons."

"Good deal," Ben said. He'd finally broken the habit of saying, "Cool." Next, he supposed, he'd be able to hold a thin china teacup and set it down without breaking the rim of the saucer (because he habitually broke fragile things, the cups and saucers had disappeared and been replaced with mugs). Manners—which his father's second wife called "protocols"—were All Important. He got that.

"Have any of you had experience on a farm?" LaVerdere asked. He seemed more relaxed, after putting behind them the case of Dennis Tito. Why did LaVerdere have to have such a wind-up to the pitch, every time they met? Did he think up his topics the night before, then professorially unload them, secretly hoping the issues they raised would soon conclude? For quite a while, Ben had been a holdout, seeing the examples as contrived. It had come as a relief to Ben when he realized the guy was probably just anxious and felt more was expected of him than he was providing. "And you, Hailey?" LaVerdere asked. Hailey was also processing the revelation about another, female LaVerdere. She had one eye and wore a convex eye patch. She was an excellent soccer player who was being recruited by almost every Ivy League college, but what she really wanted was to play the cymbals with Stiff Formaldehyde. She'd already had a baby with Stiff and given it up for adoption.

She said, "I spent some time on a ranch in Montana." (She'd told Ben about that; her mother had arranged for her to stay there during the last months of her pregnancy.) "It was owned by a friend of Ted Turner's. We watched movies in a screening room we helped build out of a storeroom. You know what was being stored? Towers of toilet paper. Our host managed to work Turner's name into any conversation. We sort of hoped he'd show up, just to give his friend a thrill."

"Who was that famous old lady who divorced Ted Turner?" Aqua asked.

"Jane Fonda," Ben replied. He knew this because Jane Fonda and his stepmother belonged to the same environmental organization. Her face appeared on every other issue of the increasingly thinner monthly magazine Elin got in the mail.

"When Hollywood gossip starts, I leave," LaVerdere said, with a bemused smile.

"If you go, we might start talking about sex and drugs," Lou-Lou said.

"Then you'd be representative of teenagers everywhere, as

most of the world chooses to see them," LaVerdere said over his shoulder. He was headed in Jasper's direction. LouLou's specialty was running away, though she stayed put on exam days. Otherwise, she was often AWOL, or grounded for disappearing. She'd made it clear she was biding time until she could move to Brooklyn. She'd written three novels—she maintained that anything over a hundred pages was a novel—and had a plan about getting an agent. Then, supposedly, the pressure would be off, and as a prolific, successful writer, she could figure out what she really wanted to do. Ben had asked her why she didn't just think harder about what that was (his father continually asked him the same thing). "Because you have to pave the way for yourself and then have a big epiphany and totally do something else to renounce all your childish dreams. It's what the culture demands."

Though Ben didn't personally find Hailey attractive, others did. He preferred LouLou. Jasper had had sex with Hailey and sort of had a crush on her, though the name LouLou Sils made his heart go pitty-pat like every other male's. The Friday-night beer delivery arrived courtesy of a boyfriend of LouLou's—this category was vague, because mostly she'd never dated the men in it.

Ben had attended quite a few cocktail parties during the summer he'd spent at his father's summer place in New Hampshire— a retreat, as his father called it, apparently thinking it necessary to summer in a more rural location than Hanover (bizarre). Elin, his new wife, rarely appeared at the parties. Ben's mother and some friends had built the porch the year he was born. He'd been told he'd slept outside in a bassinet under tinkling wind chimes, though all he remembered was later rolling out his sleeping bag and using a cushion from one of the rockers for a pillow. Their mother had been more protective of his sister, Brenda, letting her sleep in their bedroom until she started kindergarten. Now Brenda lived with a roommate in Rhode Island who'd been born missing her pinkie. She wore a finger prosthesis. Their mother had died the year Ben finished third grade. Only recently had Brenda told him that as they were growing up, she'd debated whether his closed door meant he didn't want to be disturbed, or whether he kept the door shut to avoid their father. How strange to think of Brenda hovering in the hallway before slipping away. What hadn't occurred to him was to ask what she'd wanted, though that would have been a stupid question. She couldn't have always wanted the same thing. (LaVerdere: "Observe the woodpecker. We could learn from its single-mindedness. What it does may be industrious, yet in no way mysterious, perhaps because 'animal' behavior in animals is viewed differently than compulsion would be in humans, we might assume. But does the woodpecker's action define it? Do our most concerted and observable efforts define us?")

"He just dropped it into conversation that he has a twin. Does that explain anything, do you think?" LouLou asked, when she finally drifted toward Ben.

"Everything," Ben said. "The way he looks over his shoulder when he's walking off. As if that other, ghostly presence remains."

"I like it that you've taken in so much hippie wisdom that you bring up just to be disparaging," LouLou said. "You're right, though. He does look over his shoulder."

Darius came up beside LouLou and stood there limply, in his habitual, indifferent puppet-posture, as if his arms were in someone else's control. Darius was living proof that a person could be smart and entirely lacking a sense of humor. His face had been so pocked by acne, he was scheduled to have a chemical peel after graduation. Phillip Collins's father was going to do it. Even now that the medicine had started to work and the pimple eruptions had subsided, his face was deeply pocked. His cheeks were always red.

"Gotta go," LouLou said immediately. She was usually cooler about her distaste for Darius. Her boots were nice. She looked stylish in her black tights, short white skirt, and the dark-gray hand-knit scarf she wore almost regardless of the day's temperature.

Then—appearing more like an apparition than a person—The Man, Mr. C., Jasper's father, strode across the newly installed, historically correct carpet (that, too, had a nickname: View from the Roller Coaster on LSD). Mr. C. was clasping Eleanor Rule's hand. As they'd find out later, he'd driven back to Bailey, seen Eleanor—whom he recognized, though he couldn't remember her name—and asked her if she knew where the Honor Society was meeting. She'd told him and mentioned that she felt guilty for not attending. Together they'd walked across the grass, up the stairs into the building, then entered the meeting room. Neither said anything when all conversation stopped.

"Dad," Jasper said.

"Yes, I *am*," The Man said, "and I don't know where we went off-course. If you wouldn't mind, Mr. LaVerdere? I'm here to have a conversation with my son."

"Drunk," LouLou exhaled quietly. She hadn't made her escape soon enough. Hailey touched her eye patch, the way she did when she was nervous.

"Drunk," Mr. C. said. "Did someone say I was drunk?"

LouLou looked at her boots.

"Glad to see you!" LaVerdere said. "Jasper, your father's most welcome. We should offer our guest some coffee. Mr. Cabot?"

LaVerdere's hand clasped the wrist of the other behind his back, like an obsequious maître d'. Why those guys liked to look like birds hobbled by broken wings, Ben never understood. Or why Elin loved eating at Beaujolais, though the reservation never seemed to be on the day she wanted, or at the time she preferred. LaVerdere said, with a deferential nod, "Bob Cabot, isn't that right?"

"Everything I've done is wrong," Mr. Cabot said.

"Let me get you some coffee, Mr. Cabot. What do you take in it?" Eleanor said. She wore a scarf—a scarf not nearly as fabulous as LouLou's—and red gloves lined with fur that she'd found in town, sticking up on the spikes of a fence. She had a way of finding things, but arriving with The Man had been particularly unexpected. Of course, he'd actually found her. She'd mistaken the alcohol on his breath for aftershave. It never occurred to her he might have been drinking until LouLou said the word. She pulled her gloves off slowly, as if skin were liable to come loose with each finger. Then, as if he'd answered, she strode off to get a mug from the shelf. Hailey's older sister, who'd also attended Bailey, had made the matching mugs. She'd also left behind painted portraits of a few of the teachers (including the tragically deceased Ms. Niffle, whose snowmobile had crashed into a tree), mobiles made from junk pulled out of people's trash, and a large sculpted monkey with its chest ripped open, a series of hearts morphing into a small man.

"Thank you," Bob Cabot said quaveringly to Eleanor, as she handed him one of the heavy blue mugs. "Thank you for this, and for everything." His smile was really only a twist of his lips.

"What's so fascinating?" LaVerdere asked. "Ladies and gentlemen? Please continue your conversations."

"So, when you run away next, LouLou, where will you go?" Aqua asked, loud enough for everyone to hear.

"Boston, again," LouLou said. "To continue my affair with a married man."

"Bob, they're being brats," LaVerdere said. "Pay no attention. May I join you and Jasper in those more comfortable chairs?" He gestured to a jumble of chairs with faded upholstery depicting colliding rectangles. For whatever reason, the caterer and her daughter always hauled the chairs into the corner near the kitchen door when they were setting up and left them there facing every which way, like bumper cars, when the event concluded.

"Let's take a walk, Dad," Jasper muttered.

"I'll come!" Ben said, as if the thought had just occurred to him. LaVerdere's eyes darted to Ben.

"Outta here, time to study," LouLou said.

Everyone envied LouLou her hard-soled walk across the floor, out the door.

"Okay, now we can talk about LouLou!" Aqua said.

The joke fell flat.

"Bye," Hailey said, flapping her hand as if it contained a tiny piece of laundry that needed shaking out. She hero-worshipped LouLou and would do most anything to be her devoted friend—though Hailey didn't leave; she kept touching the corner of her eye patch and seemed undecided about whether she should stay or go.

Benson Whitacre, whom Ben had forgotten was in the room, stood near the back, by the window, hiding as much as possible behind the large, potted Norfolk Island pine so that he could talk on his cell phone. Even turned off, cell phones weren't to be in evidence when they met with LaVerdere—but now Benson was chatting away inaudibly, with impunity.

"Pierre, why don't the two of us have a beer?" Mr. C. said, as if he'd just startled awake, his son standing mutely at his side.

"Sure," LaVerdere replied. "Campus is dry, of course."

"That's why we've got cars!"

"I'm *here*," Jasper said to his father. "I didn't dematerialize, or anything. The son you came to see? You come in totally unexpectedly, then you and LaVerdere decide to leave and have a beer?"

"Hey, man," Ben muttered. "TCE." It was their personal shorthand for not sweating something: Time changes everything. Instead of saying TCE, Jasper sometimes liked the long form: "You can change the name of an old song, rearrange it and make it swing . . . ." They often listened to that—country music—when they were playing chess or drinking contraband Coors. For some reason, both found the singer's deep voice funny.

"My dad holds hands with somebody he barely knows?" Jasper said. "If they want me in boarding school so my mother can suffer in silence, why not forget about me—what's with showing up to hit on my friends?"

"He didn't do anything inappropriate!" Eleanor said.

"What would he think if I showed up at his office and went in holding his secretary's hand? Nobody even knows where he's living!" Jasper said.

"That's what I want to talk to you about," The Man said.

LaVerdere steered Bob Cabot in the direction of the door, a single fingertip placed lightly on the man's shoulder. What was this? LaVerdere updating life on the Sistine ceiling?

"I've gone home!" The Man said adamantly.

All the students were grouped close together, as if they'd rushed onstage at the end of a Shakespearean play. A line popped into Ben's mind: *Our revels now are ended.* The week before, he and Jasper had listened to some famous actor reading from Shakespeare on a CD sent by Jasper's mother. They'd also eaten small, expensive candy bars she'd included, which had unfortunately melted in the package.

"Home?" Jasper said to Ben, as if the word had boomeranged to hit him on the head. "Mom let him move in again?"

"Go for a run before dinner?" Ben asked.

"Hey, Dad!" Jasper hollered, walking quickly after his father and LaVerdere.

Binnie came out and began carrying platters back into the kitchen. Hailey pulled a tube of lipstick out of her bag and began deftly coloring her lips without benefit of a mirror. Everybody had parents, so except for the particulars, the incident hadn't been hugely surprising. Like sheep who suddenly rolled themselves across safety grates all around the world at the same time, maybe Mr. C. had just been the first parent who'd unexpectedly tumbled into their midst in the throes of some existential crisis.

Ben left, but lingered outside. He did wish his friend had taken him up on the offer to jog. He could go alone. But if he did, and if Jasper changed his mind, he might miss him. "Take action. Stop thinking and take action," he could almost hear his father saying. It was what he said if you faltered for more than three seconds, trying to impale a wiggling worm on the hook. Elin had been a good influence on his father. She particularly disliked his "Take action" speech and had more or less managed to shut him up by pointing out that rushing to a conclusion didn't necessarily make that solution the right one.

The wind was blowing the tops of the oak trees.

Ben decided he'd wait ten minutes for Jasper, then go to the dining hall and worry about him after dinner. How could he return Mr. C's beret? Not that it was burning a hole in his pocket. Not like it was *money*.

It *was* cold—that stinging, fall cold that felt the way chalk on a blackboard sounded, even if winter hadn't begun. This time of year, early September, the temperature plunged in New Hampshire after three in the afternoon, though even at the end of August they'd rushed to wear their boots and their down vests at night because they had more style than limp, summer clothes. It was that time of day, twilight—Ben loved that word, *twilight*—when darkness began to pull itself around you like a shroud.

Two

Ladies and gentlemen, today Dr. Ha, though called upon, was unable to speak, so The Powers That Be have decreed that in the absence of the museum's art adviser, Ms. Alwyn-Black, who is ill, I am to say something about this painting, *The Peaceable Kingdom,* which has newly arrived at the Harriet G. and Hubert J. Felton Gallery, on permanent loan from the cousin of an alumnus." LaVerdere turned to LouLou. "Ms. Sils, if you could delay your boot repair until I have finished? Thank you kindly. To continue: It will be obvious that a version of Eden exists before us, where animals antagonistic to one another stand contentedly side by side, a small figure assumed to be the painter, Mr. Hicks, among them. Mr. Hicks was a Quaker, as you may know from the handout photocopied by Tessie. I've read a bit about Mr. Hicks, and it seems that in spite of his projected vision of peace and happiness, which makes him a premature hippie— Aqua, you are the perfect audience; thank you—he became pained as the Quaker religion split into factions: what we would call "orthodox," versus a more rural, conservative faction, with which Mr. Hicks, as a former farmer and sign painter, felt personally affiliated. In his old age, he came to believe that these differing views would not be reconciled. I suspect you will find out that this is a common attitude, one arrived at quite often by anyone who thinks, for example, that in our time the Arabs and the Jews must inevitably reconcile. This interjects a moment of current affairs, meant to jolt you awake, since I won't assume you have freely gathered here, or that you care about a depiction of lions and sheep, with a conventionally beautiful sky spread overhead. Yes, Ms. Hayashi-Myers?"

"Must we factor in that nature's beauty is impermanent, which colors perception, so to speak?"

Ben took a deep breath. To avoid answering Akemi's impossible-to-answer questions, some of the teachers resorted to calling on her classmates to respond, instead. Now, though, no one replied, though LaVerdere coughed into his hand.

"Let us look at this painting—its subject matter; our arguably unreliable information about a lack of peacefulness within the painting's creator. While that hardly makes it Munch's *The Scream*—thank you again, Aqua—may I suggest that ultimately, anecdotal information makes our contemplation something other than it might have been, allocating three to five seconds to walk past it in a museum. Or, in this case, in a Park Avenue condo. Though we cannot detect conflict, the vision portrayed, the idealization, is to my eye a bit too remote from reality to be convincing. And while I know nothing about the painter's intentions, I do know that there are sixty-some variations on this painting, which might be interpreted at least two ways: that the painter is insisting—which always makes us think we might be encountering someone's defense system, hmm?—or that the painter has a specific ambition he is unable to accomplish. Of course we would not want Mr. Hicks to say, 'Aha!' and destroy the succession of paintings leading up to this one. Yet, ironically, amid the ostensible 'peace' of the painting, its emotional underpinnings may be quite varied, among them obsession, frustration, even desperation.

"Without adding more biographical information, let me suggest that while certain writers and musicians are approved of *because* they have a so-called vision that they return to, it is also a risky endeavor, because quantity may raise questions rather than reinforcing the impact. Does one's adamancy convince, or suggest a possible struggle within the artist that becomes part of the art itself—perhaps inseparable from it? Something we are no doubt still thinking about, following our trip to a so-called real art gallery last year, under the supervision of Ms. Alwyn-Black, as I'm sure all of you will remember: another highlight of your broad—I imply no pun here—education at Bailey Academy."

Phillip Collins got it. He snorted.

"Thank you for your time, ladies and gentlemen," LaVerdere said, his face becoming animated. "Let us hope our museum director makes a quick recovery so that she can preside at the upcoming dinner thanking our benefactor. Study those animals and marvel at their slightly romanticized accuracy, but wonder whether within those depictions we don't sense a personal projection not to be satisfied by this painting, or by its reiterations."

Three

Against Ben's better judgment, on Thursday after basketball practice he agreed to accompany LouLou to see a guy she'd met during the summer when he was singing and playing guitar at a coffeehouse in Bellows Falls. As far as Ben could tell, the fascination Willy held for LouLou was that he was seven or eight years older than she and married, and had briefly been a studio musician in Nashville, where his wife remained. They were technically still married, though he wrote and sang songs about divorce. Ben and Jasper had listened to only one: Froggie got divorced from Mrs. Frog, who drowned herself under a lily pad (those weren't really the lyrics, but he could no longer remember the anthropomorphic song's story). He had an aversion to songs that condescended to the audience's intelligence, but according to LouLou, the crowd (Crowd? For a folksinger in *Bellows Falls?*) loved him. At first Hailey said she'd go along, but it turned out she had to write a paper she'd left until the last minute. Ben also thought she was skeptical about any musician except Stiff Formaldehyde.

Jasper had been scheduled to go, too, but he told Ben that he felt like he was being used, so he'd backed out. It was unusual to be invited anywhere with LouLou, because most of the time you found out about her adventures after the fact. She just went missing. If you believed her, any number of people were happy to take her in (those times she wasn't with a boyfriend), or to give her a meal. This must be a boring adventure if she wanted him along, Ben thought. Jasper's sense of things was probably more accurate: She might have wanted protection, but more likely she wanted an audience. She'd told Willy she was twenty-one.

A dark-green hatchback picked them up in front of a house a block past the school. The house was a landmark, for no good reason except that it was painted yellow. The Bailey students called the house The Big Banana. On Halloween, the young couple who lived there with their twins gave out butterscotch candies and Mr. Goodbars. The driver's name was Lee—a friend of Willy's, who seemed surprised to see Ben. The car smelled of cigarette smoke. "How ya doin', man?" Ben said, climbing in front and shaking the man's hand.

"O-*kaaay*," Lee said. Ben assumed LouLou knew Lee, until she introduced herself. "And, uh, you two go to school here? You're, like, teenagers? This is what—some practical joke?"

"We're twenty-one," LouLou said. "We have a long history of flunking out of other schools."

"You have some identification to that effect?"

"We need it, to ride to Vermont?"

"Maybe I misunderstood something," Lee said. "Your friend Willy's such a loser, he's got to import a teenage fan club?"

"I thought you were his friend," LouLou said. Willy had sent her twenty dollars that he told her to give Lee for gas.

"How are you kids getting back to school? You know I'm headed for Saint Johnsbury afterward, right? I've got a gig of my own up there, only it's construction, not music. A real job."

Well, this was certainly unpleasant, Ben thought. Though Lee could see LouLou in the rearview mirror—which he looked into often—Ben had no idea how she was reacting to their blunt, seemingly unwilling driver. How *were* they going to get back? He'd assumed the ride would be round-trip. Lee drove like an old woman, never changing lanes, braking lightly when approaching intersections even when the light was green.

"So tell me," Lee said, "what about Willy's music do a couple of kids like you relate to? It doesn't seem like a little boilerplate old hippie 'Puff, the Magic Dragon' shit?"

"It's my kind of music," LouLou said. "You're the one who seems down on it. And on your friend."

"Down on Willy? Nah. Went out of my way to pick you up, at his request, though now I'm worried I might be charged with kidnapping two kids that go to a fancy rich kids' school. Anybody'd think that for that tuition, they'd keep tabs on you. But hey, maybe those school bigshots aren't so perfect. You think they might be not quite right in the head themselves? They sure watched me where I went to school. One time I got expelled for cherry-bombing the Christmas tree." He lowered the window to pitch his cigarette. "Smoking's bad," he said. "I'm sure they instruct you rich kids in how to live a long life. Aerobic exercise, right? Jumping jacks till you feel the heartbeats in your ears. You vegetarians?"

"No," Ben said.

"Uh-uh," LouLou said.

"Tell me," Lee said. "What do you take me for? You think I'm just another adult, the way I think you're just another couple of spoiled brats?"

"You're somebody doing us a favor," Ben said.

"You don't make any assumptions, hearin' my accent? Don't wonder what a Southern boy's doin' in the north? See this tear under the arm of my jacket, here? I could use some new clothes. Surprising to me that shit-kicker boots are in fashion. Weren't when I was in high school, but they were the only shoes I had."

"We're not judging you," LouLou said. "People dress all different ways."

"Your boyfriend's so far over in his seat, it looks like he's magnetized to the door."

Shit, Ben thought. But neither of them denied that he was her boyfriend. For a few seconds, he imagined that he was. But how much sense did that make? She was on her way to see Willy. The guy driving regarded both of them as interchangeable with the charms dangling from a rawhide loop hung over his rearview mirror: little stones; good-luck charms only if he believed in them. The guy drove carefully, eyes straight ahead. "You two know Mandy?" he asked at a red light.

"No," Ben said.

"No," LouLou said.

"That's Willy's wife, back in Tennessee. She would not believe that today I'm driving my mother's vehicle with two school kids in it, heading off to some coffeehouse to hear her Willy. She thinks he's working construction with me. You can't have a marriage if you don't have any honesty with one another."

"I've got a flask filled with Mount Gay. Want a swig?" LouLou asked, rummaging in her bag.

"Drink and drive? I never do. Maybe your boyfriend here would like a drink. I can just feel his brain waves wiggling like worms. 'Who's this guy? What am I doing here?'"

"He's cool with things. He never says much. That's just Ben."

Was this true? Ben wondered. He thought of himself as talkative. His father often said he was too quiet, so it was a sensitive subject.

"I don't understand young people. I didn't understand myself when I was one, either. I broke it off with my girlfriend and took off for Asheville and played music with two different bands, the first of which fired my ass for sleeping through a rehearsal. Then I joined up with Hibernation, playing the lyricon, and one day I got so sick, I collapsed onstage. Turned out I had a heart problem. I take pills for it now. They make me feel fifty. They also affect my judgment, I guess, if I'm chattering away with a couple of school kids." He snorted. He turned on the radio. They'd just missed a song by Michael Jackson, who was appearing that night, Ben learned from the excited announcer, for a concert at Madison Square Garden. That was of little interest to Ben, but Elin would have been elated to hear the song, and even more thrilled if his father had taken her to New York. She preferred Manhattan to their home in Brookline. She loved "Billie Jean," which had gone to the top of the charts to become number one in Sweden.

Ben understood guys like Lee. They were like some of the workmen at his father's summer place, guys who tried to sound forthcoming at the same time they were judging you; they wanted to distance themselves to assert superiority and control. LouLou, from the backseat, waved her flask in the space between seats, but neither took it. Was she wearing perfume? It was probably her shampoo that smelled like the beach in the rain.

"Anybody want to take a whiz?" Lee said. "If so, I'm pulling into the service station up ahead. Get me a Diet Sprite, enjoy a couple of pills, then we're on our way, straight through, bladders empty as a pocket picked by gypsies."

What would LaVerdere make of this guy, Ben wondered. La-Verdere, who had such a facility with words, partly because he had so much knowledge to call on.

"Nobody for the can?" Lee said, pulling into the parking lot and getting out.

"Guess not," Ben said.

"Not me," LouLou said.

After the comment Lee had made about his recoiling, Ben had made it a point to center himself in the seat. He felt like crossing his arms over his chest wasn't defensive, but instead indicated that he couldn't be pushed around. If he had it to do over again, he would have stayed at Bailey and played chess with Jasper.

At the convenience store, LouLou stayed silently seated. What was he supposed to do—pretend everything was cool? Or blurt out nervous, stupid questions? "In silence, the butterfly rises," La-Verdere had once said. Some Zen koan, or whatever it was. He remembered LaVerdere's hand rising like a conductor's, with purpose. There had, of course, been only a metaphoric butterfly in the air, and LaVerdere had been talking to Dr. Ha, who amused him, or whom he disdained—Ben and Jasper had an ongoing disagreement about this. Ben looked out the window. He wished Hailey had come instead of him.

"Do you want to do a *Five Easy Pieces*?" she said, leaning forward.

"What?"

"Jack Nicholson. At the end of the movie LaVerdere screened.

The guy who dumps his girlfriend at the gas station and jumps in some guy's truck."

"Really, LouLou? We continue this adventure by hoping some trucker takes us wherever he's going?"

"He stopped so we'd split. Don't you know anything?"

"*Five Easy Pieces*? You think Lee knows that movie?"

The scarf she kept fiddling with was from an admirer who'd gone to Paris. Somebody who no doubt didn't have to mow his father's lawn all summer, who'd gone to see the Eiffel Tower instead.

"Come on," she said, opening the door. "I'll apologize later. We've got to get out of here."

"You've suddenly lost interest in this guitar player it was so important to see?"

"He's not playing. I screwed up. I thought he was confirming he'd be back in Fellows Balls, but he left a voicemail. He's in Sharon, Connecticut, playing a private party. I got my signals crossed."

"*What?* Does Lee know he's not there?"

"I don't know. Come on. Let's go."

He sprang out of the car. "We hitch a ride and go back to Bailey? Are you fucking kidding? I don't believe you, LouLou! You wanted to hit the road, but what was the point in dragging me along? Just to see if I'd do it?"

"Children, children," Lee said, walking back toward the car, smoking a narrow, dark cigar. "Let's not have a meltdown on our way to our playdate."

"He's not on tonight, according to her. What do you know about that? Huh? Is she telling the truth?" Embarrassingly, his voice cracked on the last word.

Lee exhaled noxious smoke. "Ben," he said. "Don't we all

believe that the fun is in the journey? Somebody's playing at the coffeehouse tonight. Another friend of mine, as a matter of fact. A female friend. That might be more interesting to you, I'm thinking, than meeting Willy, because what was in that for you, Ben, am I right?"

"We're outta here," LouLou said.

"Rushing off to try to catch Michael Jackson at the Garden?" He pushed a button on his key ring. The car doors locked. "Change of heart? You rich kids were really going to hear Willy play in that factory with mice running around, nothing to eat but stale pretzels and beer? My friend and I can show you a better time than that. By the way, I think we need some gas. Get back in the car and I'll pump half a tank and you can pay for it, huh, kids? I wouldn't want to take advantage."

"You locked us out," Ben said.

"What's so funny about being young?" LouLou said. "What's your story, that you stop to get two so-called rich kids, so you can get free gas?"

"That is such a disappointing reaction, LouLou. Please don't contribute if you don't feel you should."

"Here," Ben said, holding out a twenty-dollar bill he'd pulled out of his own wallet. That left a five and a one-dollar bill, worn thin and missing a corner. It had been in his wallet for some time, because he wasn't sure it was negotiable. "Sorry to have inconvenienced you, Lee. Let's not have things turn ugly."

"Let you wander away into the night, with no clear way to get back? Some *other* dude might be a child molester. I say we have a hit of LouLou's moonshine, pump some gas, and continue our exodus from Live Free or Die. I'm certainly about to be on *my* way." Lee took a few steps closer to Ben. LouLou stood outside the locked car, the flask nowhere Ben could see, her backpack dangling from one shoulder, her scarf entangled with the straps. Thank god she'd pulled her backpack out of the car behind her. What really amazing hair she had. Her nose had turned pink from the cold. But her hair—he could almost feel it in his fingertips.

A car pulled in and a woman hopped out, unscrewed the gas cap, and began pushing buttons before inserting her credit card. Someone else came out of the store, eating a candy bar. There were people around them. Lee wasn't an eagle whose talons were going to lift them from the planet. A man had gotten out of the passenger seat and was hitching up his pants while walking toward the store.

Why did Ben feel like these people, this place, might be the last things he'd ever see? Lee had turned his back and walked off. He was lifting the hose. He didn't seem dangerous. He seemed to be having some sort of discussion with himself—anybody who went to Bailey became hypersensitized to that conversational mode. All along, it had seemed like he'd been preoccupied with something else while talking to them.

"Joke's on us," Lee said, hanging up the hose. "All of us going to some sad café in Hicksville, me hoping to get laid, just like you wanted to fuck my buddy, LouLou. Wish me luck with that, huh? Ben—I think your girlfriend wishes I'd drive away and disappear."

"You have a good night," Ben said. "Sorry about the mix-up."

"Benny! You're too much! You pay for gas and now you're going to insist on getting me a package of cigs, too, aren't you?"

"Fuck you," LouLou said. "Don't do it, Ben."

He stood there thinking. Then he walked into the store and bought Marlboros, hoping the woman behind the counter wouldn't ask to see his ID. She didn't. She was polite. She gave him matches. He looked at her pudgy fingers grasping the cigarette pack and the matchbook, her hovering index finger's pink painted nail the cherry on top of the treat. She was missing a tooth.

Back at the car, he handed the package to Lee, though he'd pocketed the matches. He had no plan for them, but they seemed like a good thing to keep. Boy Scouts knew how to rub sticks together to make a fire, but he had no such skills. He also didn't think that they'd be camping in the woods. With a pretty girl, it would be easier to get someone to pick them up.

"Much obliged," Lee said, pushing the cigarette package into his shirt pocket. "Lots of loonies out there on the interstate. Best to take back roads."

The man who'd gone into the store earlier now came out, hopped into the passenger seat, and the car drove away, its exhaust fumes so dark the rising cloud turned almost green as it hung in the air. Lee got in the car. The door slammed shut. Music played loudly as the ignition turned over: Prince. Lee put the wagon in gear and drove past, without a look in their direction. Gone—back on the road. The taillights quickly disappeared. For a wavery second, Ben remembered his mother running, trying to track the disappearance of a shooting star. But maybe he really only remembered his mother on the ground, hurt.

"We have to hitch," he said. It had begun to get dark. She was looking down. He thought about extending his hand, but didn't. Something bad had happened between them. He didn't know what. He supposed he'd now become a coward in her eyes.

"We're not riding with some stranger," she said. "I'm calling Binnie."

"What?" Binnie popped into his mind as a character in a

Dickens novel. She was in her apron, leaving the Sunday social, carrying a pile of half-eaten food on a tray. The thought of food made his stomach clench.

"I'll pay her to pick us up."

"What are you talking about?" he said, as Binnie settled back into reality.

LouLou turned away—she had Phillip Collins's phone! She'd borrowed Collins's phone with the skull decal! He could hear her talking quietly as she walked farther away. She was calling the caterer's daughter? How would she even have the number? He stared at her dark mane of hair, glossy and thick. He walked up behind her and lightly wrapped his hands around a clump of it. She spun around, frightened. He was going to pull her hair out of her head, was that it? He was that angry? Because she'd told him not to be manipulated by Lee? He could hear a high-pitched voice on the other end of the phone that was recognizably Binnie's. "LouLou, tell me where you're at!"

LouLou raised her hand and grasped his, still wrapped around her hair.

"Give me the phone," he said, surprised to see tears rolling down her cheeks. "I can explain better than you."

Four

The night of the first biweekly Film Society meeting, Ms. Delacroix asked LaVerdere to reconsider and to select something less disturbing. He grumbled about "prior censorship" to Ben when she walked away. They were outside Cavendish, the building where the math students took classes. It was a standing joke that the spire on top represented their pointy heads. Two guys Ben didn't know hurried by, each muttering, "Mr. LaVerdere," not greeting Ben at all. LaVerdere raised a hand but otherwise paid no attention to the pair, who'd begun giggling, for some reason, once they'd walked past. Ms. Delacroix's ideas were not a productive way to consider art, he said through clenched teeth. Should certain art not be looked at, if people were judged to be in some particular mood, or might the argument be made that being disturbed provided the optimal moment to accept art's challenge, since the best art wasn't inert? *Guernica*, hmm?" LaVerdere said. There was no representative person, no inevitable approach to anything (except in Ben's father's mind), blah blah blah. Ben knew these thoughts well. He agreed with them. *Sophie's Choice* had been listed on the schedule, and another faculty member who would go unnamed (*Ha,* LaVerdere mouthed, moving his lips silently as he and Ben resumed walking) had said that it was inappropriate to bring up world events that had caused great suffering so early in the school year, when "positive examples of man's humaneness" had not been screened. "He isn't a stupid man. Why would he take that position? And what's Helen Delacroix doing, swanning after Ha?"

"What do you mean, 'swanning'?"

Another math major hurried toward Cavendish. He didn't make eye contact.

"Following him like a bitch in heat. If you quote me, I'm denying it."

Ben would tell only LouLou. She'd never repeat it.

"Because of history? The U.S.'s retaliation against Japan during the Second World War?"

LaVerdere paused. "I wouldn't have thought of that," he said. "You might be right. We can't overlook the obvious. In any case, I think I've figured out a plan. We won't screen just *this* movie, we'll offer it at the same time as *Gandhi*."

"Really? You wouldn't want to consider *The Sound of Music?*"

LaVerdere smiled. "It might be interesting to observe Ha—Dr. Ha—sitting through that, but no. No, I think Ben Kingsley as the estimable Mahatma Gandhi is our fellow. You did know that Gandhi wasn't always a man of peace, or however others conveniently categorize him? He was to be a barrister. He went to law school in England. He'd have been working at his job just like the rest of us, but do you know what happened? I suppose you couldn't, if you didn't know he'd studied law. Forgive me for asking a question you obviously couldn't answer. The day I take pride in that will be the day I quit my job. Whether I sometimes think my own unstated answers are superior to the ones I elicit, we won't discuss."

LaVerdere continued: "The thing was, Gandhi couldn't bring himself to cross-examine witnesses. It's sort of perfect, isn't it? When you consider that about Gandhiji—as I understand he's called in India; I'm not being a twit here—it seems more than anecdotal that his personal belief system resulted in his being unable to do something that—had he met the challenge—would probably have robbed us of experiencing the teachings of one of the great men of the past century. And then, of course, we have Sophie, who had to decide something profound, when it was a terrible decision to ask any human being to make. Ever seen the movie? It's been around for a while."

Ben shook his head. "Meryl Streep?"

Twit hung in the air.

"She won the 1983 Academy Award. When people haven't read the book or seen the movie, they assume it takes place at a concentration camp, but Styron was cleverer. It takes place years later, at a boardinghouse where Sophie's lover is a Jewish man. Life's ironies, hmm? Ben Kingsley also got an Academy Award for *Gandhi*. Until I ordered the film, I hadn't realized both awards had been conferred in the same year. Please don't tell Dr. Ha that I confided in you. I know you won't."

"Of course not," Ben said.

"As long as we're buddy-buddy? I heard that you and LouLou hit the road. The Powers That Be are still considering how to respond to that, as I'm sure you're aware."

"Shit," Ben said.

"My thought? Since my job is vaguely defined, which is an advantage to those same Powers That Be, so that I am never exactly not working, to state a double negative? There are real risks associated with what you did. Everyone has his horror story. Mine's that a childhood friend was picked up where he'd been hitching on I-95 and forced at knifepoint to drive the car up to Canada, while the guy who'd been driving sat in the passenger seat and sang along with Little Richard tapes for five hours until they had to stop for gas and my friend got away. Funny now, but in the moment? I've been known to put out my thumb, but I know better."

"Maybe you're overthinking the movie pairing, if I can say that," Ben said.

"You're being educated to speak your mind. Develop your point."

"They might think"—what might they think?—"that you're sort of pandering, maybe, by giving them the choice of watching some saintly person, like an antidote, or something, to the other movie? Everybody's going to say they want to watch *Sophie's Choice*, even if they don't."

"Is that your concern? I assure you *Gandhi* isn't a mindless celebration of a saint. Would Kingsleyji star in a movie like that?"

"Maybe you should run them sequentially."

"Then Helen would complain that I was keeping everyone up too late."

"What do you care what she says?"

They stopped to look at a fire hydrant painted to look like Princess Leia. The spigots were like coiled braids and the eyes were eerily perfect. It crossed Ben's mind that Jasper might have had something to do with the alteration.

LaVerdere said: "If a dog wanted to take a piss, it might hesitate because it would be passing judgment on one of our iconic cultural artifacts."

"Do these things just pop into your mind?" Ben said. "Is irony the way you make sense of everything?"

"What an interesting question," LaVerdere said. "I suspect I depend on people's being interested or amused—disarming them, I mean, rather than having to talk about things of more substance."

"You're not kidding?"

"No. You asked a serious question. I bore myself," LaVerdere said. "That's why I read books, listen to music, travel when I can, watch movies, and largely avoid people. A teaching job allows you to make a retreat that seems public at the same time it's actually private. Not to say that my deeply valued students aren't people, but of course there's a built-in power imbalance that allows me to have the last word. You won't hitch again, is that correct?" LaVerdere said, stopping dead. "Though since LouLou was out there in the middle of the night, I'm glad that at least someone capable was with her."

A kind word! How often did LaVerdere say anything that verged on being complimentary? His strategy was usually to pretend that everyone was in the muck together, with understatement and irony the only escape ramps. Ben felt almost fond of LaVerdere. His father would have punished him if he'd found out what he and LouLou had done, and he couldn't imagine what his father would think if he heard how LaVerdere regarded Ms. Delacroix.

"We were going to hear music in Vermont," he said.

This was followed by a long silence. Ben had run into LaVerdere when he was leaving the library. They'd fallen into step and now Ben was simply walking to be with LaVerdere, hoping he wouldn't be asked where he was headed. He saw a white balloon deflating in a tree, then a paper cup on the sidewalk—such an offense at Bailey, he wouldn't have been surprised if the grounds-keeper dusted it for fingerprints when he found it.

"I considered becoming a composer," LaVerdere said. Some-times, his remarks came from left field, but as Hailey had pointed out, at the end of any exchange, everything LaVerdere said, as well as in what order he delivered the information, made perfect sense. "I have a friend, a fellow named Maw—last name, Maw; it sounds like a character in Dickens, doesn't it?—who's finishing an opera based on *Sophie's Choice*. It's to be performed next year in London at the Royal Opera House. I've been invited to the pre-miere."

"So you'll go?"

LaVerdere considered. "Probably not," he said. "Maybe some regrettable feeling of envy."

"You should do it," Ben said, though he was surprised he blurted it out. They stood in front of the building where LaVerdere lived on the second floor. Ben had never seen an opera. Or Lon-don, in spite of his nickname.

"Good evening," LaVerdere said, slightly retracting his chin.

"Evening," Ben replied. At Bailey, you might or might not shake hands when you met, but you never shook hands when you parted.

Five

The response paper Ben had written for LaVerdere had been stupid, and he doubted he'd even turn it in. Each term, you were excused from writing two weekly papers without having to give a reason. Jasper always made it a point to skip the first two papers, to get LaVerdere's attention, before he got onboard and wrote all the others. Jasper knew how to make people pay attention to him when he wanted that, and, an even greater skill, how to drop off their radar when that benefited him more. LouLou wasn't the only one who ran away; this early in the school year, Jasper had already spent a night in a motel with a girl he'd gone to kindergarten with, after he'd run into her in a health food store. Jasper had never been as happy at Bailey as Ben had, and Ben still vacillated about Bailey, though, as his father would say, he'd "voted with his feet." Should he have stayed with his old man and Elin and gone to the local high school, where he'd have had much more free time, even if he'd felt Elin would smother him and really wanted him gone (okay; he hadn't felt she wanted him out of the house until LouLou explained it as Elin's real motivation for being so hyperattentive)? Years later, he'd think the obvious: Even if his mother hadn't died, his father wouldn't have been a very good father.

That morning, three days after stupidly going along with LouLou on her road trip, he still felt humiliated, which didn't have so much to do with getting caught as with feeling he'd somehow failed her. It had called his attention to the fact that he didn't yet have a driver's license, though if he had, he wouldn't have been able to drive, because no student at Bailey was allowed to keep a car. That was why they were preoccupied with cars, whether it was Dr. Ha's amazing machine or AB's (LaVerdere's nickname for Ms. Alwyn-Black) white Toyota with the driver's side and the passenger side deeply dented, as if the car were a well-squeezed tube of toothpaste.

Jasper had asked Ben how, exactly, he thought he'd failed Lou-Lou, and all he'd been able to say was that he'd bought a pack of cigarettes out of cowardice, and that they'd never even made it to Vermont. He'd said nothing about the musician's not even playing that night, though when he'd given a quick description of who the man was, Jasper had said, "Sounds like a loser. What's with her, thinking every older guy's hot?" Even that had made him feel better, though he had to discount a lot of what Jasper said because Jasper was too much on his side. "Maybe LouLou failed you—did you ever think about that?" Jasper had said, pressing the point.

When the wall phone rang in his room, he'd picked up the receiver hoping it was LouLou, and if it was, that the awkwardness between them was over. Not only was the caller not LouLou, it was the worst person it could possibly be, his father. Which meant that word of the road trip must have reached him. His father rarely called except on Friday evenings, when he got off on pretending Ben was going to be having an exciting weekend. It was not good news that his father was on the phone.

His father asked how his studies were going, whether the Film Society had met yet, what his "flamboyant" teacher was up to. Could his father possibly not know?

He told his father about LaVerdere's cleverness in screening two movies simultaneously to make an end-run around another teacher's objection to showing depressing movies, which was a continuation—he suddenly realized, even though he was still half asleep—of LaVerdere's fixation on "The Lady, or the Tiger?" That, he didn't say. It would give his father an excuse to ruminate about his "liberal education" and how he wanted Ben to concentrate on "something real" in college. His father rarely mentioned Elin, so Ben didn't, either, though he was aware that there was a pattern of his stepmother calling exactly one day later, sometimes to the hour. His father said that it already felt like September was "whizzing by." The way his father talked always made it seem like the old man had to dig in his heels while various tornadoes whirled through. When they said goodbye, Ben felt almost as relieved as if LouLou had called.

As he headed toward the bathroom (empty, not a good sign; he was running late), the night before came back to him. They'd ordered pizza. They'd had some bourbon mixed with Pepsi, then the last of the brandy Phillip Collins's brother had mailed to him wrapped in a pair of ugly pajamas for his birthday. It hadn't been long before Darius, who could hardly tolerate food, let alone alcohol, began puking out the window, the sound as likely to bring someone running as a pulled fire alarm. The vomit had been nothing but a slush of pizza and booze puked down into the rhododendrons.

How was it, he wondered, that he and LouLou could talk half the night. He talked about things that worried him, while she pretended that she had everything figured out, under control. If she didn't—every instinct told him that was true—why did he feel so relieved to be with an impostor? Was she more a habit (as Jasper thought)? Did Ben rely on her as much as Darius relied on Lou-Lou's "boyfriend" (she was the one who always jokingly identified the man as her boyfriend), who dropped off cheap vodka—some guy's attempt to seduce her with a present she cast off to her friends as quickly as the Dalai Lama renounced worldly possessions?

He was going to be late for the Sunday social, held much earlier than usual because of a cello concert that evening. He dressed and picked up his backpack. Impossible to zip because of the things sticking out of it. He slung it over one shoulder so he'd be aware if anything dropped out, closed his door, and hurried across campus. He arrived after the bell rang, slipped quickly into an empty chair, and was overwhelmed with misery about where he was, as sure about how the next hour would go as if he'd been stopped in a time warp, LaVerdere, yet again, standing in front of them. When he lowered his backpack, half the contents spilled onto the floor: books; a half-empty bottle of lemonade; a scarf; notebooks; a softball that rolled up the aisle and stopped just behind Akemi Hayashi-Myers's heel. LaVerdere watched the ball but said nothing. He loved that. He loved those moments when he withheld any remark at all, and let you know that he knew he was doing it. Akemi began to nervously twist the ends of her hair, as she realized his focus was on her.

Ben looked down. There were carpets everywhere at Bailey. The only wood floors were in the bathrooms. The pattern of this rug was truly crazy, the complex pattern becoming ever more complicated before resolving itself into familiarity as it repeated, spreading out like something in a horror film. He concluded, in LaVerdere mode, that the rug expressed the regularity of irregularity, that it might have been manufactured to express an inherent paradox.

Being sick of LaVerdere was like being sick of the hands of a clock. Of course they studied him to see what his mood was, while trying to appear uninterested. *Uninterested* and *disinterested* were words that expressed two different emotions. As Ben would later think of their fascination with LaVerdere, they were simply too young to be disinterested; they couldn't possibly think of personal advantage when they'd really accomplished nothing.

LaVerdere might be on the rebound from as bad a night as some of them had had. It was a way of thinking that Elin, with her good intentions, had instilled in him: that he couldn't easily understand his father because he didn't observe his father's off-moments. He didn't; his father, at most, loosened his tie at dinner and wore his jacket winter or summer. The long, thick bathrobe Elin had given him as a gift hung on the hook of the bathroom door. It was used only for hand drying.

"Ladies and gentlemen, politics. This American politician gave a now-famous televised speech in which he admitted accepting a dog from the then-Russian president."

"Who is Richard Nixon?"

"When he left the White House, he got all teary and thanked everybody, but he didn't thank his wife," Hailey said.

"He and Henry Kissinger should have been tried for war crimes," Aqua said. "Even my father thinks that."

"Ladies? Gentlemen?" LaVerdere said. "This is not a blurt-out-anything-that-occurs-to-you occasion. If we may continue?"

"Just go on, Mr. LaVerdere. Ignore them," Phillip Collins said.

"Literature. This play that premiered in the U.S. in Miami Beach was billed as a 'laugh riot,' and involved two characters waiting for someone or something that never appears. Ms. Sils?"

"What is *Waiting for Godot*?"

"LouLou always gets the easy ones," Jasper said, disgustedly.

LaVerdere scanned his eyes over the group sitting on large cushions on the floor. Earlier, he'd joked that he felt like a pre-school teacher; he'd wondered aloud—in that super-wry way that still made some of the girls wonder if he was gay—if *Jeopardy!* should be followed by nap time. The shiny blue cushions, edged in multicolored fringe, had been a gift from the same woman who'd arranged for the donation of the Edward Hicks painting. No one had an explanation, however, for why the series of very large boxes had been shipped to the school from Bloomingdale's. LouLou had pronounced them "cool." When she sat on one, other girls instantly did the same. Finally, more people had joined her, though Ben sat in a chair. LaVerdere said, feigning fatigue, "Jasper, as with everything else in our universe, the cards have been randomly shuffled."

"The real point of his asking that question was so he could shock us by dropping in the information that *Godot* was considered a comedy," Phillip Collins said.

"I will take that as a compliment and continue," LaVerdere said, "though you might also consider that the question contained disdain for Miami Beach as well. We move again to the category Philosophy." LaVerdere gestured. "You're up next, Beltz and Whistles," he said to Darius. Ben looked quickly over his shoulder. Toward the back of the room, which Ben had passed through quickly, Darius was on the floor, weight on one hip, propped on his elbow. This, like the softball, was something LaVerdere was obviously not going to comment on. Dried mud caked the soles of Darius's shoes. He must be sprawled there with a terrible hangover.

"A philosopher famous for saying, 'What needs to be said is best said twice.'"

"Could you say that again?" LouLou asked.

"My mother," Hailey said, simultaneously. Several people cracked up. Ben smiled, though he was preoccupied; he was still thinking over what Phillip (a.k.a. "Tom") Collins had said. Though nobody paid much attention to him, the guy certainly was astute.

"Em—" Darius Beltz said under his breath. "Who is Empedocles?"

"How would you know that?" LouLou exploded, turning toward Darius.

"I don't know," he said. "I read a lot." In his room, Darius had a framed letter, handwritten, from his second-grade teacher to his parents, saying that he was reading at the sixth-grade level. None of them knew what to make of it—whether, by framing it, he was boasting or joking.

"Kindly refrain from digressing into personal conversations, ladies and gentlemen. Aqua, might you stop looking around like someone has taken us hostage?" LaVerdere, expressionless, reshuffled the cards.

"Science. A famous scientist said about quantum mechanics that if you thought you understood it, you did not."

"Who is Richard Feynman?"

"Too obvious, Mr. LaVerdere! You're obsessed with Feynman. He's your default scientist, like Dostoyevsky's always the most important writer."

"One more interruption, and I lecture on *The Peaceable Kingdom* again," LaVerdere said.

Silence in the room. Again, the cards were shuffled. Ben noticed that LaVerdere's ears had turned bright pink. He seemed to be in a particularly bad mood. It had been Dr. Ha's turn to preside over *Jeopardy!*—that is, if he didn't come up with an alternate idea—but he'd canceled late the night before because of a sore throat. Ha had been lying, Ben thought, when LaVerdere announced the change of plans, with his characteristic straight face.

LaVerdere nodded in the direction of one of the two math majors who were sitting in today, for no reason anyone could understand. Later, Jasper would nickname them "Tweedledum and Tweedledee." The next question was directed at Tweedledum.

"Shakespeare. Identify the play that contains the line 'I have of late, but wherefore I know not, lost all my mirth.'"

"What is *Macbeth*?"

"That is incorrect. It's *Hamlet*. Let's try again, Mr. Amasett.

"Our next category is Famous Americans. Mr. Amasett, ready? For those of you who don't know Grover Amasett, whose studies include an emphasis on math, he has decided to join us today. Let's see if we've turned up a question about Einstein for him." LaVerdere cleared his throat.

"Famous Americans. He said, 'I'm the most cold-hearted son-of-a-bitch you'll ever meet.'"

"Who is Ted Bundy?" his friend Tweedledee shouted.

"Who *is* Ted Bundy?" Akemi Hayashi-Myers asked.

Tweedledee turned to look at her. "A sociopath," he said. "He murdered at least thirty women. Nobody knows the real number. He was born in Vermont. He went to the electric chair."

"Very good, Mr. Duquell. Please excuse me for neglecting to introduce our other math student, Mr. Duquell. Since we're going off-script today, I recommend to you, if it might have escaped your attention previously, an amazing painting—a painting by Andy Warhol, a.k.a. Warhola, of Campbell's soup can fame; numerous paintings, I should say—of the electric chair. But let us continue, as I'm sure we're all eager to enjoy our"—he looked quickly around the room—"unhealthy snacks, which will affect our glycemic index at the conclusion of *Jeopardy!*"

"That was really in the category 'Famous Americans'? Darius Beltz asked. "Don't we want to have a debate as to whether, morally, murderers should be considered 'famous'?"

"In spite of what you imply, Beltz and Whistles, I am not a pedant," LaVerdere said. "So the answer is no. Though perhaps in our next debate we can take sides about whether interruptions are helpful or unhelpful.

"Literature. In this twentieth-century novel, a character attends a sparsely populated funeral after the protagonist is found dead in his pool."

"Who is John Cheever?"

A groan went up. "*The Great Gatsby*," LouLou said, then clamped her hand over her mouth. Heads nodded in agreement. *"Gatsby!"* also escaped someone else's lips. Aqua had bumped over and put her arm around Akemi's shoulder, continuing to explain who the serial killer Ted Bundy was. There were no teams—the worst you could suffer was personal embarrassment—though for Akemi, a mistake was always devastating.

"Entertainment. This movie by Robert Altman had a haunting musical score that only occurred to the director *after* filming concluded."

"What is *McCabe & Mrs. Miller*?"

"That's his Holy Trinity: Dostoyevsky; Richard Feynman; Robert Altman," Darius Beltz said.

"I will ignore that remark—though it does express my own excellent taste, as well as my ability to understand the underpinnings of our culture. Tom Collins, I feel sure you were thinking the same, even though you are surreptitiously consulting your phone, which is against the rules of Bailey Academy. But now, following Big Ben's triumphant answer about Mr. Altman's film, let us conclude by wishing Dr. Ha a speedy recovery—though we need commit these thoughts only in our hearts, as former President Jimmy Carter informed us he did, when considering adultery."

It was too convoluted, Ben thought; LaVerdere could easily be a one-man band, but when he played the synthesizer, the audience quickly lost all sense of what was going on. He agreed with LaVerdere about the brilliance of Altman's revisionist Western, though. He also knew another interesting fact about it: When filming, they'd decided to continue when it began snowing, and the snow went on and on and on. He'd never seen such real-looking snow as in that movie and later he found out why. He conjured up Julie Christie, her face on a pillow, stoned.

"Dr. Ha," LouLou said solemnly, standing, touching her palms together, her fingers pointing up, "our condolences go out to you today, though we understand that, really, you're somewhere in your sports car."

LaVerdere cocked his head. He said, "Perhaps you could let us in on the secret of how you're sure Dr. Ha is not at home, ill?

Would that be because you looked out your window and saw him driving away?"

"Okay, I didn't *see* it," LouLou said after a long pause.

"I did," LaVerdere said. "Though I do admire the man's chutzpah."

Six

O n 9/11 LouLou was the town crier, banging on her classmates' doors. It took Ben some time to realize that he hadn't been awakened from a nightmare. Mrs. Somersworth, the school nurse (rumored to have had a drug problem herself, when she was their age), handed out tissues and herded them into the TV room to look at the shaky footage, the incomprehensible smoke in New York.

Oh, Ben thought stupidly. *They've wheeled a TV into the solarium.* The solarium had no plants in it because the baseboard heating had killed all of those that Binnie and Tessie hadn't rescued and put elsewhere. The corner room, hung with portraits of the school's founders, was used for faculty meetings, with extensions fitted into the big oval table. Someone had pushed the table against one wall. The TV had been brought in from somewhere else, its back trailing extension cords. It sat angled toward the two sofas. Some people sat on the rug, or on the few folding chairs Tessie had dragged out before she stopped and sat down, drawing her daughter in close to her side.

Everyone's real affiliations immediately became clear: Lou-Lou did her best to comfort Hailey, using some patois of baby talk, holding her face so Hailey had to look into her eyes and focus her attention. Eleanor (Ms. Rigby, to LaVerdere) refused to sit and backed up against the wall near Darius Beltz. Darius's eyes kept darting toward her. No one touched Darius. He'd ask you not to, if you did. Mrs. Vale, the history teacher (who always corrected you if you called her "Dr." Vale; only LaVerdere did not stand corrected), walked over to be with her star pupil, Eleanor, trying to sniff back tears. "I can't explain, it's a horrible accident, a plane went off-course and flew into the tower, that has to be what happened," Mrs. Vale said dully, drowning out the more interesting speculation on the TV, as she went to sit down.

"Fuckin' hell," Ben said.

Tessie, Binnie's mother, sat beside Mrs. Vale on the low, red leather couch, fingering colorless rosary beads, her lips moving silently as her big-knuckled fingers—worse even than Benson Whitacre's—worked themselves over the glass. Tessie's slip showed—it often did—but today none of the girls pointed it out.

Darius Beltz had left the room. He stood in the corridor, fumbling in his attempts to button his shirt. He looked like a crazy man exploring his body for imaginary insects.

"What are you doing?" Aqua said. "Go bang your fist against the wall or something, Darius, but *don't do that.*"

"Aqua, come sit with me," Mrs. Vale called.

"Where is every other person in the whole school, like *every teacher?*" Aqua said, her shoulders heaving with exasperation.

"I'm a teacher," Mrs. Vale said quietly.

"She's the history teacher," Ben echoed. Hearing his own voice, he wondered why it sounded so high. The minute he spoke, he felt like everyone had caught him in an enormous lie. Worse, that he was falling back into his pattern of echoing his father. Elin had discussed that with him privately. "You don't have to repeat what your father says, if you disagree," she'd said. "You shouldn't just echo his words." What she didn't know was that by echoing, he was simultaneously erasing, in his own mind, what his father said.

He rubbed his hand over his forehead and his uncombed hair. He was standing there in his socks—socks! Stiff and dirty, worn since basketball practice the day before—but he'd forgotten to put on shoes, LouLou's cries had been so disturbing. Who knew there was anything between Aqua and Darius—or possibly he was imagining it. Right now, she was clasping Darius's hands (amazing!), their arms swaying the way someone would show a child how a metronome worked. Darius's shirt remained unbuttoned. Ben was stunned at what white skin he had. He'd been in the locker room with Darius . . . why, suddenly, did his ribs protrude? Was it the angle from which he saw Darius's body?

Adults floated into the room. They came from nowhere, like ghosts blowing through empty castles. Even if they were crying—or maybe because they were—they said little. No ghost greeted another. They hadn't been there when LouLou started screaming, or when blank-faced Binnie—Binnie, who'd rushed out to rescue LouLou; Ben had been entirely incidental—turned on the TV. No matter how hard Ben tried, Binnie wouldn't make eye contact with him.

Where, though, was LaVerdere? He was the person you'd expect front and center, he was the one who could be counted on to provide some perspective, to involve everyone in a discussion.

Dr. Ha stood in the doorway in black Lycra shorts and an oversize Nike T-shirt. Had he fallen? Quite possibly, since he was holding a pair of broken glasses. "What's happened? They told me at the post office," he said. He glanced at Mrs. Vale, though he quickly looked away. She shook her head in disbelief, but the baffled silence continued, all attention riveted to the frightening image on the television, which Mrs. Vale abruptly muted. Confused, she continued to stare at the screen; eventually, she held out the remote to Dr. Ha, who said, "Do you mind?" and turned the volume back on, watching her out of the corner of his eye as the sound came up.

The second plane hit. The new picture provoked a moan from Tessie, whose slip had a thick strip of lace at the hem, though you could see where the lace ended and the dingily colored nylon began. Satin, nylon, polyester. Polyester. Elin had once gone on a rant against polyester, and his father had made a joke, trying to be cool, asking if that wasn't the name of someone who'd hung around Warhol's Factory. Elin was attractive, though her startled eyes didn't reassure anyone. Her eyes would certainly be huge today. He could understand why his father had married her, though she spent almost as much time instructing him as she did Ben. Her own daughter, from her brief first marriage, had died in infancy, long before she married his father.

In the hallway, Darius held his shirt against his chest like a flimsy shield. He and Aqua had stood apart from the TV watchers so long, whispering, that it wasn't clear they'd ever join the group. With ribs protruding that sharply, better that Darius cover up, since adults were flipped out by seeing ribs. There were worse things to worry about now, though. It truly, really, completely, totally did not matter that Darius, pitted by acne, was also anorexic.

"I do not believe even one plane has flown into the World Trade Center by accident," Dr. Ha said.

"Pray for the people," Tessie said, tugging her hem.

"What's happening?" LouLou said, her voice more desperate than when she'd been running down the hallways.

Dr. Ha continued to cast sideways looks at Mrs. Vale. She paid no attention to him, even when a piece of cracked lens fell out of his glass frames. Ben picked it up and handed it silently to Dr. Ha. Dr. Ha looked at the lens as if it were the most unfortunate thing he'd ever seen.

Ms. Alwyn-Black appeared, frowning. "My god," she said, not realizing that no one was talking. "A plane? It went out of control? With all those people aboard?"

"Two planes!" Darius Beltz said, then went back to biting his thumbnail.

Ms. Alwyn-Black was joined by Ms. Delacroix, who was obtuse, absolutely unlike anyone else at the school. Ms. Delacroix had majored in women's studies and volunteered several nights a week at a shelter for abused women. Recently, a man had shown up at the shelter—Ben knew this from a discussion with LaVerdere, who, in bringing it up, had seemed genuinely interested in what Ben really thought—wearing a curly wig and lipstick and begging for a place to stay to escape domestic violence. That had really gotten LaVerdere's wheels turning. Ms. Delacroix had been Eleanor's first confidante after what did or didn't happen with Phillip Collins in the potting shed. Ms. Delacroix was married to a judge in Albany whom she saw only on weekends. She was nice enough, though sanctimonious. "I serve as I can," she often said. The day was lovely, warm compared to the previous night. The world might be ending (Hailey's bluntly stated opinion: Her eye patch was askew; Ben had once seen that the place where her left eye had been was a shallow indentation).

"Madmen hijackers," Ms. Delacroix said, her big butt collapsing onto the couch so that Mrs. Vale rose up as if they were on a seesaw. Tessie—who'd been clutching her daughter's hand all the time they were riveted to the TV—walked away, shaking her head, her back mercifully blocking Ben's view of the burning buildings. Tessie and Binnie had a dog that they sometimes brought to work. Otherwise, their neighbor, who lived above them in the town at the crossroads, looked after it. The dog was old. Dilly, it was called. On the ride back to Bailey, Binnie had told them that the dog was fourteen years old and sick, but that putting it to sleep would be a mortal sin.

Ben had spaced out. He only realized he had when LouLou re-entered the room and he was startled to see her. She looked at him—it was such a relief; her eyes met his and again he felt their instant connection, the peaceful one that had nothing to do with talk.

"Macbeth doth murder sleep." What did that mean? LaVerdere had asked. And more important, was that Shakespeare's best thought about how to express those sentiments? Who but LaVerdere would think to ask that? Even in Shakespeare's day, LaVerdere continued, there was circumlocution, "so might the playwright have sought a poetic way for the character to express his thoughts—and when I say 'poetic' it would be naïve to assume the word was synonymous with something inherently good, hmm? Ask yourself: Was the character being clear, or was he hiding behind what some might call 'highfalutin language'? If there was intentional ambiguity, what would be gained by choosing those exact words?" Ben rubbed his hand over his face. Skin not ruined by acne. Rubbing your eyes only made it worse. It seemed the TV would be turned on forever, and his eyes would never stop burning.

Tessie pulled LouLou down beside her. She whispered to her as she continued to pray her beads. Ridiculous! Everything was ridiculous, people dying, plants dying, a response paper he'd worked on about *Macbeth* late into the night that he knew he'd never turn in. Why was LouLou sitting where she was, her arm around another person's shoulder? He couldn't stop thinking of the line "Macbeth doth murder sleep." Maybe it meant nothing. Sleep was sleep. Inanimate objects and states of being couldn't be murdered—that was an erroneous concept, as silly as personification. *Twit,* he thought, angrily. He hated it that LaVerdere could analyze anything and transform its clarity into ambiguity.

Where was LaVerdere?

"I told you no phones!" Mrs. Vale said sharply to Phillip Collins, though she hadn't. He turned it off and pushed it into his pocket.

Dr. Ha had walked to the window.

Ben left to find Jasper—he assumed he'd be called back, but no one took notice. He was so upset, though, that he took a wrong turn and almost collided with a man who turned out to be Ms. Alwyn-Black's brother, who'd come looking for his sister (though he called her only "Lauren," so Ben had to ask twice what her last name was). Ben could certainly see the family resemblance. Out the window in the corridor, Ben could see what he assumed must be the man's car idling with its door open and the hazard lights blinking. Pointing, Ben explained how to find the solarium. Yes, he could confirm that he'd just seen Ms. Alwyn-Black. The man looked enormously relieved as he rushed away. Years later, there'd be security. People would no longer be able to show up and go wherever they wanted on campus. A cousin of Binnie's would be posted as a guard in a kiosk inside a locked gate. But that day, no different from any other, the grounds seemed to exist apart from the world.

"Jasper?" Ben said, knocking on his door.

"Ben?" Ms. Delacroix said from behind him.

"Hi," he said, startled. He hadn't seen anyone coming. "Just checking out Angelina." The TV had been turned louder, though this far away, because of all the voices talking over whatever was being said on TV, it was impossible to hear anything clearly.

"You're what?"

Ms. Delacroix's face was pale. At first she'd seemed on the verge of tears, though when he spoke, her expression resolved itself into a frown.

"It got my attention," Ben said, pointing.

Old tape marks, as well as new photographs Jasper had been told to take down (LaVerdere had let Jasper know that he thought the students should be able to put anything they wanted on their door) that Jasper had gradually snuck up again and were lined up, just above eye level: a page ripped from a tabloid of two actresses wearing the same dress, the viewer asked to decide who wore it better; photographs purporting to be about cars, subliminally orchestrated to sell sex; a photograph of Angelina Jolie, dangling a vial of Billy Bob Thornton's blood from a necklace.

"I can't believe this, I truly cannot," Ms. Delacroix said. "We are gathered together to comfort one another as this horrible moment unfolds, which is sure to change air travel in our time, and you have walked off to stare at a photograph of an actress? Wasn't that junk supposed to be taken down?"

It didn't seem the time to tell Ms. Delacroix that Angelina

Jolie's politics were liberal, that she was one of them. She'd had a rift with her father—nothing new there—some actor famous for a movie he'd acted in with Dustin Hoffman. Ben's mother had watched it many times on TV, crying at the end every time.

As Ms. Delacroix fled, shaking her head, Ben knocked again, trying silently to send Jasper the message that he was the one knocking. He empathized: If Jasper knew that something horrible was happening in New York, but he was already on sensory overload because of his mother's health problems and The Man, why open the door and admit one more thing? All those contrived stories like "The Lady, or the Tiger?," of people having to decide what was behind a door and what they'd risk by opening it—it worked the other way, too; when you were inside, you had to decide who'd come knocking, which might range from Mormon missionaries to the Red Death, the Grim Reaper, or your friend Big Ben, not as tall as his father and not likely to be, recipient of one of LaVerdere's uninspired nicknames. Though the worst thing was to have no special name.

Ben gave a last, two-knuckled tap. His next idea was to slip a note under the door. Jasper was determined to have privacy. Or maybe he'd decided to go for a run. That was more likely. He should go to his own room and put on the dirty clothes from the night before and set out, see if he met Jasper on the trail. Everyone their age was skilled at making something intentional appear coincidental; Hailey just happening to find herself next to LouLou so often—whether in photographs, at relay races, or just standing around on the insane wall-to-wall carpeting at the Sunday social; Darius Beltz leaving any room into which snacks were brought because a thought had just occurred to him that he had to write down immediately. (Jasper, noticing the same thing, had drawn a cartoon that looked very much like Darius, transforming him into a lightbulb.) Ben wondered what he, personally, would have done if his father had shown up drunk, holding Eleanor's hand. *Die,* that's what.

When he left, went down the hallway, and opened the unlocked door to his own room, he saw—though he hadn't before—his name on an envelope that had nearly slid under the bookcase. It was unsealed. "Mom's in the hospital. Too much chemo," Jasper had written. "Binnie's friend Ray is dropping me at the bus to Hanover. Don't tell anybody, including LaV. Whatever my dad told LaV, my mother doesn't know anything about his coming home. He's probably still drunk. If he comes back, you don't know where I am." No signature. There was a quickly drawn figure below the message. The face looked remarkably like The Man's, but after giving careful attention to the face, Jasper had drawn a stick figure, the torso's long vertical line pierced with arrows. Ben put the note back in the envelope, then pretended it was a puck and toed it under the bookcase.

When he'd first seen it, he'd feared it was a note from LouLou, saying something he didn't want to hear.

Seven

Now everything in the world was going to be rethought ("defamiliarized," to use one of LaVerdere's favorite words). For a while, Ben's dreams made him awaken confused, as if he really had been on the bus with Jasper. He'd think he could smell the tires' burning rubber, hear the bus driver's announcement of "a problem in our country," the ripple of astonishment drifting down the aisle like Sarin as the driver pulled onto the shoulder and communicated through his walkie-talkie. That was when 9/11 became 10/4, as Jasper had said to Ben.

At times, Ms. Delacroix's look of incredulity would come back to him, as he'd stood in front of Angelina Jolie's photograph. Of course he hadn't been looking at it. There'd been nothing anybody with any courage could do but lie, rather than blow a friend's cover.

Things had turned out so very badly, anyway. During his wife's hospitalization, The Man had had a drink with LaVerdere, then gone to the house and left a note. Apparently, he hadn't known where his wife was. In the note, he'd written that he'd spoken to one of their son's teachers, "a sensible Frenchman," who'd agreed that making a clean break in their marriage might ultimately be best. After thinking about it, he realized that the marriage really was over. He'd be taking a train into the city to see a lawyer, as she'd asked him to do when she threw him out. Perhaps she, too, might consult a lawyer, if she hadn't already. He wrote down his lawyer's name and number. He'd leave it to her to tell Jasper.

The lawyer's address was One World Trade Center.

She found the note on the kitchen counter when she returned from the hospital on September 14. She called the school immediately. Who was the French teacher her husband had talked to, and what did he know?

There was no French teacher. There was a Spanish teacher, but there was no French teacher.

Tessie's cousin Dolores was the school operator. She was doing her best to be helpful.

Then flip forward: Suddenly everyone knew The Man was dead. The information spread quickly. People never seen outside their offices clustered all over the grounds. The useless Bailey headmaster—it was an open secret he had dementia—appeared for what he kept referring to as "a press conference" beside the statue of Dr. Martin Luther King, Jr., stumbling through a reading of a Wordsworth poem and refusing to let either his grown son or the school nurse lead him away. Ms. Alwyn-Black broke down in tears when someone came into the art gallery and asked to see "inspirational art, instead of this pointless junk," and had to be

driven home by Ms. Delacroix. All of Bailey became one big, dys-
functional family. Even the groundskeeper went to church for the
first time in years. Although he kept his head down and never
talked to anyone, he told this to Hailey outside the cafeteria, tears
in his eyes, and for some inexplicable reason, she'd shouted,
"There is no god. You're fooling yourself. Everybody's just going
to die and disappear." Eleanor gave Jasper a blowjob. Dr. Ha went
to be with his brother in Storrs, Connecticut, leaving no one in
charge of his classes.

Jasper's mother's attempt to see him had compounded the
problem. She'd passed out in her friend's car as she was being
driven to Bailey and had to be taken to the ER, so that as the
teachers and students were awaiting her arrival, prepared to join
the family in a quickly arranged memorial service in the art gallery against a backdrop of *The Peaceable Kingdom*, her panicked
friend was at the hospital, trying to think what to do. She'd called
Jasper, trying to downplay his mother's collapse ("It was a little
too soon, so maybe we should try another day"), crying herself.
Getting the most recent bad news had put Jasper into a tailspin.
He'd handed Ben the phone the same way he'd handed him the
bag with his medicine in it from the drugstore, then disappeared.
After talking to Jasper's mother's friend—rather, listening—Ben
had turned to LaVerdere for advice, catching him walking out of
the restroom. The two of them, grim-faced, had headed quickly
toward Jasper's room and its yet-again closed door, like a team in
a cop movie, LaVerdere muttered under his breath. They'd crossed
paths with Aqua and Ms. Delacroix, rushing toward the art gallery still empty of its director, carrying a box of devotional candles in small glass containers. Dr. Ha appeared, wearing new,

black-framed oversize glasses. Everyone was going off in various directions as if they'd been launched by the pinball machine outside the cafeteria.

The memorial service was delayed, the same way everything planned had misfired, for what seemed like forever. The devotional candles were put back in the box, unlit. The girls got in a huddle, and Hailey burst into tears, because somebody always burst into tears. Word spread about Jasper's mother the same way it had with the awful news about The Man's death. The newly installed spotlight above *The Peaceable Kingdom* was turned off by Tessie. She looked so solemn, it was as if it had become her personal responsibility to turn off the sun. Ms. Delacroix was red-eyed. A bracelet fell from her wrist and she didn't know it had until one of the girls handed it back to her. The clasp had broken and she couldn't put it back on. Dr. Ha took it from her and put it in his pocket. He handed her a bandanna that he explained he hadn't worn when he'd gone running. She buried her face in it.

Jasper had become crazier than Darius Beltz about not wanting anyone to touch him. He frowned fiercely, insisting on terrible scenarios about his mother's health. He had some theory about how The Man's neediness had caused his mother's initial collapse and then, in her weakened state, she'd succumbed to cancer. His reasoning was far from scientific. Then another phone call had come from the ER. Nothing but bad news. His mother's blood pressure was abnormally low. She'd been admitted to the hospital. "What do you think, this is just a little setback?" Jasper said sarcastically to Ben, dismayed at his friend's stupidity. Jasper turned and left the room.

"Blowing off steam," LaVerdere said to Ben as the spring-loaded launcher was pulled back and released. Pinballs began flying: There went Dr. Ha; here came Binnie; there went Phillip Collins, calling, "Jasper, man, c'mere, I've got something to say." The door closed in his face. Phillip Collins's hair was slicked back. He'd put on a suit for the memorial service, which made him look years older.

After 9/11, everyone at Bailey perfected staying out of other people's way, leaving them with their own thoughts. Attempts at false cheer had become depressing. Were Dr. Ha and old Ms. Delacroix having an affair? They were, weren't they?

The box of candles fell and broke. That meant nothing, really, in a world where no one would ever care about minor breakage again—or at least that was the way it seemed. They might never know, though—as LaVerdere later remarked on graduation day— whether, if the world hadn't appreciably changed on them, leaving Bailey would still have resulted in a backlash of regret. It was another one of his questions that, as he himself pointed out, hinted strongly at its answer by being posed. Or, as Benson Whitacre came to think, he was insidiously cueing them to be adolescents instead of adults, because that way he'd remain in their minds.

Once they'd graduated from Bailey, what bonds *would* make them keep their friendships, their infatuations, their animosities? Would some still tell one another their dreams, or would they become embarrassed by such obvious symbols? They'd be going out into the real world—a place LaVerdere, the person many of them respected most, thought was only another cultural concept that was inevitably politicized, with so-called national pride worn as blinders, doled out like 3-D glasses at the movies to keep the citizens of the world thinking they were seeing reality, when all they saw was an optical illusion.

There was a rumor that Binnie had had an abortion over

Christmas break. Aqua knew it wasn't true; she'd had a D&C because of gross fibroid tumors that made her menstruate almost nonstop, Binnie had confided. Aqua told LouLou. LouLou told Ben. If anyone else found out, it wasn't because he repeated it.

In their last semester, Darius Beltz began going to church with a family friend, who came in his Mercedes and took him to Episcopal services in the only affluent town within radius of Bailey. The friend was a former alcoholic, though he'd recently gotten a job and had his driver's license reinstated. Rather than hiding this information, Darius announced it proudly. "Don't you think it's weird there's no church at Bailey, just the stupid Spiritual Studies building that's a wing of the art gallery, with the Buddha jumbled together with statues of Mary, and music playing that sounds like the music played on the *Titanic* as it went down?" Darius asked Ben.

Ben hadn't thought about it. Attending church services was optional, and since they were presided over by a rotation of three math teachers, of course Ben had never bothered to go. His father hadn't gone to church after Ben's mother died. Even his wedding had been a civil ceremony. After 9/11, the Spiritual Studies building had been set up to offer psychological counseling. Hailey had had a meltdown there, talking not about the terrorist attack, but about the necessity of being reunited with Stiff Formaldehyde, though Stiff had a restraining order against going near her. She'd emailed, she'd called, she was sure he wanted to get together again, but nothing was happening, her whole life would never happen, it had already happened and she'd given her baby away to someone else.

Phillip Collins was accepted at Harvard. His mother and father separated, though they attended his graduation together. His father had moved into a house in Redding, Connecticut, with his graphic designer girlfriend, who also dealt in anime art. She was not at graduation, though her dog was, a malamute, tied to a tree, who behaved perfectly throughout the ceremony. "A true representative of *The Peaceable Kingdom*," as LaVerdere said, scratching the dog's ruff afterward.

Barbara Ehrenreich was the commencement speaker in June. Ben and his friends had rushed up to give her high fives—the girls, especially, though immediately afterward Jasper had faded away. Ben had noticed that as the last semester wound down, Jasper acted like someone who'd already put Bailey behind him. He didn't even want to play chess anymore. He jogged without asking Ben to go along. He'd been talking a lot to his uncle. He'd be going to Stanford. He was thinking of declaring himself premed.

Ben suffered much indecision about whether he should go to college. Jasper had had little tolerance for his self-doubt. It had been to LaVerdere's credit that he'd taken him aside in May and told him he was sure he'd sort it out. He'd been rejected at Yale, which had really disappointed his father, wait-listed at Penn and Harvard, and accepted by Georgetown and Cornell. He spent so much time the summer after he graduated working around his father's place, he thought of becoming a landscape architect. Since indentured servants didn't exist anymore—technically, they didn't—Ben hoped simple exhaustion might provoke an epiphany. He spent his days chopping and stacking wood, for both his father and his father's elderly neighbor (a former federal judge, who'd written a letter of recommendation on his behalf to his alma mater, Cornell), pruning bushes, removing and reglazing windows cracked by winter storms, then scrubbing them down with newspaper soaked in vinegar, the fumes stinging his eyes, making sure he got rid of every smudge when he rehung them, snapping on latex gloves he pulled out of a dispenser like tissues.

At night, bored, he read books about famous gardeners and tried to imagine being one of them, but he realized how demanding and how relentless the work was. Devoting his life to physical labor began to seem daunting. With few variables, it was easy to know what to expect, and when you knew the way things would go, who could help but wish them gone? He talked it over on the phone with Jasper, and invited him, at Elin's urging, to visit on the weekend. Jasper said he'd like to come, but at the last minute he canceled, claiming allergies (drugs). He'd gotten quite glib with his lies, Ben realized—later vindicating everything Ben thought by confessing that he'd met a girl in Harvard Square and gotten stoned with her. She'd invited him that same weekend to her brother's house on the Vineyard. For a brief period of time (brief only in retrospect) what seemed most important was getting laid.

Eight

Ben met a girl he liked at the hardware store during the summer. Since she'd flirted with him, he assumed she might be easy. It was equally possible that she was a little crazy: insisting on stroking her mascara wand over his eyelashes, then laughing; dropping black plastic flies in his lap during a movie, so that when the lights came up, he jumped out of his seat. The warm-up to sex was making sex a joke. Next, he had sex with someone named Bea, who had a tanned, muscular body from working as a lifeguard at the country club pool. They struck up a conversation and it turned out that she also loved documentary photography. Did he know the work of Bob Adelman? Adelman, who did those amazing civil-rights-era photographs? She gave him a copy of *Let Us Now Praise Famous Men*. He first learned from her about Margaret Bourke-White, who'd been at Cornell, but Bea thought only because it was where Bourke-White's first husband had studied.

The evening of the day they met, after fooling around by touching each other's wrists and quickly interweaving their fingers and squeezing, they had sex in the women's changing room after hours (Bea was trustworthy; the pool manager had given her the key). They had sex the second time inside one of the outdoor showers, with him cradling Bea's ass as she faced him, thighs bracketing his waist. They were sheltered by a tall bamboo curtain missing a couple of pieces, suspended from a rod in a tree, and later, as the moldy-smelling steam dispersed, they shared a joint outside the shower, making a game of exhaling smoke in the area where the steam had dissipated.

Instead of listening to her advice (she thought he shouldn't worry about what to major in; he could just make money because he decided to), he had sex with her on top of beach towels sharp with the smell of Clorox, a smell that seemed to Ben to permeate the whole world. The towels were stacked in a cart ready to be rolled to the front counter the next morning. Then, because he hadn't found a way to tell her he had other plans, he left without saying goodbye to board a bus so he could crash with LouLou in Somerville. LouLou had started calling him late at night, saying she missed him, putting down their classmates at Bailey, people he knew she'd really liked. She'd decided that Aqua had been exhausting and that Hailey was a drama queen. LouLou was in the process of breaking up with her married lover, who was trying to reconcile with his wife, though LouLou still had the keys to his secret apartment. Ben stayed for a week. How could he? What would he have done or said if the boyfriend had appeared, since men never believed that other men who were with their girlfriends were just friends? But his luck held, and he never once encountered the man, who still existed for him as a slightly blurry photo-booth picture cheek to cheek with LouLou, and a box of condoms inside the medicine cabinet. True, that made the guy seem a little more real, though he felt better when he thought of him as a figment of LouLou's imagination, so he did. He'd never doubted that LouLou had a lot of sex with some jerk who cheated on his wife, who was said to be an up-tight, Catholic New Englander who worked at Harvard University Press, but he'd never imagined LouLou and the man having a real life. The sparseness of their apartment underscored, even by Ben's low standards, how much the relationship was about the bed, since there was nowhere to sit except the two uncomfortable Goodwill chairs pulled up to a scratched kitchen table. "Champagne and pizza," LouLou had said, opening the refrigerator door to prove it. She was essentially telling the truth, though the pizza was stacked in boxes in the freezer, and the Champagne was something called prosecco.

The bed had no headboard. It had been pushed against the wall so people could sit on it sideways and lean against the wall with the boarded-up window as they talked. The nicest thing in the apartment was the neighbor's beagle, Mrs. Robinson, called simply "Robinson." There was a water bowl for the dog, a soup bowl (he found a stack of those in the cabinet, but no plates). LouLou told him her lover had removed them from his grandmother's place when she died. Someone else in the family had taken every plate, and every bit of flatware, but somehow the tower of mismatched bowls remained, so he'd put them in a box and carried them out. He'd meant to take the rug, too, but the door had closed and locked behind him. He'd considered that his message that his work was finished. The message from his wife that the marriage was finished had been more than a little cryptic. Every piece of furniture had been loaded out while he was at work. When he returned, nothing remained except her symbolic goodbye: her diaphragm on the side of the sink, so mangled that he mistook it, at a distance, for a dreamcatcher.

Nelson Goodhart was the lover's name. Why not think of the man by his name? Maybe in part because such a name was hard to believe. Nelson and his wife had recently gotten back together and were in counseling, and LouLou at least acted as if she didn't care what they decided about their marriage, since she was going to California. LouLou liked her summer job at an outdoor-clothing store. She'd traded in her feminine boots for clunky lace-ups she'd bought at a big employee discount. She'd also had her beautiful hair cut and wore it in an asymmetrical bob that she called her "flapper look." Good luck to anybody who still thought it was the 1920s.

Seeing LouLou, though, he realized how much he missed talking intensely, how important it was that another person shared his frame of reference about so much, in part because they'd experienced so many things together. Yet she still surprised him with what she knew that he didn't. Binnie had had an abortion. She'd been wrong, she'd been stupid to accept Binnie's lie; Hailey had confessed that she'd gone with her to the clinic, so Hailey had been a liar, as well as self-dramatizing.

LouLou's clothes were strewn around, though she'd been one of the neater people at Bailey. Her bra dangled from a drawer pull in the kitchen ("What do you do when you wash your underwear?"), and her shoes were jumbled in the corner near the never-used, upside-down recycling bin with a lamp on top. She was reading a book by Ronald Firbank—even the name was slightly silly—that made her laugh. LaVerdere had put her on to him. Ben picked up the book and read a page or two, but found nothing funny, though he realized that if he'd been the one to whom the book had been recommended, he might have felt differently.

When he left, she didn't come outside with him to say goodbye. She feared the two women who lived in the downstairs apartment, who always wanted to talk to her about investing in the stock market. He'd encountered one of them, or thought he had, though their conversation had been about the problem with the pipes clanging every time the upstairs shower was turned on.

He went south again, as he'd agreed he would ("Of course you're still my friend, I just didn't know how to say goodbye," he'd told her, quite honestly, on the phone), to hike part of the Appalachian Trail with Bea after her summer lifeguard job concluded. "A lifeguard?" LouLou had said to him. "Isn't that maybe a little too symbolic?" It was August, and to Bea's parents' dismay, she hadn't responded to Yale. (She was later admitted by an administrative waiver.) She dumped him in Lexington, Virginia ("I'm sorry. I just didn't know how to say goodbye"), after flirting successfully with a VMI cadet they met along the trail and deciding to continue the rest of the way with him. The guy had won her over with protein bars and loose talk about Kierkegaard and the importance of making a leap of faith. Where she went from there, before New Haven, before the psychologist, he didn't know. In Lexington, splitting a pizza just before she ditched him ("Why not order large, if it's only a dollar's difference?"), she'd said he was selfish and immature, as she slid more than her share of the pie's melted cheese in her own direction, though none of her accusations had been persuasive. He should have agreed that they'd both forget about school and live off the land and make documentaries about rural musicians. What rural musicians remained undiscovered? Who'd buy the movie camera?

After their split-up he set out to visit Darius in Washington, getting a ride as far as Charlottesville from a friend of the VMI cadet on his way to visit his mother in Sperryville, who informed Ben that he'd been fucked over by someone who'd never been worthy of him. Ben had worried that the guy might be gay, but what he said had only been his honest opinion. At the little brick train station below Main Street, Ben boarded a train to D.C. It seemed sad to him that the guy had waited with him and waved as Ben boarded the train. Why were some people so awful and others so sad? Anyone kind made him feel sad.

He lasted in D.C. only a night, sleeping in a filthy Foggy Bottom apartment where the still-thin, smooth-faced Darius— who never mentioned religion, though there were theology books scattered around, including some wedged in the wooden napkin holder—and his roommate played solitaire, separately, late into the night, ignoring the shiny black, nearly Ping-Pong-ball-size roaches skittering across the floor as they shared a coke-laced joint Ben declined a hit of, followed by a red wine chaser he was happy to join in on. It became clear that the roommate was a trust fund kid whose great-grandfather had patented something Ben could make no sense of, which had been used, before it got into wider distribution, to reinforce the Alaskan pipeline. Gee, maybe he could buy me a movie camera, he found himself thinking, though neither of them cared what he did, let alone had anything invested in Bea's idea that he become a filmmaker. His father, though, most certainly cared what he did; nothing would do but that Ben enroll in college, with his major already decided upon. Elin, who had a bloodhound's ability to sniff him down, never failed to attempt neutral, friendly calls, barely disguising the pressure she was under from his father to get answers.

Ben joined in as Darius and his roommate threw darts at a bull's-eye enlargement of George W.'s smug face that hung on the back of the apartment door—such a nonentity; such an establishment puppet, incapable of even holding a book right-side-up for a photo op—where the cracked wood above El Shrub's left ear let in light from the super-bright bulb in a metal cage dangling in the hallway.

They dumped freezer-burned ravioli out of a bag for dinner. Darius had plunked down a half-empty fifth of cheap vodka on the table, which he poured over ice the same indifferent way Elin overwatered houseplants. Darius and his friend exchanged in-jokes without giving Ben any context, wildly amusing each other, sloshing more vodka into their glasses than his after they'd finished the bottle of wine. Basically, they let him know he wasn't part of their world, whatever world that might be, and in some ways their bond was so convincing that he felt like he'd invented his friendship with Darius, and even that Bailey itself had been a different place than he remembered. The name of the school never came up.

He slept on a mattress you inflated with a pump that Darius told him, proudly, they'd found in the corridor when they'd moved in. Dog or cat hair had hardened against it. It looked like eczema. He tried not to closely examine the sheet Darius pulled out of a closet, with a note in an envelope pinned to it, from Mrs. Beltz, telling him it was "for the Thanksgiving table." That was so stupid that they'd all laughed, agreeing that the tablecloth was more useful as a sheet. The top covers were Ben's own clothes: his shirt, his jacket. The bed was, to use the roommate's favorite word, gross, but he was tired and felt stupid and uptight for being shocked at the way Darius was living. It made him suspect that Darius was doing more drugs than he wanted to admit.

The sleeping arrangements made LouLou's seem palatial. He closed his eyes without wanting to think about what might be skittering around and sharing his space, three inches below, on the floor. In the bedroom, Darius and the roommate had a pillow fight, or some muffled encounter with thumping that made the floorboards squeak. What was so funny? What could be so fucking funny? Drifting off to sleep—or trying to, while the broken ceiling fan hummed without rotating in the kitchen, he remembered how really anguished Darius had been when his parents were the first ones to arrive at Bailey after 9/11. They'd insisted on taking him to Mount Kisco, where they had a summer house. Darius hadn't wanted to go. LaVerdere had stepped in, trying to appease the Beltzes, saying that Darius would be safe at Bailey and that it would be better for everyone if he stayed. As the car pulled away, the back window had rolled down, Darius's head leaning out like a dog's, the sound he made equally as high-pitched. Ben had been up early, heading off to the trails to go jogging. He'd had to check his own response to run after the car.

The pillow fight in the bedroom went on and on. In the morning when he woke up, both of them were gone, though he hadn't heard either one leaving. He played with the notion that he was a character in a novel. He'd imagined all of it: his being excluded, Darius's anger, Darius's bizarre opinions. On his late-night walk with the roommate to get beer when the vodka disappeared, the guy had joked that he might toss Ben down the *Exorcist* steps as they passed Prospect Street.

There were empty beer bottles on the counter in the morning, so he must have remembered correctly that the two of them had gone out to get beer. He left everything on the floor and got out as fast as he could. He would have showered, but there was only tepid water. He was glad to go. At Bailey, on 9/11, he'd experienced claustrophobia for the first time, in spite of the fact that he was free to move wherever he wanted. It had all seemed like an impossible game of chess, though, because there'd been no good move to make. Was there anywhere his presence was truly wanted? The odd thing was that when you were in school, your presence was demanded. When you left, it was up to you to find out where you fit in, if you belonged anywhere at all, or if you could convince people you belonged when you didn't.

Ben never rode the Crescent again, though he liked its name; he'd rarely smoked a joint since that night, when the roommate had puked, and they'd all taken aspirin before going to sleep in anticipation of being awakened by headaches. Now, if he drank too much, Ben took B vitamins, washed down with Excedrin PM and a tall glass of water, waiting fifteen minutes to be sure to piss before even trying to sleep. Were you getting old when you had an automatic remedy for hangovers?

He had, though, to his surprise, delayed any decision about college and spent the next year in Washington. Sitting on a bench in DuPont Circle, he'd been approached by an old man who turned out to be Ms. Delacroix's husband, the judge. He must look bad, he realized, when the two of them were seated in a hotel dining room, having breakfast. "I never worry about any student who's graduated from Bailey Academy," the judge said. "Anything you like, son," he added, as the waiter approached. Ben ate eggs Benedict (a favorite of Elin's) and drank cup after cup of coffee. The judge ate scrambled eggs with a double order of sausage. When breakfast ended, the judge made a phone call and Ben was introduced to a man not much older than he, a graduate of American University, who needed someone to answer calls at an apartment complex and to send and receive packages for the residents. "You can write plays in your spare time, and have them staged at the Kennedy Center," the judge said.

"I don't write," Ben replied. (Even LouLou had stopped writing after 9/11.)

"Well, you'll be so bored, you will. Or you'll study the clarinet. Or maybe you'll enroll in a night-school program, over there at Georgetown, did you say it was? See how college agrees with you. I don't worry about a Bailey boy," he repeated. "You might end up a judge."

He did not. He lived in an apartment on Tunlaw Road, where he quickly learned how to answer three incoming calls simultaneously and also picked up extra money doing errands he wasn't required to do. Henry, one of the residents, taught him to drive. In the man's car, he practiced at night in the parking lot, or sometimes they bumped through the grounds of American University, and eventually they drove around circles and parallel-parked on Connecticut Avenue. He borrowed Henry's car to take his road test and got his license on the first try. His father had been such a prick, not to teach him to drive. "I specialize in being everyone's perfect father," Henry joked. But in May Henry was transferred to Oklahoma, and when the job got too boring and the heat settled in, Ben began to think about his father's place. He'd almost gotten in touch with LaVerdere to tell him what an odd thing he was doing, though he never had. There was every chance that LaVerdere would have been disappointed in him. Why should he feel defensive? Why was it necessary to explain himself? On the phone, he and LouLou—it seemed she was halfway across the world, in Berkeley, California—agreed that underlying so much of their education had been the implicit demand that they not only have knowledge, but that they understand themselves. Their teachers got to posture, to hide behind the façade of Bailey in order to give the impression that they understood themselves, Lou-Lou said.

Though he assumed he'd run into Darius again, he never did, and he realized that he'd disliked his roommate so much, he didn't call. Even stranger, when Henry left for Oklahoma they had a beer together at a bar on Wisconsin Avenue but never talked again. The judge, also, seemed like a figment of his imagination: an old, male Tinkerbell whose magic wand had arranged for, well, the status quo. LouLou was right when she said he needed to get serious.

He thought he might go to Cornell in September, which he told Elin on the phone. When she expressed excitement and went to get his father, he hung up. He'd been offered a scholarship, if he could get it reinstated. If not, that would be soon enough to speak to his father.

Talking to his sister, Brenda, was even worse than talking to his father: It didn't matter so much about undergraduate school, she said; he'd have to go to graduate school. Personally, Brenda had never imagined he had the temperament to do anything in the arts, since he liked instant gratification. That one had really stumped him, until he realized how long they'd lived apart, how little she knew him. Also, he hadn't said anything about what he might major in. What genie had he let out of the bottle? She regretted that he hadn't majored in math at Bailey. Some artists, Brenda said grudgingly, who were obsessed, might have lived to create, but who thought effort guaranteed success?

The judge died. Ben didn't know that until LouLou found out when she was talking to Binnie, who'd called to tell her she'd gotten engaged. "Thank god there were some real people at Bailey," was what LouLou had to say about that. She'd moved with her roommate to Oakland, which was more real than Berkeley. In May 2003, he flew to California to visit her.

She lived four flights up, with a Ph.D. student just as wired as she'd described: The woman didn't even stand to say hello. She twisted and sucked the ends of her hair as she worked on her computer. She was wearing striped pants and looked like a convict, he thought. Maybe an old-fashioned ball and chain kept her anchored to the chair. She dispelled that illusion when she carried her Mac into the bedroom to let them have the living room. "Unless you'd rather use the bedroom," she said, then blushed and hurried off before receiving an answer. LouLou laughed; he felt awkward, as if they'd both been rude, when she'd tried to be considerate.

LouLou handed him a beer from a refrigerator that stood in the passageway from the living room to the tiny kitchen, and they immediately started talking. The subject was the cover of *Entertainment Weekly,* on which the Dixie Chicks had appeared naked. Natalie Maines was LouLou's hero for what she'd said about George W. Bush. D.C. had been so oppressive, Ben said, with the young Bush bureaucrats everywhere. LouLou called them "Gregor Samsa cockroaches." The only problem, she explained, was that everyone else had to wake up, too.

Nine

fter he graduated from Cornell in 2007, he crashed at his former classmate Arly's East Village apartment, servicing her twice a night and working as a poorly paid photographer's assistant by day. He wasn't thrilled when he learned that Brenda planned to visit. She'd be in New York on business, but she set aside time to see him on the weekend. Of course he couldn't invite her to the small one-bedroom walk-up, but he didn't really know where to go with his sister. Also, though Arly clearly cared nothing for his friends or family, he'd be in trouble if he excluded her. A walk? A simple walk somewhere?

He decided on the obvious: Central Park. Once there, Arly immediately ran into one of her grandmother's friends and stopped to talk. She'd been surprised to hear that the man had moved from Rye to New York. The two warmly embraced. Ben and Brenda waited on a bench—it didn't seem like the sort of conversation they could easily enter into, since she and the man had such a long shared history. While they were sitting side by side, a squirrel fell from the tree—how often did that happen?—and landed in between him and Brenda. They gasped as it scrambled away.

"Fucking filth!" his sister exclaimed, jumping up and brushing her jeans as if the rodent's hair had been instantly ejected, like porcupine quills. (Ben silently corrected himself: The porcupine has no way to send its quills out of its body; it is the animal's flapping its tail that embeds the quills.)

Arly and the man, Michael, had rushed over when Brenda screamed, but by then everything was okay—or Ben thought it was. No time to turn it into a joke, or a family story—in fact, in their family, there were no family stories. Anything bordering on nostalgia was sneered at.

Arly and Michael's conversation resumed, out of earshot, until Michael came up and shook their hands before tipping his hat brim and taking his leave. Michael had had two oranges in his jacket pockets, one of which he'd given to Arly, and he'd insisted on giving the other to Ben and Brenda to share. They'd gotten not only the orange, but a lecture on Christopher Columbus, who'd ostensibly planted the first orange tree in the New World ("New World"—wasn't that a phrase out of F. Scott Fitzgerald?), though initially oranges and lemons hadn't been valued. That had come later, Michael had informed them, using the same condescending intonation an adult who knew nothing about children would use when reading a fairy tale. Oranges had initially been imported from Sicily. Old people were so proud of their knowledge, but their information so often only created a twisting path. Whatever old people said was news brought from a vanished land.

The day was intermittently sunny as they walked past Strawberry Fields. Of course one of them—in this case, he—mentioned John Lennon. His sister uttered an irrelevant slur about "the great Yoko Ono," ironizing "great" with a roll of her eyes. Arly took exception. She was like a cigarette ash, her grudges tiny, glowing embers waiting to flare, though she addressed the subject only when they'd crossed the park and stopped to have coffee. She felt he and his sister were "a unit." They'd been rude, or borderline rude (he'd argued the point), to an elderly gentleman. "He didn't want to talk to us," his sister said dismissively. "We thanked him for the fruit."

"Are things that happened in the past ruled out as a possible topic of conversation?" Arly asked. "You knew—the way your brother knows everything—that oranges were imported from Italy?"

Arly had dropped out of Cornell without graduating. Her job at Macy's put her in a foul mood. Some days she just didn't show up for work.

Brenda looked at Ben. She said, "I assume she's kidding?"

"Arly—sorry if we didn't seem sociable enough. The gods got even by dropping a flying rat on Brenda's lap, okay?"

"*Please listen,*" Arly said. "Anything you want to say, you can say directly to me, Brenda. There are various interpretations people have when reacting to something that has just happened."

"Especially true if the other person's intent on bullying," his sister replied.

In the coffee shop, Arly smiled falsely at the waitress as she put down an espresso and placed coffees in front of Ben and Brenda. The waitress also smiled, sliding the container of sugar to the center of the table.

Brenda considered her coffee mug for some time, then moved it aside. "Is my presence disturbing you lovebirds? Is there some problem with my being here, Ben? Arly?"

"Oh, we wouldn't want to talk about *the past*," Arly said. "Let's talk about the present. That's the time period in which your brother lives, so let's not talk about anything that isn't happening right this minute."

Ben cleared his throat. He said, "You're taking this too far."

"You might apologize," Brenda said. "You're sort of ruining our afternoon."

"I happen to believe it's better to talk openly. I don't apologize, but I do regret being a bit hypersensitive. In the world I grew up in, you should include older people, make them feel comfortable and valued."

"The day of good etiquette," Brenda said. "Think of all we can learn."

"I doubt it," Arly said. "Whatever happens in your family, you'll do whatever it takes to remain an insular little group, even if you don't approve of one another. And 'approve' means 'silence.' Nobody would ever want to say anything real. You haven't talked about one thing that's important to you, Brenda. I know you withdrew after your mother's death and that you have as little to do with Elin as possible, and that you're gay, even if you don't say so."

"Wow," Brenda said. "Ben, really. An amazing choice you've made here."

"Why are you doing this?" Ben asked Arly.

"Oh, I'm insecure because I'm two years older than you and flunked out of Cornell—don't you think?"

A little boy in his overalls, bib and forearms streaked with ketchup, had caught the flash in Ben's eye. He squeezed his fingers toward his palm, a kid's wave. Ben's raised hand acknowledged it. The boy shyly turned away.

"How would you know anything about my relationship with Elin, Arly?" Brenda asked.

"Because unlike you, and before I gave up, I tried to have a relationship with Elin. Just by telephone—I wouldn't want to transgress and actually interact with someone in your hermetically sealed family. And Ben, don't get upset, because it wasn't about *you*. I tried to talk to her woman-to-woman about how she felt, whether she might like to have a more substantial relationship with someone who cared enough to relate to her and who was important in her stepson's life."

"Really? What did she say?" This was the first time he'd heard this.

Brenda took a sip of coffee. The way she pursed her lips reminded him of their mother. Her hands, with their long fingers, were their mother's hands.

"Sadly, she just couldn't do it. She obviously doesn't feel she can trust anybody. It's why he married her, don't you think? Your mother was lovely—I'm assuming she *was,* because that's what I've always been told—but after she died, apparently second-best was someone who'd keep her mouth shut."

"Did it ever occur to you that she might have thought she was dealing with a nutcase?" Brenda asked, surprising him by defending their stepmother.

"She certainly wasn't going to admit that he killed himself," Arly replied.

Ah: She'd just been warming up. His sister was looking at him. He could feel his face's rigidity, any expression absent in proportion to how much pain he felt.

New cups of coffee and espresso were put down by the waitress, though no one had summoned her. "Refills are free," the waitress said, as she walked away.

"I read the autopsy results. If you read between the lines, it's pretty clear 'pneumonia' is listed as a technical cause of death."

"How did you see our father's autopsy results?" Brenda asked, her hands clasped tightly. If a madman had locked his sister in a windowless cell that she might talk her way out of, she could not have decided on a more judicious tone of voice.

Well, Ben thought, Arly would have done it because she had little sense of personal privacy, whether it was leaving the bathroom door open when she was on the toilet, or reading someone's mail. She'd confessed to ripping up a parking ticket he'd gotten when she'd preceded him back to the car, because it would have spoiled their afternoon. To throwing out a summons for jury duty because "They send those things out like coupons."

Elin had told him how his father had died. So what was the truth? Was Elin deluded? Arly malevolent? Did one preclude the possibility of the other, as LaVerdere had been so fond of asking?

Outside the restaurant, Arly said she was sorry for them: Hansel and Gretel, no match for the evil witch. When Arly extended her hand before leaving, Brenda shook it. It was the same way you'd deal with an insane person who did something improper as you left the asylum. Then Arly turned and left. She did have a beautiful ass. He stood with Brenda, who, he knew, needed to return to Grand Central.

"Was she serious?" Brenda asked.

"I don't know," he said. "Please don't take it personally. She was completely paranoid about that Michael guy. She's opened my mail. I thought it was harmless. It wasn't like she hid it after she opened it."

"She's poison," Brenda said.

"I'm so sorry. We'll find out. Nothing she said was really about us. It was all about her."

"You knew I was gay?"

"Sure."

"It never crossed your fucking mind."

"No," he said. "It didn't."

A cabbie ducked his head to see whether they wanted a ride. All those split-second decisions everyone was always making in the city: Were that man and woman drunk? On speed? Had he just told the funniest joke imaginable, or was his friend having a heart attack? Then the cab was pulling away, and of course the driver would no more remember them than the waitress would think about her miserable customers one minute after she got off work. Was he going to go back to the apartment, to Arly? Would she be gloating? Furious? Had she accomplished what she'd set out to do, packed her bags, and gone off to crash with a friend? He'd lived with her for long enough that he knew if he returned, so would their routine. They'd go to midnight movies, set roach traps around the apartment in places they stupidly thought weren't noticeable, they'd spend more money than they should on wine, have arguments neither was willing to concede. They'd try to be healthy and jog on weekends, on Sunday morning they'd listen to Lou Reed sing his spookily seductive "Sunday Morning" as they ate muffins drizzled with honey, get mugged on Essex street (Arly), see a cat run over by a truck in front of the Strand (Ben), buy stolen down pillows (Arly) from a vendor on Houston Street.

He'd rent a car and begin looking at property upstate, whose potential purchase would underscore his inability to keep on keepin' on. Whatever its advantages, it would also announce the end of something, and if that thing wasn't youth, it was nevertheless related to age, related to a world you'd renounced, extending its never-dormant tendrils to pull you back.

Metaphor. It was insidious. You had to ignore that way of thinking, the same way you had to understand that your dreams contained straw men rather than real omens, the way you were obliged to admit your neurotic fears lacked legitimacy. Strangely, to admit you lacked intuition, that you realized symbolic stories were inert, that you had no special abilities, no second senses to go on, meant that you had achieved a sense of power.

He was determined not to go into the drawer where he kept his birth certificate, which he'd needed to show on so many occasions, and the letter Hailey had sent when she was drunk or stoned, and the coroner's report. What good sense Elin had, not to befriend Arly. Arly was the oven, if he and Brenda were Hansel and Gretel. She was not merely the witch.

Ten

Had he thought that, because he'd done the exact opposite of what he intended and opened the death certificate and seen that "complications of pneumonia" was listed as the cause of death and called Brenda and told her, and apologized again, that Brenda wouldn't call Elin?

He was sitting in a bar he liked, Redz, off Avenue A. Bars were a lot better than his so-called home and also provided a soundtrack. Any minute, Arly would come through the door, but until she did, he could brood about the whole miserable situation. The same night, after she'd dropped the bomb, after his worst fight with Arly ever, she'd insisted he go to the psychic. Why bother, since she'd found all this out, he'd said. In a rage, he'd told her he didn't know how charlatans worked, how some psychic had discovered things about his past. (God, the woman even knew he'd been a chess player.) Maybe she'd gotten access to the coroner's report, for all he knew. Who knew or cared how people who preyed on others sneakily got their information, then described their visions and bizarre notions to gullible, desperate people.

The surprise was that Brenda had succeeded where Arly had failed: After some hesitation, Elin gave his sister information he and she didn't have. It later emerged that Arly's precious psychic had described a vision she had while grasping Arly's hand (not so unusual that somebody would flirt with Arly, though the psychic had probably learned her gestures from reading the cartoons). Her "vision" was of a man, sick, climbing a mountain, trying to arrive at the top. Arly had never seen his father, so how could she know who the "tall, frail, bald-headed man wearing a stocking cap" was? The man, according to the psychic, was either Arly's relative or related to someone close to her. Someone she knew very well who was unable to make crucial decisions, who was blocked because he was under the influence of the person—a man who wouldn't come into focus—who was climbing the mountain with him. Might the bald man need to make a decision between life and death? There were other problems, more mundane problems of living in the world, but in addition to that, the man felt pain, either in his lungs (by then, Arly had been reading from notes she'd jotted down in a little notebook) or in his stomach. As she spoke, Ben's stomach also began to ache, but not as much as his head. Had his father's problem been in his stomach? He'd been in his last year at Cornell when his father was operated on. Had that been the site of the surgery?

Ben wasn't in a good mood. Earlier (on his second drink), he'd decided he'd never have the talent, let alone the luck, to run the business his boss had. He was doomed to be someone who answered the phone. There was another much more talented assistant where he worked, who'd been there for years. He set up the lighting and took test shots. Ben made the appointments and cleaned up at the end of the day, filing, confirming appointments, calling FedEx. He was nothing but a glorified janitor whose job was to damp-mop terra-cotta floors.

Arly came into Redz with her red leather bag slung over her shoulder. She could seriously hurt anyone she swung it at, she liked to say. The thing was loaded with essential Arly paraphernalia: a Swiss Army knife; a large Hershey bar; a cosmetic bag with enough products inside it to transform the faces of every woman in the bar and on the block, and probably in the neighborhood. She carried extra tights, a light jacket, flip-flops, a black scarf. Once, helping her look for her missing keys, he'd upended the bag. Out had come a bag of marbles, a can of Mace, and a tube of KY jelly.

She swooped down and hugged him. "Forgive and forget" she said, instead of hello. She was on her way to an evening mani-pedi with her friend Sharon. Before he even had time to ask if she wanted a drink, the other woman came into the bar. Arly pulled the jacket out of her bag, put it on, and bent a second time to say goodbye—this time by tongueing the top of his ear. As usually happened, Sharon stayed at a distance and held up a hand to bestow a silent farewell. ("Nixon" was his nickname for her, behind her back.) If she'd greeted him in the first place, he'd been looking elsewhere.

He was glad they left, because he couldn't stand hearing any more about Sharon's upcoming wedding, which, as one of four bridesmaids, Arly was obsessing about. He had no idea why women thought that their bridesmaids' dresses had to be a style they could use for other occasions.

He ordered another drink, unable to get the image of his

father out of his mind. He'd tried not to register his father's thinness the last time he'd visited from Cornell; it was fine to see him in bed, with covers piled on top, but when he'd had to help him to the bathroom and he'd felt his father's ribs, far worse than Darius's, he'd felt faint. Apparently, he was so light that Elin could move him with little trouble, though when the chemo concluded and he could gradually eat again, Elin had been so happy to tell Ben that he'd begun to put on weight. Hiking? Wouldn't that be a bit too much of a challenge? His father preferred to sit on the screened porch at his summer place as he aimed his binoculars at the birds at the feeder. Where would he have hiked?

"Noanet Peak Trail in Noanet Woodlands," his sister told him days later, pronouncing each word distinctly. Elin had told Brenda she had not been able to disabuse him of the notion he must go hiking. Unless he could reach the top, which he'd take as a sign (His father was superstitious?), his decision was not to continue with the next round of chemo. He had a bad cough. Tears ran from his eyes from eyedrops he had to apply three times a day. She'd begged him not to even talk about such foolishness, but there was a warm spell, and it seemed true that with the new medicine, he was getting some of his energy back. He'd become convinced that because he'd had the vision in a dream (yes; okay, everybody was nuts), he'd received a message. Elin was distraught. His doctor told him to rest.

Sometime in the night, that same night, another night, who knew what night, Elin had gone to check on him before daybreak. His bed was empty. She knew what he'd gone to do. She rushed to her car to follow him, though she worried that maybe it wasn't her decision to make. If she took away hope, that would depress him so much that he'd have no reason to go on. He feared more treatment, more nausea, and the horrible weightless feeling he couldn't find the words to describe. He'd actually walked around wearing ankle straps filled with sand that she'd bought the year before as a way to develop her calves, after seeing the weights on TV. Elin hesitated. As she sat in the driver's seat, classical music came on the radio. Of course he wouldn't make it, but if he realized that and turned back, Elin thought, that might be the end of his terrible idea.

It was as if the music hypnotized her. She blamed herself, she certainly did, for sitting passively while her husband might be in the process of killing himself, but she just didn't go anywhere—nor would she have known where to go. She never started the car. She sat there crying for what seemed like an hour, maybe it had been an hour, or only half an hour, or maybe the worst twenty minutes of her life, and by the time the sun came up she decided that she, too, could think symbolically: that any moment she'd see him. His car would appear. He'd apologize for his foolishness, they'd return to the house hand in hand. No, she never thought any of that. She was making it up after the fact, she knew she was, she was rationalizing. The truth was, she didn't know what she would have done if she'd been the one to receive such a diagnosis. Not strike out on a hike, that was for sure, because she'd become agoraphobic; during his illness, it had gotten more difficult to drive anywhere.

Brenda told Ben that Elin had wept, insisting on her own inadequacy. Their father hadn't died on the hike, though he hadn't made it far. Whoever was with him had summoned help when he'd doubled over, choking, blood running from his nostrils. He'd been unable to take another step. When Elin next heard, he was in the ER. She didn't go there, either. Because by then, she thought that the hike hadn't been about living, it had been about provoking his death, and how humbled, how embarrassed he must be that all he'd done was further sicken himself. She didn't have the courage to see him. Or to drive. So she'd taken a cab—she'd done that the next day before he was discharged, after speaking to a psychiatrist he was to continue seeing twice a week. What time had he left the house? How had he crept out without her hearing? Where was this park? Angels had lifted him out the window, he'd replied facetiously. Who'd gone with him—or had he gone alone and lied about having a companion?

Someone, a neighbor, had come to stay with them at night when he returned. Elin was afraid to be left alone with him. The cough quickly worsened. So many doctors were being consulted. And then he had a heart attack. The medics stabilized him in the ambulance. They were preparing to do a procedure, one they put on hold after consulting with the senior surgeon. The pneumonia had set in fast. She saw no reason to tell his children about his folly and didn't want to risk diminishing him in their eyes, with his crazy talk of birds and mountains to conquer, as a young, exhausted-looking resident deliberately avoided making eye contact with the doctor standing beside him at the foot of the bed.

After work a few days following his conversation with Brenda, Ben gave the revised, short form of his father's suicide—what he now described as his father's deliberately exhausting himself—to Gerard, the photographer's talented assistant. He and Gerard had worked together for almost a year. They went to bars entirely different from the ones where he met up with Arly. He told Gerard that he had trouble feeling the same way about Arly, because she'd opened the whole can of worms. Gerard thought that maybe if they left the city they could get their relationship back on track. Ben didn't think that was likely. There was no use now in trying to think whether he wanted to know about his father's bizarre, debilitating journey, because he knew.

"Look at it this way. At least you were in Ithaca when he had surgery. At least you didn't have to observe everything, blow-by-blow. My old man's looking better by the minute," Gerard said. He lived with his father in West New York, New Jersey. His own constant personal debate was whether to continue living there, remaining closeted, or to move in with his boyfriend, a doorman on the Upper East Side who appeared in porn films, and break his father's heart.

"Maybe the chemo did something to his brain," Gerard said. His usual drink was either white wine or a margarita, if he felt like splurging. Ben had bought them both a round of Patrón Silver margaritas. "I feel like there's this shit coming down—you know what I mean? Downtown's nothing but rubble. All day we see people whose egos are bouncing around like Ping-Pong balls, then we get out of work and they're weaving all over the streets in their fucking limos. You know, Ben, this place could sop up your tears with a sponge. Maybe some distance is needed. Maybe we've got to put it on the line, you know? What would Barack Obama say? Wouldn't he say that if we're not rallying the people, we should at least quit our jobs and do something more meaningful?"

"You think Obama would want us to be unemployed?" Ben asked. The salt was gone from the rim of his glass. The tiny chunk that had fallen on top of the bar looked like cocaine. Another pleasure of the rich. Outside the restaurant, a black stretch limo waited. A rumor started in the bar that the Olsen twins were in a private room in the back. Ben overheard a guy whispering this to the greeter, a super-pretty woman who stood next to a greeter-in-training, who was even prettier. Both women looked confused when anyone walked in for a reservation. A reservation? In *their* restaurant? Was this April Fool's Day, or something? Had they called or booked on OpenTable, or what? Next, whomever stood in front of them would be asked whether they were actually there to *eat.* Only with lengthy tapping of the keyboard, as the couple huddled together on the other side of the high-topped barricade, did the greeters' concerned frowns sometimes diminish. The few times that happened, both lifted the menus—it seemed as if there were at least three pleather menus to be piled atop one another per person—as if they were made of lead.

Gerard noticed him looking. "You're not going to get laid by either one of them," he said. "The short one's going home to paint sparkle stuff on her fingernails like her friend, and her friend's gonna shave her legs and do some shots. Or maybe she'll do the shots first and nick her shin. All these new razors, they never improve. What do you say the two of us, we go in tomorrow and quit?"

"Gerard, you can't quit. You're as talented as he is. Your old man will die, and you can go live with what's-his-name."

"It's a made-up name," Gerard said. "You don't have to remember it."

"Tell me again what it is."

"I've told you ten times. You don't want to remember."

"Give me one more chance."

"Duncan," Gerard said. "But his real name's Gunther."

They both cracked up. Gerard almost choked on an ice cube. It jumped out of his mouth and flew across somebody's lap and shattered on the tile floor. The startled look on the woman's face wiped the grins off their faces. When Gerard started laughing again, it was contagious.

Ben ordered another round, including a cosmo for the startled woman. It went without saying that Ben didn't mind if she thought of it as a flirtation. Gerard, of course, was completely indifferent. After a "thank you" and one sip, she got off her bar stool and went to a table, where a man who'd just entered the restaurant converged with her. The bartender put her drink on a tray that a waitress carried to her table. She was seated. She didn't look in their direction. In a movie, that wouldn't have happened, Ben thought. At Bailey, even The Brains wouldn't have snubbed him that way. He'd started to become aware of women's sideways glances, expressing interest. The drink had been meant as an apology—didn't she get that? Or were no apologies accepted in the presence of her boyfriend?

He quit before Gerard did. He quit the next day, when Gerard was merely late for work.

Eleven

Before Ben was in any position to repay Brenda the money he'd borrowed while the old man's will was in probate, he'd taken a job in the financial district that was less exciting but paid more. The great perk of the job was that his boss was letting him live in his brother's never-occupied pied-à-terre on Hudson Street. As he'd realized at Cornell, he had an aptitude for coding, though he couldn't have predicted that he'd end up focusing on legacy software; all you really needed was to keep up your own interest, to be able to sit staring at your screen for hours as you tweaked decade-old algorithms, and to be amused that you were writing a language no one used anymore—one your company would also eventually give up on. Though he liked his boss, and enjoyed the bento-box lunches he often treated him to on Fridays, he'd been honest about saying when he took the job that he was considering going to NYU Law School. He'd announced his intentions to Elin. Then, on the verge of taking the LSATs, he'd gotten an unexpected phone call that had resulted in a detour: a trip to the Museum of Natural History, and a sort of proposition, more an apology, no, not an apology, a paraphrase of a book that apparently argued for negative experiences being ultimately more helpful than positive ones.

Arly stood in the lobby, holding two tickets. She wasn't wearing a bra. Her hair was in a chaste bun, though, as she fingered her thread-thin necklace, which caught light like a mirror.

Amid schoolchildren and crowds of adults, they'd lingered by the dioramas, later linked fingers when looking at the dinosaur skeleton, like people sharing a moment of awe at the Grand Canyon. Well, in a way it was, it was just the Grand Canyon of Tyrannosaurus Rex. The next surprise, which he could take or leave, absolutely his call, involved more tickets. ("I don't know your social. If you want to, I mean *only if you want*, we can pick up your ticket at LaGuardia.") That evening he and Arly flew to Miami.

It was just for the weekend. One last time he'd decided to have with her, since he couldn't remember the last time he'd had sex. He'd been to Florida once, Destin, Florida, where his father's favorite cousin lived. His mother had gotten the flu and couldn't go, so his father had taken him instead, leaving Brenda at home in tears. He'd tasted crab for the first time with his cousin, who told him about his time working on fishing boats and told him never to parachute-jump. That was why he had fused vertebra that meant he'd have to walk with a cane the rest of his life. But Ben knew enough now to know that Miami had changed from whatever it would have been in those years, transformed by the money tornado that had whirled it closer to god, so that it became *Miami*. As they were leaving MIA in a cab (How did she suddenly have money?), she put her hand on his knee, and he looked at her fingers and thought *crabs,* and then he thought about reading T. S. Eliot at Bailey, though the only poem LaVerdere really liked was "The Waste Land." Probably nobody dredged that up to read anymore.

Stretch Humvees passed them by, two in just a few minutes. Arly was scrolling through her phone, stopping to read a review of a Cuban restaurant that had been reviewed the week before in the *Times,* so it was probably not even worth trying to get in. No yellowfin carpaccio with macerated lingonberries in their future, as she'd put it. After five minutes on the highway, coming in in a cab, Arly said they should find a way to move there, because New York was too expensive and not enough fun—and that opinion was just based on the weather, and the vibes she picked up, looking out the window.

Ben, who'd insisted on paying for something, had been in the driveway, waiting for change from the cabdriver, when Arly walked off to check into the hotel. When Ben walked across the lobby, up to the desk, the guy behind the counter was complimenting her on her dangly earrings (a paired moon and sun). He'd already upgraded her to a junior suite. The desk guy's flirtation resolved itself in a nasty stare when Ben appeared. She loved situations like that, moments of others' optimistic misunderstanding, because they provided an immediate reshuffling of power.

After they went to the room and she undressed him and they had sex on the floor, knocking out the barrette so that her hair fell in familiar waves around her face, he stood, then fell on the bed in exhaustion. The last thing he knew, he'd been looking at dinosaur skeletons on a cold day in New York City. Eventually, he got up to take a shower. She followed him into the bathroom and didn't look at him as he tested the water and stepped in. Through the frosted glass of the shower enclosure, he could hardly see her; he swiped a streak on the thick glass—some of the problem was steam—and saw her as if looking through a Lichtenstein brushstroke from the other side of the mural. She wondered aloud if she should get into the shower with him, but instead peed—did any other woman pee that way, with one leg crossed over the other?—then gave herself a whore's bath from an Evian bottle that stood with two glasses on a small tray beside the sink, pouring water into her hand, then splashing it into her armpits and crotch, wiping herself dry on a white towel thicker than his camel's hair coat—his Christmas gift from Elin. She dried him off when he stepped out, and after that knelt on an irregular pink island of bath rug and took his penis in her mouth. Whatever was going on was going on.

They went to a different restaurant from the one she'd heard about, a longer walk from the hotel than it appeared on the map, where Jaguars and more Humvees clustered outside. The valets wore camouflage jumpsuits. Inside, the bartender was famous for serving mojitos with a dusting of gold leaf that Ben thought looked repulsively like pollen. The gold leaf supply, he observed, was kept locked in a safe under the bar. They had two drinks that cost as much as an entrée in a classy New York restaurant because they had no reservation and had to wait. The faint flecks of gold above her top lip were much more intriguing than cappuccino foam, so maybe it was true, what Bea had thought, what Arly thought now: Money was sexy. He told Arly they should order food at the bar; clearly, they'd never get served. "We'll get a table," she said. "I gave her two twenties."

"Have you come into an inheritance, or something?"

"Not exactly. Only into good luck," she replied. Long afterward, he'd find out the good luck had a name, worked at Deutsche Bank, and paid for sex.

In the garden of their Deco hotel the next afternoon, after they'd had sex in the room, he asked her what she thought had gone wrong between them, and she brought her thumbnail close to one nostril and looked at him with Bambi eyes, sniffing. Her face was more expressive when she thought he was dumb than when she was having an orgasm. He considered her pantomime— had she used a lot more than he realized, was that it? They sat in the garden, drinking the last of a bottle of Cristal she'd shoplifted the night before from what should have been a locked case in a liquor store where nobody spoke English. She'd pointed out the dangling padlock with as much joy as a lepidopterist seeing a rare butterfly on a leaf.

When he came back to their room the next night, carrying an expensive little pizza whose topping smelled more like ammonia than mozzarella, to find her in bed with the bartender from the previous night and another guy, he didn't panic. He was relieved— okay; that wasn't his first emotion, but he felt that a burden had been lifted, soon enough—because otherwise their relationship would have gone on and on. The bartender jumped from the bed, his erection a bright-pink magic wand, and locked himself in the bathroom. The other guy went right on, like a jackhammer.

Ben sat in the lobby, flipping through a newspaper, then asked directions to the News Café from the Asian woman behind the front desk. She must have been asked that as every third question. He walked there from the hotel, though the heat made the walk unenjoyable. There were cars everywhere. Everything seemed to be happening in slightly speeded-up time, like the sex in the bedroom. The speed with which the bartender had shot out of bed suggested he'd played football before spending his life pollinating mojitos. The notion of the world speeding past Ben, everything too frenetic, had begun the second he opened the door. Now, in a reaction so delayed he doubted there could be any connection, he felt his penis begin to stir. At the café, he ordered only an iced tea. If they'd sold aspirin, he could have used a couple of those, too.

The woman sitting across from a man at the next table had a little dog in her lap who kept staring at him, panting. More interesting things to look at inside the hotel rooms, doggie, he thought. He reached out and squiggled the top of its head. The woman, in an accent he couldn't at first place (Russian), told him the name of the breed, which he hadn't asked and didn't recognize. Was he on vacation? Yes, he replied, from New York. Where were they from? Pompano Beach. The woman lowered the dog to the sidewalk. It retreated under the table. A tall black man with a bandanna around his forehead that was wider than his Speedo streaked by on a skateboard. Yeah, right—they should live in Miami. It really was more Arly's kind of place. She could dance all night wherever she was, but by midnight he was always exhausted. Once he'd found a bottle of Jack Daniel's he hadn't known was in the apartment, on the top shelf of the closet, but he'd never found drugs.

"Have you been to the beach?" the woman asked. The man said nothing. He wore wraparound sunglasses, so that his eyes were invisible. He'd taken out his phone and was making a call. Ben caught sight of several bracelets on his wrist. He turned slightly away from them. The woman seemed on the verge of saying something, and Ben didn't want to talk to her. He didn't even want to notice as much as he did: that her high heel rested in a puddle of her dog's urine, her other leg safely crossed over her knee. In the bathroom, when Arly had risen, her knees had been so pink, they'd both thought dye from the rug had rubbed off on them.

The Russian woman looked down when she caught the smell. "FrouFrou, bad!" she said. "Very bad!" Ben turned away again, trying to indicate lack of interest—if he might not have looked as indifferent as he hoped back in the hotel room, at least he could be unfazed about some dog taking a piss. The woman stood in a puddle of piss; where were all the famous *Vogue* photographers when you needed them? She began jerking the dog forward on its shiny purple leash.

"The dog is a pig," the man said, when she got to the sidewalk.

At this point, he didn't realize they were trying to pick him up. Not that the dog could have been made to pee on cue, but whatever it took, both were waiting for a way to warp whatever happened into an invitation. He got it the second the woman returned, when she told him they kept a condo in Miami Beach and asked if he'd like to go there: "Drinks are free." Maybe she thought he'd ordered iced tea because he didn't have much money.

"No, sorry, my wife's waiting at the hotel," he said. Even the lie scared him—the mere possibility.

The woman was at least forty-five, tall, pretty, her hair dyed the color of Mercurochrome. Her husband—he had quite a collection of bangles on his arm—older. Ben had never slept with anyone older. In a way, it might be the perfect ending to his big Saturday night in Miami. If he'd been fucked up, he *might* have considered it (yeah, he was a little angry, but worse than that, everything that was happening now made him feel like he was bogged down; it all seemed lugubrious, there was no middle ground between speed and near-narcolepsy now that everything had stopped happening so fast), but the woman stank of perfume.

"Hear about the new trend of putting gold dust in drinks?" he said, testing to see how she'd react if he started talking to her husband.

"True also in Japan. They've been putting it on pastry for years. Like shaved chocolate," the man added. Ben pulled his chair over to their table. "What do you drink?" the man asked, his eyes not at all visible through his sunglass lenses, signaling the waitress, then miscalculating, running the toe of his shoe up Ben's ankle.

After that awkward moment, Ben spent the night walking, sitting somewhere, if he could find anywhere to sit, every now and then testing himself. He thought about whether there could be any way to go back to the hotel, but that seemed impossible. It was as futile as trying to strike one wet match after another. Not one thought lit up. At dawn, he decided to leave the things he'd brought in the room (so did she; he never saw them again). He counted his cash, then called a cab to the airport. She'd bought round-trip tickets, but he couldn't imagine being on the next day's flight with her. Paying whatever fine they demanded for leaving early might actually cost him less than spending money for a night on his own at a hotel.

In the men's room at the airport, someone made it clear he had drugs. Drugs: Well, that was another possibility. Instead, he bought a fresh-squeezed orange juice that tasted, oddly, like a lump of coal. He drank it slowly as he stood in the long security line, wondering if he'd have been able to fuck the Russian woman while her husband watched. Not likely the guy wouldn't expect to be included, since he'd toed him.

The junior suite had looked like a tornado had blown through: clothes tangled with towels, bathrobes in a heap, pillows tossed like huge hopscotch stones on the floor, shoes knocked over, drinks spilled, one woman on TV mounting another, whose skirt was bunched at her waist, the soundtrack so loud you'd have thought someone would have knocked on the door or called the front desk.

He closed his eyes and tried to remember exactly what the room had looked like, but, disconcertingly, what popped up in his mind was the room where the Honor Society met at Bailey Academy—how truly absurd; from another lifetime—where the disorder was artful, like the rug, pre-fab disorder meant to reassure with repeated patterns. Not that anybody ever figured out why Binnie and her mother always made a mess of the chairs they dragged into a corner.

Tessie and Binnie. My goodness, he thought, Tessie and Binnie.

Before he boarded the plane, he called the hotel switchboard and asked to speak to the front desk. "I'm in room four-oh-four," he said. "I know this is going to sound strange, but I opened the window and a tornado came through. Can you send someone up from housekeeping?"

"Sir? Did you say a tornado?" the male voice asked. It was sort of heartbreaking that people didn't realize the things that betrayed them: The voice sounded young, unguarded, truly surprised.

"Yeah, it broke the windows. Really, you've got to send somebody up. It's a mess," he said.

"Four-oh-four," he heard the person say, in a muffled voice.

"Hello?" another voice said. "There's a problem in your suite, sir? Are you calling from within the hotel?"

"Four-oh-four," he repeated emphatically, letting his voice veer out of control before disconnecting.

In the seat next to his was a large man wearing a black eye patch. He was reminded of Hailey. All the way to New York, the man read copies of French cooking magazines, studying each page intently and, with shaking hands, folding over almost every corner, then becoming transfixed again, as he fingered nonpareils out of an oversize box sitting upright between his legs, enjoying his candy masturbation.

It had been a major miscalculation to fly to Miami on Friday. He was going to have to do some fancy talking to explain his absence to his boss. Maybe he could arrange to get mugged. Maybe he could mug himself. He was pretty good at that, he thought. When the plane landed, he called his boss from the airport. A woman on her knees, struggling to make her son face her so she could zip his jacket, looked at him, red-faced, as the child shrieked and twisted away. Maybe he should take off after the kid (the boy was now running at full speed; the mother was scrambling up) and just not return, he thought. He and the child could be on the lam together. Oh, sure. They could morph into animated figures in a cartoon. Maybe if the Road Runner raced in, they could all jump up and down chaotically, moving toward the edge of a cliff. Or the escape could be the beginning of a movie that would either be satirical or sentimental, you'd never be able to tell. Something a French director would make.

His boss was on the line. "Yes?" he was saying, wearily, as Ben stood with the phone to his ear near baggage claim. Of course, he had no baggage. He'd just found it necessary to make the call before he even exited the airport, apparently. "I'm really sorry. I won't lie to you," he said. He could feel his hand shaking. "It was a spur-of-the-moment thing. I'll work this weekend. It won't happen again."

"'It' being what?"

A long pause. "Okay, you're right. More Arly shit. It was Arly. We flew to Miami. I'm going to have everything you need completed by Sunday night. I'll give it to you Sunday night."

"I see. Should I drop by the apartment? Would that be convenient? My brother's apartment, which is fucking huge for a pied-à-terre, let me tell you that, so I consider it a really nice apartment. One you won't be living in anymore."

"I apologize. I sincerely apologize."

"It sounds like the fucking world is ending. Where are you?"

"LaGuardia."

"Stupid question. You went to Miami, where might you be? Oh, you might still be fucking your girlfriend or sipping a drink served in a pineapple, while I'm here busting my ass. Sure—why wouldn't you be at LaGuardia? But get this, Ben: You can live at LaGuardia. But you know what you can't do? You can't live in my brother's nice, big apartment for peanuts anymore. And you can't come to work. Well, apparently you blew off your job, so you already made that decision for me. I thought, Well, maybe the guy's really nervous about the LSAT, maybe he flipped out. Maybe he's . . . it doesn't matter what I thought. It only matters what you thought. And you thought, No apartment! No job! And certainly no obligation."

His boss hung up on him.

He thought for some time. Then he called Benson Whitacre. The guy's mother had bought him a condo in Kips Bay, even if it wasn't a very nice one, and asked if he could stay with him for a couple of nights, trying not to sound desperate. He was exhausted. He no longer had anywhere to live. How was he going to get his clothes back? He fell asleep in the cab.

Benson buzzed him in. He had dinner waiting: take-out chicken and a container of mashed potatoes he must have bought for himself, unless he also ran out for food. He should explain himself to Benson, but as soon as he started, Benson held up both hands. "Don't want to hear it. I'm your friend, whatever's happened. Let's have dinner. You can tell me later."

It brought tears to Ben's eyes. Benson had called twice in the past year, and both times he'd put him off. No time even for coffee. They ate in silence. He was surprised at how hungry he was.

Later, it would be Benson who'd help him pick up his things, piled in boxes in the lobby of the building on Hudson Street, but he didn't know that then. As they were finishing the meal, he started telling Benson about the spontaneous trip, losing his job, his frustration at Elin for always insisting he become a lawyer, how stupid he'd been in his previous job not to take on more responsibility, how demeaning it had felt to sweep the floor at the end of the day.

"Listen," Benson interrupted. "I can be a reference for you. Or maybe you can get your job back, I don't know. If you can't after your breakdown—"

"What?" he said. "A breakdown? I'm not really up for being mind-fucked, Benson."

"Well," Benson said. "Whatever you'd like to call it. But the thing is, you'll get another job. Obviously you will. But the thing is, inconvenient as this is right now, somebody's coming over in fifteen or twenty minutes, and if you could get lost until, oh, about midnight, so I can have as much fun with my girlfriend as you apparently had with yours? Okay, just kidding. Ben, I don't have a spare key. But get out of here and come back later. Since you're not in the middle of a breakdown, that shouldn't be difficult."

It was the first time he'd seen Benson smile. A faint smile, but a smile nonetheless. He nodded, put his napkin on the table, found the bathroom, pissed, and left.

Then, to his surprise, he picked up someone when he stopped and asked her if he could help as she consulted a map. What profession he might devote his life to disappeared from his mind. He imagined not so much that the girl might be his future, only that if he was slightly worse off, he could think that. They walked across town and went to a bar in Chelsea, where, going in, Ben heard "Lawyers in Love" blasting over the sound system.

A gym rat sat on a bar stool. He'd cut his sweatshirt sleeves so you could see his arms, every muscle defined. He still wore his sweatband and leather sneakers without socks. Two younger guys were flirting, sipping a drink the color of pond scum through thin straws. The place had a slightly gay vibe, though he hadn't known that before he'd gone in with the girl he'd just met. It was humiliating, but Benson had given him a fifty. He had money in the bank, some money, but he didn't know where his cash card was. He feared he might not have as much as he thought in his account, which was certainly not a worry of lawyers. But really: He wanted that? He wanted to practice law? Hooked up with somebody like the pretty, pointless woman who sat on the bar stool next to him? He'd conjured up the taste of a mojito, though he'd forgotten the name of the drink and confused it with a margarita. He looked past her, out the big windows of the bar. Chelsea, it seemed, was no longer Chelsea. And then, the tip of his tongue rubbing the inside of his cheek, trying to taste mint when there was only the residual sourness of the Guinness, he thought about doing the *Five Easy Pieces* he and LouLou hadn't done that night they'd been headed to Vermont.

LouLou. The way she'd told him, so matter-of-factly, that she'd made a mistake, that the guy wasn't even playing that night because he'd been hired for a private party. How fucked up was that? In fact, how fucked up was Bailey Academy, and Binnie, who everybody pretended spoke the same perfect English they did, somebody they'd conveniently assumed wanted to be there doing what she was doing at her mother's side, her not-so-bright, religious mother. Binnie Mouse, with her plates of cookies and brownies, lemon bars and cupcakes, homemade fudge and date bars and bunches of seedless grapes, slices of banana dipped in chocolate and frozen, Hershey's Kisses with their fragile paper wicks protruding, and Tessie's famous pecan pie, apple pie, or custard. Custard: There was an onomatopoetic word.

He was hungry. When he went back to Benson's, he'd see what was on the kitchen shelf, the one kitchen shelf, bolted to the wall, because the cabinets had been taken out by the landlord for refinishing and had never been brought back, as Benson had complained.

He excused himself and went to the men's room, then exited through the kitchen, where he scared some dark-skinned man who no doubt didn't have a green card almost to death as he swept by—yeah; he did that—and from the alleyway he exited onto Eighth Avenue. What was being stuck with the bill for somebody else's Guinness to her? She'd been looking for a tailor's shop! What the hell, he still had a place to crash for another, what, three or four days, before he had to move on.

Outside Benson's building, he chatted with an elderly lady preparing to take her poodle for a walk, who asked him if he could see what was wrong with the clip on the leash (nothing; she had no strength in her fingers). He scanned the row of mailboxes behind where she stood, as if one might belong to him. She used her key to open the front door, when he patted his pockets and said to the woman that he'd eventually find his keys in one of his many pockets, but would she *please*... In the elevator he started to cry, wanting the girl in the bar, wanting—fuck!—wanting a dog, wanting the poodle, though he hadn't been so crazy he'd wanted the sixty-year-old woman. As the elevator doors opened, a man who was waiting glanced at him and stepped back, making a split-second decision not to get on, sounding like Mr. Magoo, muttering that he'd forgotten something. Well, everybody was forgetting everything, weren't they? They couldn't thumb open a hook, or get into a building, or find their *tailor* to slightly adjust their hem, or to move a button a fraction of an inch. The man's expression said it all; he must look more disheveled than he thought. Four-oh-four popped into his mind. Hungry and messed up, his eyes so red he could feel the color, the draught's tinny aftertaste constricting his throat. It was making him cough.

Lifting his fingers to wipe away spittle, he glanced at his Swatch. It was not quite ten p.m. Well, the joke was on him. Or the joke was on Benson. Or on the naked woman at Benson's. Or the woman back at the bar, the one he'd met coincidentally, because such things could happen when you stopped to talk to a stranger. She couldn't be deluding herself any longer that he was taking the longest piss in history. It got confusing, but the joke was definitely on somebody.

Twelve

A few months later, with a letter of recommendation from his former employer ("Ben, I hope I don't insult you, I ask only out of concern. Have you noticed that when life's going well, you seem to feel a compulsion to shake things up? I've been thinking, Ben. Would it be an incentive to stay if we switched you to a more time-sensitive program?"), as well as Benson's letter of recommendation, flawlessly typed on company stationery by his secretary (who was transitioning from male to female)—this, even though he'd told Benson he'd just be sending the letter by attachment—Ben had landed an entry-level position at a place where his job was to write code helpful for running the numbers for companies considering expansion and, basically, to test and to extend other coders' work. This, he told himself, was not as boring as law school. The paycheck, not star pay, but certainly adequate, allowed him to get a second credit card, leather shoes that fit almost as well as his running shoes, and to have a box of Teuscher truffles sent to Elin for her birthday. Twice, probably three times, he'd met Gerard for lunch at the cheap, delicious noodle place near where they used to work, but Gerard had decamped as soon as his father fell and had to go into a nursing home. Gunther had broken up with Gerard the same day he heard the news. Ben was only surprised that Gerard had been surprised. Gerard went into a slump, depressed that their former employer wouldn't write him a letter of recommendation because he said Gerard always got to work late and had a negative attitude. As far as he was concerned, his negative attitude was primarily directed toward the photographer's ex-wife, an out-of-work model for whom he could never do enough; the boss had made Gerard the fall guy, urging him to tell her that he wasn't there when he was, silently sanctioning Gerard's hanging up on her when she called in a state. As Gerard said, it wasn't exactly the studio of Richard Avedon. Though Gerard talked about going back to school, he left abruptly for Kansas City with a guy he met at a club one weekend—an older man who promised him he'd buy him the best steak dinner he'd ever had in his life. Ben had gotten Gerard's scared, maudlin farewell call from Newark Airport just about the time he went full-time and was given a larger desk crammed into a slightly larger office with a mysterious smell of mothballs that nobody could figure out until the desk broke and, for no reason anyone could comprehend, mothballs were found piled like Pez inside the hollow wooden legs. Gerard's call, with all its background noise, had come in just as a call beeped on another line, minutes after he'd already had to tell his initial caller, Elin, he'd need to call her back.

Where other people had hung their diploma, or a photograph of their son or daughter, he displayed an autographed photo of Mama Cass, enormous in her shapeless hippie dress, microphone in hand, the photo cropped at her knees, that she'd inscribed to some other Ben ("To Benny with love. Tell me you'll miss me!"— what a find). He'd bought it at a flea market on Sixth Avenue when he and Benson had gone poking around. It was slightly disappointing that no one who came into his office walked over to look at it, that everybody was so focused on work that they couldn't see and often couldn't hear; five minutes later they'd be back, rephrasing the same question. The best steak dinner of someone's life. That sounded like one of those banal, suddenly funny, deranged thoughts in a Roz Chast cartoon.

Before he left the city, Gerard's final gesture of friendship and goodwill had been to give him the key to a former boyfriend's studio apartment on East Seventh Street, now empty because the boyfriend had paid six months' rent in cash, in advance, to get it, then had the good fortune to be hired as a sax player touring with a band opening for Wynton Marsalis—first stop, London.

Friday night, alone, Ben walked out of a photography gallery on the West Side that he'd gone to as much for the high-end hors d'oeuvres as to see the art. He'd been invited by a PR person, a friend of Gerard's, who seemed irrationally afraid Gerard might kill himself in Kansas—at least, she could provide no reason for what she feared. He saw the girl—the one he'd left in the bar— hailing a cab, a red umbrella threatening to blow inside-out. Did she ever have good luck? She didn't see him. Actually, maybe that was the good luck.

Time passed. He had his shoes resoled. He almost never thought of Arly. He got a call from Gerard, who said Kansas wasn't bad. Gerard was going to take a course in hotel management, reconceive his career. Ben had never heard him use the word *career* and suspected the older man, whatever his name was—too embarrassing to ask—had planted the idea. Fine idea. Sure. He, too, was acting on an idea, which was that he could act. He made it to work on time, even if it required setting two alarms, but he began to feel claustrophobic in his office, not just in the elevator. He felt as if—how familiar was this?—he were being squeezed by the buildings of Manhattan, that really they were huge, fisted hands, even when he sat working inside, increasingly certain he was going to have to pop out of the grip or be crushed. Images of people jumping from the Twin Towers sometimes flashed through his mind.

The opening he'd gone to had featured an artist whose sculpture dangled from near-invisible wire and depicted contorted forms in midair. A well-known vodka manufacturer—the stuff had been so clean, it had tasted like nothing—was bankrolling the reception, because the sculptor was the owner's brother. All over the floor, there'd been plaster dust and broken glass.

The idea of looking for a place to live outside of the city made him feel less anxious. Benson begged to differ: Every time Ben talked about "getting out" he seemed more agitated. He'd done so well, it was great what he'd done, getting an alarm clock, getting a job. It wasn't acting to do what he was capable of doing. Okay, it wasn't ideal, but people had jobs so they could move on to other jobs. He should take pride in being able to locate other people's errors.

"It's easier than truffle-sniffing your own," Ben replied. "What you really have to understand is that human error is just that, except for the times people deliberately build in weird shit or fuck up parts of the code, for their own reasons."

He'd accepted an unopened bottle of vodka from Jamie Renquist, the PR person ("Just put it in my Strand bag! Don't be silly, take it. I'll see you again!") and gotten together with Benson—Jesus; had Jamie thought there'd been something between the two of them?—when he left the show. Ben's regret about the girl in Chelsea—his being obsessed with finding her, and apologizing—showed that he *did* have a conscience, Benson insisted. (What was he supposed to do, apologize twice? Say he needed double forgiveness because he'd seen her grappling with an umbrella in the rain, and he'd walked away?)

That weekend, in *The New York Times*, he'd read about the sculpture show, which was called "Memories of Meteor Showers." The critic's review was titled "Memory's Shards." Was the critic playing along with the artist's title, intended for some reason to throw people off? The review ended without suggesting anything the artwork evoked, let alone mentioning the obvious, 9/11. The photograph, though, had taken some time to decipher, which was why he'd been so caught up in the image, he'd almost missed the review. You always heard that the photographers worked separately from the writers, and it was a very interesting photograph, though it hardly gave a feel for the actual show, as—he figured out—the shadows of the ostensible meteors bled into one another, orbs made more abstract, all of it a mishmash of shadowed shape on the floor, amid glistening glass. ("Broken plastic. Of course they wouldn't use real glass!" he heard Jamie saying.) She'd called him twice, once asking him for coffee "because I just happened to be in your neighborhood." He had no interest in her, but he met her anyway, just to double-check his perceptions. Yeah, she wasn't all that bright. When he'd talked about the sculpture show's allusion to 9/11, she'd called him "morbid," punching his shoulder as if she could dislodge the truth and jostle sane thoughts into his head. "Nobody would put on a show about that now," she'd insisted. Oh. Did all painters paint battles when in the midst of them? he'd asked. "Stop it!" she'd squealed. He'd pressed his point: "There's a statute of limitations on trauma? Because it was years ago?" Their meeting for coffee had been followed several weeks later by an email invitation to another show in SoHo, with a personal note: "Unless you think an artist who paints horses is just doing it to remind us the frontier is gone!" At least he'd managed to plant a seed of doubt in her compulsive cheerfulness. He made no response. Strand bags were incredibly low-priced.

The glass—it had been glass on the gallery floor, come on—there was no other reason to rope off the area; Arly's knees, reddened by the pressure of kneeling on the rug; his mother's body, flattened by the tree root; the carpet at Bailey, so scattered with cake and cookie crumbs it looked like someone had mistaken the students for birds; urine running in a little yellow puddle from under the table at the News Café. No wonder when people paused they looked at what was in front of them, or up—wasn't it a tendency to look up?—to look into the distance and see the sky those times you could, when buildings didn't lean in, blocking the view.

How strange that it took him some time to figure out that he was experiencing claustrophobia. It wasn't just present-day New York that was oppressing him, it was its recent history. Because everything and everyone had a legacy.

He left his businessman shoes on the closet floor and began wearing his Adidas to work again. He read with interest pieces in *New York* magazine about people his age, or just a bit older, who'd decided to set up camp outside New York City. He admitted to Aqua, when she called unexpectedly ("The guy where you used to work gave me your number"), that he felt restless, as if he'd been captured. Saying that word had surprised him, because it was the first time he'd put a name on his anxiety. Her response had also surprised him: "Didn't you win at chess more often than Jasper? I mean, even before his parents died?"

On a weekend in late March, Ben rented a car to explore outside the city. Granted, other people had pregnant wives or husbands who'd lost their jobs, who'd always wanted to be beekeepers. (Sure. That came right from the mouth of one of his most forthcoming, intelligent female colleagues.) Elin had been noncommittal when he told her what he was thinking about. In a way, he appreciated her not saying what she really thought—maybe she'd be good at titling art installations—but at the same time he wished she'd be less guarded, less intimidated. In that, she was totally unlike any woman he knew. LouLou and Arly, if not always perfect friends, were perfect examples of women who never hesitated to tell him what they thought, to let him know in what ways he was deficient. It was sort of amusing that Elin was a little afraid of him, or at least of losing whatever closeness they had.

The last time he'd spoken to her—such calls were always at Elin's instigation—she'd asked if he'd ever seen *McCabe & Mrs. Miller.* "I don't remember," he'd replied, not sure why he hadn't wanted to simply say yes.

It was spring, but he could close his eyes and feel the snowflakes, as if he stood among the actors in the film. He had a feeling he couldn't figure out, except to identify it as recurring. It was as if he'd stepped out of something, call it "reality," and into another life where, because he'd lost something, he had no credibility. The closest thing he could compare it to was a bad waking dream. He had plenty of those, too—anxiety dreams in which he was going to be called on when he hadn't done his homework, or—this one was really strange—as if, instead of the way things had happened, he'd abandoned LouLou in the parking lot and returned to Bailey alone, only to find that no one asked after her, no one said, "Where's LouLou?" As if no one believed she'd existed.

Elin had seen the movie on television. Her own thoughts were pretty inarticulate. He'd stopped in a rest area to check the tires, because the rental car felt bumpy. He was leaning against the driver's door, satisfied that nothing was wrong that he could see, when her call came in.

"It was too sad!" Elin continued. "But I couldn't turn it off. It's a Western. Your father loved them. Well, it was a strange movie. In the end, Warren Beatty gets shot. You never think he will, because he's Warren Beatty. And Julie Christie—do you know who she is? I think she was his girlfriend in real life. She plays Mrs. Miller, and when everything's lost, she smokes opium—I felt like I was suffocating from carbon monoxide poisoning, in my own house! The camera just lingers on her face."

"Entertainment" popped into his head. He remembered so clearly what his classmates had looked like at the Sunday social, who was sprawled or sitting on those weird floor cushions that were never used again, as well as where he'd sat slightly apart, yet still in LaVerdere's peripheral vision. The correct answer, stated as a question, had been "What is *McCabe & Mrs. Miller*?" That was the problem: The answer could so often be remembered. You could act in accordance with the answer all your life, but what happened when the answer took the form of a question?

Was that true? He was watching a robin pulling up a worm near the curb. He looked up and saw another bird in a tree. A grackle? Or was the bird too large to be a grackle? It wasn't the first time he was aware that he'd begun noticing things.

"Hey, man," Benson Whitacre said, when Ben—eating lunch

at a diner—took his call. "Hey, something I want to ask. Jenna and I are getting engaged. I told you that? I didn't? I must think you're still crashing with me and I tell you everything. Okay, so, but, we are."

"Congratulations," Ben said.

"Yeah, well, probably she's the one. I mean, she *is* the one. She's great. You like Jenna, right? I thought so. Okay, it's not an engagement party, there's no ring, we're thinking maybe only a major statement wedding band, she's got such little hands. Her older sister wants to do a lunch thing up in Hudson, where she and her husband live. That's not going so well, but that's another story. There's no third person. The thing is, I thought I'd invite you."

"Great. Thanks."

"But meanwhile, today's my birthday! It is. I'm thirty. You know what? Where are you, by the way? Is this an okay time to talk?"

"Eating lunch. Go on."

"Don't you want to wish me a happy birthday?"

"Sir," the waitress said, pointing to a sign asking people to please turn off their cell phones. "If you could comply, I might not lose my job, please."

He stood immediately and walked outside.

"Happy birthday, Benson. How can you be thirty, though?"

"You knew I was older. I had that skiing accident that kept me out, then I didn't get back to Bailey until my dad died, right? That's why we were in the same class."

"I remember. Bladder cancer."

Cars whizzed by. He could hardly hear. He felt sure the waitress would throw away his food and coffee. She hadn't liked him from the moment she'd seen him.

". . . in with Jenna. In . . . msburg. You've gotta . . . before you marry 'em, right?"

A semi rattled by.

". . . didn't have to live to see the World Trade Center come down, which would really have upset him, after being . . . and such a patriot and all. Flew the flag in front of the house his whole life."

"He was a lieutenant," Ben said. He felt like it was his obligation to spout Benson facts, though Benson obviously hadn't forgotten his own life. No. It was something else, that other thing, the one that scared him: the parallel reality in which he knew an answer, but not the question.

"Okay, I've got to get going. We can continue this conversation later, okay? I'm—it's great about the engagement, it really is. Happy birthday, man."

"Where are you?"

"I just had lunch at a place off the Taconic. I had to get away."

"So this is like that . . . you're riding the Taconic like it's the streets of Boston?"

"What?" Ben said.

"Is somebody with you?"

"No. No."

"You rented a car?"

"Yeah."

". . . did? You rented a car?"

"Yeah. From Avis. Why does that matter? I don't know anybody who has a car."

"Oh. I was going to invite you to Bowery Ballroom tonight. Hey, I've got two tickets and Jenna can't come. Will you be back in time?"

"No. I don't think so. But thanks."

"Why won't you tell me who's with you?"

"Benson, nobody. I told you."

"Just more of your crazy idea that you've got to get out of the city everybody else wishes they had the bucks to afford?"

"Benson. You've never heard of anybody needing a break? Needing to get some distance on things?"

"Right," Benson said. "Call when you can."

They hung up. What was wrong with that conversation, he wondered, as he went back to find everything where he'd left it. He paid the bill and overtipped, hoping at least the waitress would have a good impression of him when he left. When she was at the other end of the counter, pouring coffee for another customer, he left. Something seemed very different. Where had the birds gone? There'd been so many. There'd been the robin (though the American robin was really a thrush), and now there was only a squirrel. What was with Benson's hypersensitivity? Why had Benson's voice changed so suddenly? Back on the road, as the grilled cheese sandwich sank heavily in his stomach, he wondered who was at Bowery Ballroom. What he might be missing.

The real estate agent he talked to at the first town where he decided to stop was a single mother who joked that the influx of people trying to get out of the city was sure to increase her marriage prospects. There was no chemistry between them and they both knew it, but she flirted anyway.

Soon after 9/11 formerly unlikely places like Portland, Maine, began to quickly absorb people in their twenties and thirties, but as time passed, the seepage spread locally. It never stopped. People Ben's age fanned out over the Hudson Valley. Three miles down the road—after 9/11, even the dirt roads were named—a developer had bought the land behind a greenhouse that had itself

gone on the market for an astonishing sum, the real estate agent
had told him. There were plans to build a series of houses on half-
acre lots that the planning board had so far resisted, but the person with the greatest clout had died over the winter, and his
middle-aged son, who'd worked with him, had moved with his
family to Saratoga. That left the niece-by-marriage of one of the
developers—*quel scandale!*—along with a bunch of do-nothing locals who chose to consider the threat standing right in front of
them an opportunity. Money.

After more investigating, just after New Year's Day, 2011, he
bought—in a different town, farther away, from a male real estate
agent who asked to be called "Zippy"—his fixer-upper two hours
from New York City—okay, two hours and twenty minutes—or,
to be honest, two and a half. He put in an offer, agreed to the
counteroffer, on Zippy's advice ("It's a great time to buy, with
those Bush scumbags out of office, just to give you a hint about
where I stand, politically"), and was able to move into a house
before the area became fashionable and people began selling their
barns and carriage houses.

To his surprise, Elin approved of his leaving the city, though
she'd been a little surprised that he'd be living alone ("You think
I'd tell you about buying a house, but not a serious girlfriend?"). It
perplexed her that he hadn't found a job he could fit into comfort-
ably. He'd been honest about that, too, when she asked if he'd be
taking the train all that way, five days a week.

Thirteen

rly reappeared in his life, not something he wanted, something he'd almost managed to avoid, even calling Brenda to ask her to remind him that Arly was poison. "If you're a masochist, there's nothing I can do," Brenda had said. "I don't want you to think I'm Miss Conventionality. I like nasty sex sometimes. I know what it is. I just don't drag in my family and friends, if the fallout's going to extend to them. You went to that fancy school where everybody played to everybody else, so you came out thinking the whole world wanted to be your audience."

Arly seemed different when they met for coffee, but still herself, still edgy. She'd dyed her hair brown. She said she had a job selling cosmetics downtown at M•A•C. She apologized for what had happened in Miami, though she absolutely denied that one of the men in the bed had been the bartender. It seemed like a pointless lie, though in insisting she was telling the truth, she told him the man had been the friend of a guy she knew who'd paid her to have sex with him. At first, he thought she was lying. He cut the discussion short, saying he had to get back to work. "I understand why you don't want to see me anymore," she said. "What's that look for? I do!"

"Bye," he said, and left.

He'd lied about still having a job. He had something in the works—something that might or might not work out, though he'd managed once more to get a great letter of recommendation, and he hadn't even had to hit up Benson. He'd given in and met Arly only because he had to be in town that day anyway. He'd driven in to see his dentist. He had no plans for the afternoon, but he commended himself for meeting her at Starbucks rather than a bar, and for leaving when he thought there was nothing more to say. Why should he be surprised she had sex for money? That probably happened a lot more than he knew. He walked through Union Square, found an empty bench (he could hear Benson saying, "You have to be careful of lice"), and sat down, vaguely remembering some poem they'd found hilarious back at Bailey, though that one had been about fleas. All he could remember was "And so, *ad infinitum.*"

He was looking but not really looking at pigeons, who had absolutely no personality, none, unless you projected onto them. She texted. Of course, he thought, though he hadn't expected that when he'd walked out and forced himself to breathe deeply, as if he'd left a smoke-filled room, then turned toward the park. BAR OFF LOBBY GANSEVOORT. Half an hour had gone by since he'd left her. The phone pinged again: PARK AVE, NOT MEATPACKING. Maybe she'd up the ante and have someone there to mug him.

He ignored the text and sat for some time—it was chilly, but

spring was on the way—watching a dark-skinned woman in a tur-
ban chat with another woman who wore a visor and sweatsuit and
pushed a sleeping baby back and forth in a stroller; they spoke ani-
matedly in Spanish. His tooth—what was left of it—was throbbing.
That was why he was squinting. Discovering the reason relieved
him. He had a prescription for a painkiller in his wallet from the
dentist, "just in case." He walked to a CVS and dropped it off, gave
them his address, wandered through the aisles as he waited for it to
be filled. He picked up a Toblerone on sale—some consolation
necessary. He could let it melt in the good side of his mouth. As he
was deciding, a young woman picked up a bag of candy and dropped
it in her purse. She saw that he saw she'd done it. He glanced around,
looking for the security cameras. Nervously, she followed his eyes.
She picked up one more item and turned away.

He wandered into the aisle stocked with antihistamines, decided on the CVS version of Benadryl. RM 816, the next text said.
She must be sleeping with lots of guys to be able to afford a room
at the Gansevoort. When he finally got the prescription, he picked
up a bottle of water and bought that, too, placing it on the counter
along with the candy. He did not have his CVS card. The woman
spun the bag as she handed it to him, as if it contained dog shit. He
expressed this thought. "Use that word again, I'm calling the manager," she said. Instantly, the Indian man at the next cash register
began to scrutinize him. He walked away, but once outside opened
the bag and threw it away, along with printed information about
the drug stapled to it. The bottle contained only four pills. He put
one on his tongue, unscrewed the water bottle cap, and took a
slug. He put the bottle by his feet as he removed two Benadryl
pills tightly sealed in plastic and took them as a chaser. Then he

went to a bar he and Benson had once gone to after a free outdoor concert, where, because it was still early, he managed to get a seat. "Mojito with gold leaf," he joked.

"Gold leaf, did you say? Sorry, I don't know that one."

He thought about it. About the wrecked room at the hotel. He'd had to pay a steep penalty for changing the return ticket. He was breathing through his mouth, almost panting, angry at Arly all over again, and most of all at himself. The Miami adventure had been a stupid idea. They weren't the kind of people who'd go there and have a great time. What had he imagined—that they'd rub suntan lotion on each other's backs, cavort in the waves, that she'd take his hand under the table as they sat side by side and waited for their perfect dinner to be brought? That scenario was bullshit, as farfetched as any fairy tale. The next ping of his phone he ignored, but he did make a tiny exploratory gesture with the tip of his tongue, and land on a not-too-sore spot where he dared not push. "A margarita with Cuervo Gold," he said. "Sorry. Bad day."

"Absolutely. Comin' up," the bartender said.

Inducing a slowed-down version of time, he thought, was sort of interesting, as opposed to being caught in it like a time warp. The beach. Miami. Prufrock. The crab. "I should have been a crab." Maybe people took poetry too seriously. Or maybe poetry was like any other drug—it could sometimes make you feel one way, sometimes another. He dug his fingernail into the package again to release one more Benadryl. LouLou's recipe for sleep, when you had nothing better. The bartender set a glass of water in front of him, then turned and began to pick up bottles. It was great to have the throbbing lessen. If Arly was really his friend, he could tell her about the root canal in mid-process, ask if he could curl up in the bed and sleep, though he didn't mistake her for a friend.

Who was his friend? He hardly ever talked to Jasper. And Benson. Not that he'd ever been that close to Benson, but that strange phone call, when Benson had been so paranoid. What had Benson thought, that he was off with his fiancée? WAITING pinged up. No further message. Well, good. As was the margarita on the rocks ("You said rocks, right?" He might have), the ice delightful, though something to guard against getting near his upper teeth, the pain now having subsided to a mere ringing in his ears.

A woman slipped onto a bar stool three seats away. She ordered a glass of Chardonnay and a glass of water. The bartender began to scoop ice into a glass. Ben should have taken the train. His car was parked on Twentieth Street, pretty far west. On the other hand, the Gansevoort was on Twenty-ninth. It might be amusing, or if not amusing, a weird form of retribution, to go there and to be impotent. Guys were probably thinking that as they sat on bar stools all over the city. He found himself funny. He smiled. "Sorry?" the bartender said. His blond hair was cut in layers; every way he moved his head, some different clump of hair went into motion. A middle-aged man with a beard approached the bar stool next to the woman, asking her perfunctorily if the seat was empty. That was the thing: Etiquette required that you had to leave plenty of space when it was available, in order not to be thought flirting, but when the bar started to fill up, there was no such assumption.

"Refill?" the bartender asked.

He looked at his drink. The last quarter-inch of liquid was melting into the remaining ice.

"Just the check, thanks," he said. The drink's iciness had started another, lesser throbbing, radiating into his head from his ears. He'd hold off on taking another pain pill until he got to the hotel. Then he'd pull his prank and pass out—even if it didn't seem ideal to be asleep when she was awake.

"Ben?" a woman in a velvet baseball cap said.

"Hi," he said, though he had no idea who she was. Her eyes turned slightly down at the corners, as did her mouth, after she spoke. Maybe she'd already had a few.

"Lauren Black," she said.

"I'm really sorry," he said, noticing her slightly raised eyebrows. He couldn't tell if she was hopeful or skeptical. She was attractive, and she knew him and he didn't know her.

"Lauren. I mean, Lauren *Alwyn*-Black, as LaVerdere liked to say. A sin that I didn't keep my maiden name, so he added it for me."

"Oh, sure, so sorry, hi, hi," he said, swirling off the bar stool. "Man, I'm no good at all when I see somebody in a different setting. *Sorry.*"

"Well, yeah, it's a bar, so I guess that's a different setting, all right. I live near Gramercy Park. I got divorced a couple of years after you left Bailey. I recently married a lawyer."

"Oh, well, hey, that's good," he said. "Or, I mean, I hope it is. We all had—" What did they all have? "Of course we all had these fantasy lives going on about the faculty, but I'm sure you didn't have any reason to be thinking about us. I mean, not that you didn't care about us."

She smiled slightly, nodding. "I work at the Morgan Library now. Pretty close by. I miss Bailey, sometimes."

"Yeah, we were lucky. I realize that. So it's great you're living in the city. I was here for a while, but I've moved upstate. Just in town for some business. I guess it doesn't look like that, sitting in a bar."

"Well, I'm saying hello in a bar," she said, nodding to the

bartender as he put a Bloody Mary down in front of her. "Anyway, good to see you, Ben, and I hope everything's going well. A friend's meeting me," she said, lifting her drink as if offering a toast to the empty table behind them.

"Good to see you," he said. The effort he was putting into talking exhausted him. If he was lucky, some spell he'd felt under might have broken, like a cold front bringing in lower humidity. If he was lucky, his interaction with Lauren would mean he'd given up on the idea of seeing Arly.

Ms. Alwyn-Black—*Lauren*—reached out. She briefly placed her hand on his shoulder, without saying anything. He smiled and clasped his hand over hers for a second, then released his grip, turned, and left the bar. All of this, he could see, in his peripheral vision, was being watched by the bartender, who thought that juggling glasses would mask his interest. Ben didn't expect her to follow him out—he didn't think he'd seemed as off-kilter as he'd felt—and she didn't. Only in the sunlight did he remember her brother running into him in the corridor on 9/11 and think, with a sigh, that somehow they'd all gotten through that.

He turned the corner onto Lexington. He walked past Indian restaurants and a wig store, and passed several old ladies walking little dogs. A taxi driver who'd been moving fast turned on his light, braked, and bent forward to peer out the side window. Ben realized how slowly he'd been walking and picked up the pace. *Lauren.* Had he ever even known her first name? The sidewalk was almost empty. Someone had dropped a slice of pizza, which he stepped around. Two girls in high heels and short skirts were climbing into the backseat of a car. The taxi had streaked off, and an enormous truck rumbled behind it, followed by another stream of taxis with their lights off.

In the lobby of the Gansevoort an enormous guy wearing a wire checked out the people approaching the elevators, pretending to be holding open the doors, while eyeing them for familiarity, or their room cards. Ben saw the man's newt eyes flicker in his direction, though the man said nothing.

Cindy Crawford walked in, passed under the pink chandelier, turned left at the elevators, her high heels clicking, taking the lobby entrance into the bar. The security thug was an enormous horror-movie fly with multifaceted, glinting pupils. The guy pushed a button as Ben approached to let him on the elevator, indicating acceptance at the same time he indicated contempt. You'd have to work out hours every day to get a body like that. His hands were the size of melons, the skin just as stippled. One other person, a man, also rushed forward and got on, reaching around Ben to push three. Elevators presented a problem. If you were a man and you reached around another man, he might think you were coming on to him. Ask the other man to push the button for your floor, though, and you became a wuss.

By the time the doors opened, he was thinking again of the wreck Arly had made of the Miami hotel room—not something he and she had done in her apartment, in spite of their not exactly hanging up their clothes and placing their shoes side by side. By the time the elevator doors opened on eight, his erection was pushing against his pants.

The door to eight-sixteen was cracked open. What awaited? He walked in, realizing with relief there'd be a minibar, he could have a drink and calm down even if it was too late to rethink things. He could catch his breath.

She lay naked in bed, turned toward him. Had she been crying? Was he looking at an object, not even a real person, an inflated, weeping emoticon that might blow up and drift away like a hot-air balloon . . . a rubber? She thought they had time for *that*? In this pornographic dream? It was real Gansevoort behavior; somehow he'd managed to sleepwalk to her room, filled with so many possibilities. "You get it, you get it, you get it, Ben gets it," she repeated in a muted, sweaty mantra as he fumbled to undress. There was Arly, moaning the second he climbed on top of her. She arched her back. "I thought you wouldn't come," she said. Just hearing the word forced him to fight against the cue to his body, though it was no use. If he'd taken poppers instead of pain pills, he couldn't have come more intensely, though as her tongue trailed down his body, a little rivulet from the stream, trickling down his legs in the middle of a dream, as she was grabbing him like a drowning person and his ears filled again with relentless buzzing—hey; he wasn't going anywhere!—he was hard again, inside her, though they'd somehow slid from the bed to the floor. Something was hurting his spine. It turned out to be the Toblerone. "Wait," she said, "wait wait wait." She wiped her fingers over his lips. She'd been concerned, he realized, because she'd noticed a little bubble of blood at the corner of his mouth.

In the next few months she brought a dominatrix back on the last train of the night. Another time, she flew to Vegas with a friend who'd gone to Bard and lost a thousand dollars—her entire savings—playing blackjack. He didn't want to listen to the Velvet Underground with her anymore, though. She did coke and, worse, lied about it as well as never sharing. She hinted about a more permanent relationship. She'd found out that the sister-in-law of a friend had been killed, a woman she'd liked, who'd been part of a bridal party, who'd put her hair in a French twist. Her super's brother had died—a fireman who'd had to retire after 9/11. She understood life was fleeting. They had sex three times the first time she visited, though he'd made her promise no sex, that they needed to talk seriously about what was, or wasn't, going on. He noticed she didn't say anything about her feelings for him when she said she loved his house, the yard's loamy smell, the birds and chipmunks, the voles, everything but the skunks. The next week she made an apple pie (he'd assumed when he first came in that she'd bought a scented candle). He found out she'd been seeing another man in New York because the guy called at odd hours. She lied about that, too. Finally, if she hadn't told him she was leaving, he would have asked her to go. He came back one day to find all her things gone. In the bathroom—she'd watched too many movies—she'd lipsticked the mirror, GONE FUCK YOURSELF. Examining it closely, he realized she'd painted the mirror with menstrual blood before throwing the tampon in the trash.

At least she hadn't gotten pregnant during all that unprotected sex.

Fourteen

It was always nice, but strange, when Elin visited. He'd never thought of her as a parent, but neither was she a friend he felt relaxed with. She dressed as if it mattered what she looked like. When the New York exiles and weekenders arrived, they continued to dress in black. Only Elin wore a skirt with a neat pastel sweater set and a pearl necklace. It made her seem older than she was, as did her hair, which had turned white. ("This happens prematurely to everyone in my family," she said, self-consciously touching the ends of her hair before she'd even taken off her coat.) Her conventionality made him wonder if his father had sought her out because she was a conformist, whether that had made him feel safer. Ben's mother had cared nothing about stylish hair or makeup, though she'd been—or at least, his sister insisted she'd been—a natural beauty, with her prominent cheekbones and the same almond-shaped brown eyes Brenda had. His sister would have had something disparaging to say about Elin if she'd known she was there. Of course he mentioned Elin as little as possible to Brenda, the same way he avoided mention of any other woman.

In his kitchen, he brewed some rose hips tea for the two of them. He put out the sticky jar of honey and the little wand with the curlicueing end that had been a gift from little Maude, the neighbor's child, on his last birthday. Adults loved to find presents to bestow that seemed like toys and made everyone realize their inherent childishness. Who better to give such a gift than a child?

He and Elin talked about her life. Things were often reversed, in that he took the initiative and asked to hear what was going on with her, whereas (except when she was on the telephone) she was tactful to the point of silence when inquiring about his life. After his father's death she'd decided to sell the house in Brookline and go somewhere different, not too far away. She'd thought about Concord, New Hampshire, but instead she'd moved to Portsmouth. Did she still like it there, even though everybody said Portsmouth was overrun with young people?

"Yes. Certainly. You've seen where I live. It's nice, I think. I like the secondhand bookstores. And it's becoming quite sophisticated, with all the new restaurants. The young people come only on weekends. And now. Summer."

"Then that's a yes?"

"I don't know," she said, fingering her pearls. "I like seaside towns. I never liked being inland at your father's place. There was the pond, but I prefer the ocean. New England winters are no pleasure, but what would I do? Move to Florida?"

"I don't think I have much of a sense of what your daily life was like with him," he said, surprising himself. He really didn't want her to enumerate the tedium of their life. He hated small talk. It didn't matter what Portsmouth was like. None of what they were going to talk about mattered. It was as if his sister hovered in the room, proving to him that Elin was vapid. So of course Elin turned the tables. She said, "I never told you, Ben, but once your father hit me. I mean, he didn't knock me down, but he hit me, and then he was so sorry. His shame was worse than being struck. I believed him that he'd never do it again. I really did."

So much for small talk. He said, "He hit you once?"

"Yes, of course. Only that one time, but he was so unhappy. It made him so unhappy to have done it. You look shocked. I'm sure it doesn't compute with you any more than it did with me. I can only think that he was frustrated in some other way. That whatever we were arguing about, which I've blocked out entirely, I really have . . . that, you know, he just did it, did such a thing, that he knew was terrible."

"I'm so sorry. I don't know what to say."

"I shouldn't tell you when he's gone, but that did pop into my mind when you said—what was it you said? What our daily life was like. We did what other people do. Errands! We always had our evening meal together, and we discussed—did you know we talked about having a foster child? Perhaps opening our home to, well, to a foster child. That might have been what our disagreement was about."

"No. I didn't know that."

"It wasn't a particular foster child. I mean, we never met the child. We just discussed it."

"Where did he hit you?"

"Here," she said, pointing to the side of her head.

"That's really awful, Elin. I had no idea he'd ever do anything like that."

"I shouldn't have told you, but I've always felt we've had a special connection, and I suppose . . . What am I saying? I don't want you to dislike your father for doing it, I just felt you should know. We should move on to some more pleasant subject."

He frowned. He said, "My former girlfriend Arly—you remember Arly. I think she's psychotic, actually. She wrote on the mirror with—" He stopped. "With blood. When she left. I'm really, really glad she's out of here. That the two of us are having a cup of tea, and those crazy vibes are out of the house. It was stifling."

"Something seemed strange when I walked in," she said.

"Excuse me?"

"There seemed to be some, I don't know, some tension in the air. I picked up on it the minute I walked in."

"Really?"

"Yes. I wouldn't say so, otherwise. I knew something wasn't right."

He could hear Brenda's voice in his head: "You don't think *she's* the one who's off?"

"So, I don't know, you're okay?" he blurted out. The question circled the question he wanted to ask, but he hadn't been able to think how to phrase the real question, or exactly what it was. He was thinking that when women viscerally disliked other women, you could never convince them otherwise. Was it some survival mechanism? Something left over from caveman days, when the men went out with clubs and the women were skeptical of one another?

"It's none of my business," she said, "but that other girl, J.J. The one who came with you to Thanksgiving. Did you hope things would work out between you?"

He remembered that visit. He'd told Elin there was nothing romantic between them. Still, she'd been surprised when Ben made clear he'd sleep on the sofa. Which he was very glad he'd done, because in a less frantic way, J.J. had turned out to be every bit as crazy as Arly. He'd been the last to figure out that she'd wanted more than mere conversation, but for him there'd been no real attraction. He'd never slept with her. Being with Arly had messed up his mind about what attraction was, though the more distance there was between them, the saner he felt, and the saner, the lonelier. It was very nice to have Elin sitting with him at the kitchen table, though he had no idea how to explain to her what had gone so wrong with J.J. It had ended shortly after she met Elin, when she went to San Francisco and met a Japanese painter who'd confronted Ben, demanding to know why he hadn't slept with J.J., saying, "She is a beautiful woman, with great talent. What's wrong with you?" Now, the man's aggression seemed funny. Which was more than he could ever say about Arly's.

"She got together with a Japanese guy. I met him once," he said. "They're living in California, I think. She and I just didn't have any chemistry."

"I see. Well, I understand that. No one wants to have sex with someone they're not attracted to."

He was so taken aback, his cheeks started to burn. He said only, "The guy she got together with was really strange. I saw them in *Architectural Digest,* as a matter of fact. They had on skinny jeans and matching shirts, and had a little dog with hair flopped over its eyes. They were standing like paper dolls on some perfectly level yard outside their house in Marin, I think it was. It made me feel better about being in a doctor's waiting room."

"Do that again," Elin said with delight.

"Tell you about them again?"

"No. Do that gesture with your fingers, when you made it seem like their little dog was with us in the room. You really are funny, Ben."

"No," he said, embarrassed. He took a sip of tea. For a few seconds, she continued to look at him hopefully. Then she also took a sip of tea and changed the subject. "I like the new man who's come to work at the firm. I think I told you about him. He has a very nice wife who's a nurse. They asked me to dinner a month or so ago, at a vegetarian restaurant. He insisted on picking up the check. I had a lovely evening. I don't know why I don't reciprocate, because I really should."

Had they really returned to the banal subject of good dinners and friendly people? He looked down. He'd been looking at her, puzzled. He took a sip of tea he didn't want. It had cooled enough that steam no longer rose from the mug. He smiled insincerely, raised his mug as if there were something to toast.

Elin clinked the rim of her mug to his. She looked so hopeful. About what? That he'd stumble into asking another loaded question?

"We don't have anything to toast, so let's toast that!" she said. "To nothing important to say. To quiet rapport!"

She tried so hard to be forthcoming, it brought tears to his eyes. The other question, he supposed, was something she might not know, and if she did, would she admit it? Had his father ever struck his mother?

Fifteen

W hat the fuck!" Ben's neighbor Steve said. "You've got one woman after another coming to visit, like they're doing one-person interventions. Your stepmother just comes out with the news that your father hit her? I mean, it's very sad, but is there anything women won't say to you?"

"How would I know what they don't say?" Ben asked. He'd wandered over to Steve's house to get untethered from his computer for a while, hoping they could hang out. His own house always seemed emptier when someone visited, then drove away. Steve and Gin stayed away when they knew he had company. He'd heard Steve's loud voice outside when he went out to get the mail the day after Elin left. Two men were loading a new gas stove into Steve's house. They said they'd return later with an electrician. They'd already discovered there was the wrong kind of outlet in the wall behind the stove. Steve, as always, was reciting his "Nothing is easy" mantra. Ben's story about Elin's visit, though, effectively distracted him. They went into the kitchen and sat down.

"She just comes out with, Oh, she can understand not having any sexual attraction! Man, that was not a heart-to-heart I would have had with my mother, god rest her soul."

"She wasn't wrong that J.J. was interesting. I could tell that was who Elin wanted me to get together with. She was actually a very original thinker, even if she did decide to marry a loser."

"And she has her new boyfriend debrief the old one, huh? Are you kidding me? Also, tell me one original thought the woman ever had. Do you remember even one? Their thoughts disappear when they do, I've discovered. I love Gin to pieces, but at the end of the day, I don't know what she's been talking to me about for hours."

"She thought it might save the reefs to do transplants. Introducing plants that repelled certain bacteria that affected living coral. That idea's started to catch on now, but she was the first one I heard it from."

"*Reefs?* You remember that she talked about transplanting stuff into reefs? I mean, can pillow talk get any more exciting than that?"

He'd pretty quickly become friends with Steve and his wife, Ginny, though Steve was as skittish as a kicked dog who couldn't resist wanting affection, at the same time he was poised to recoil. It was Ginny who'd sworn Ben to secrecy about Steve's losing his previous job. Ben took it in stride that Steve had something invested in seeming paternal. That the imbalance of power always tilted Steve closer to the sky, when Ben's end of the seesaw clunked on the ground.

They moved from the kitchen into Steve's den, which made Ben feel old, and as if he was failing because he'd never smoked and didn't drink during the day. Neither did Steve. It was all about staying fit, playing tennis, not dwelling too much on his only moderately successful career outside the city. Earlier in the week, they'd played tennis while Ginny was at yoga and their daughter had been dropped off at a playdate.

"*Reefs*," Steve said again, indignantly. "I always forget you had that fancy education that made mush of your brain. Listen, Ben: You've gotta look at people and think, Might these people be about to move to Marin? And if they are . . ."

Steve would have loved living in California. Gin had told him that.

"I don't pass judgment on you for being a stockbroker who helped sink the economy, Steve."

"I'm gonna let that goose and the egg it mighta laid pass right on by, Ben. Not even worth shooting down."

He and Steve had gone the week before to Steve's father's house when the old man needed advice about an addition he was having built. There'd been an enormous fountain on the front lawn and, in back, an Arts and Crafts studio where he went to carve wood instead of what he'd called "wasting my time with insomnia." He spent time in the studio in the winter, sitting under special lights that relieved his SAD, but in summer he was always in a better mood. It had been interesting to see how courtly Steve acted toward his father. There'd been little joking. A small woman older than Steve's father, Ernestine, had brought a tray with sugar cookies on a plate and a teapot brewing tea. The cups reminded Ben of the ones he'd habitually broken at Bailey, where the solution to his clumsiness had been not to embarrass him, but to replace the cups with mugs. What a strange place, with people going out of their way to make sure the students weren't embarrassed, at the same time they hired LaVerdere to teach them.

"You should get together with Gin's sister. Give it a chance," Steve said.

"I've already told you, she's fine but there's no chemistry."

"Gimme a break. I'm not your stepmother that you've got to explain yourself to. And anyway, that's just shit you *tell* yourself. Stop thinking of yourself as an empty beaker some magic chemical's going to boil up in, abracadabra, perfect bliss and endless orgasms. You had 'chemistry' with that Arly woman, who went Helter Skelter. As Gin says, we're willing and able to audition the next girlfriend. Hey, we can help you decide whether or not you should let her slip away to Marin. By the way, do you want our old TV? She tried to donate it to the school, but they didn't call back. Really rude, so fuck 'em."

He didn't want their TV. It was fine with him to watch repeats of *The Sopranos* at The Spotted Rick. (He'd had to explain the joke implied in the bar's name to Steve, who never picked up a pun. It didn't help that he'd never heard of the dessert.) Rick—their pal Rick, with two-for-one wine and beer nights whenever a TV series routinely brought in a crowd—had a goiter and extreme freckles. Rick had been flipped out when a writer for *New York* magazine came to write about him and his bar; to Rick, such attention signaled the beginning of the end. He'd avoided talking to the guy, as well as begging his regulars to keep quiet.

After tapping his iPhone several times while considering their making a Monday tennis date, Steve said, "Lemme call you. Getting some free time might be harder than I thought."

"Sure. Let me know," Ben replied.

He and Steve hadn't instantly taken to each other. Steve had sent Ginny alone to welcome him to the neighborhood. Even after that, they hadn't gotten to know each other until Ben, working at home one day and looking out his back window, had watched a guy who came with Steve's lawn service launch toy rockets half the day when he should have been working. After some hesitation, he'd called Steve and told him what had been going on. Then, later that same day, he'd run into Steve and Maude (long ago, those days she'd hidden from him) at the library one town over. They'd been coming down the steps, Steve holding his little daughter's hand, and suddenly Ben had felt more warmly toward him. The next evening, Steve had invited him to the house ("I like spontaneity") and they'd had a beer in what Steve called "the den" and his wife called "the library." He'd never before seen a child take pillows off the furniture and fall asleep sprawled amid the adults, sucking her thumb, her mother's cardigan pulled over her, but that, too, had seemed charming.

Though Ben had tried and pretty well succeeded at pushing thoughts of Arly out of his mind, today was her birthday. She'd played dollhouse with Maude a few times—an activity Steve insisted killed brain cells—and once at a playground she'd looked for a long time at a little girl hesitating at the top of the slide. The child had finally twisted around, maneuvering to descend the stairs to the ground. "Smart kid," Arly had said. "It's not like *Alice in Wonderland* awaits if you get to the bottom." Back then—before then—Steve had finally told him that Gin had misjudged Ben. She'd thought he was very guarded. *Standoffish* had been her way of expressing it. Probably a trust fund kid, she'd told Steve. She was suspicious that he lived alone, had wondered aloud to Steve about whether he did drugs.

He remembered that conversation well. "You don't answer questions unless you're directly asked, do you?" Steve had said, after summarizing Ginny's initial reaction to him. "No, I guess I don't," Ben had replied. Which cinched it, oddly. Some time had passed in silence there in the den—Ben was never really good at judging time—during which time Steve himself must have been figuring out if he liked Ben or thought he was an asshole. Not long after that, they'd played tennis. Soon after that, Steve had mentioned the possibility of Ben's setting up a better program for his father's nonprofit.

When he left Steve's, he decided to go to the store and get his errands over with. He was a little surprised to see a hidden camera aimed at the miles-long shelf of toilet paper—especially when the packages were so enormous they looked like shrink-wrapped football fields. When he'd first moved in, he'd had to drive fifteen minutes to get to a convenience store. Now, after a five-minute drive, he could get a lawn chair and a bottle of red with a *Wine Advocate* recommendation and a rating of 90.

He checked out with soap, black pepper in a disposable grinder, paper towels, and a container of grated Parmesan after a long delay while the customer in front of him waited for a price check on gummy worms. He drove home in the fading light listening to NPR—always a melancholy time of day, but now no longer a time when talk ceased. He remembered how much he'd once liked the word *twilight,* how delighted he'd been with the word *gloaming* when he read it. He'd still never heard anyone use the word in conversation. Certain words seemed to remain magical, in part because they belonged to the language of stories. Outside that realm, they weren't heard, like perfect Victorian children.

"Ben!" a woman called, as he was unlocking his car door in the parking lot of the convenience store two days later. He'd left the milk out and it had soured. He never thought ahead.

He didn't know who she was. She picked up on it immediately. "Claire Morris," she said, extending her hand. "Tatiana's mom. You—"

"I know!" he said, too late. "Sorry. I was lost in thought."

God, he'd spent an hour with the woman at Ginny and Steve's a month or so before. They'd had a very interesting conversation about, of all things, space travel, because her late husband had been a physician to the last astronauts. He'd died of a brain tumor. Their child was a year older than Maude. The girls had been playing in the dining room, where they'd tented the table, giggling and tumbling as the adults drank a glass of wine on the back deck.

"What were you thinking about?" she said.

He saw himself as she saw him: somebody living inside his own head.

"Hey, I didn't hear until after you left what a great tennis player you were. Would you be interested in playing doubles?"

"Maybe" she said, after a slight pause.

"What I was thinking," he said, digging himself in deeper, "was about Lincoln. I just finished reading a biography. One of the reasons he was apparently so good at debate, the complete opposite of all the talking heads now? He took a lot of time restating his opponent's ideas, so he seemed very reasonable and he disarmed his audience. Then when he began his own argument they were so tired of hearing the initial assertion that they considered him generous and rational, and they listened. People were often persuaded to his side."

"Lincoln," she said.

"Hey, would you like to come over for a drink?" he asked. "Or we could go to Rick's. You know Rick's?"

"Who's he?"

"Isn't it supposed to be charming if guys fall apart in the presence of a woman?" he said. "I realize I'm doing very badly here."

She looked even more puzzled.

"I had a nice time talking to you at Gin and Steve's the other night, so I thought—I mean, since we've run into each other—you might come by for a drink. Or we could try to round Steve up for an impromptu game of tennis on the clay courts, if you want. Instead of drinking, I mean."

"It's dark," she said.

"Well, then maybe something else? We could show up together and pretend we thought we'd been invited to dinner. Are you good at keeping a straight face?"

She walked so close that if he hadn't reached out, she'd have head-butted him. "Kiss me," she said, closing her eyes.

It was like the improbable, final minute of a movie that demanded you view the ending as uplifting, he thought miserably, though they stood in the convenience-store parking lot, where super-bright lights glowed with an intensity rarely seen outside of interrogation rooms.

He kissed her. Would they live happily ever after, have the most unusual How-We-Got-Together story of all time? Who would have thought, as their lips touched, even when his bag containing the half-gallon of one-percent milk, a bag of granola, trash bags, and a package of batteries kept banging her back, that she'd tell Gin he needed to be on medication?

"Wow," she said, raising her hand but dropping it before she touched her lips with her fingers. "This place is *much* stranger than Gin said."

"If you don't want to come to my house? Rick's is a bar."

"Thanks," she said. "But I'm going to have to think this over."

"You *were* daring me."

"What else do you do if you're dared?" she said. "Jesus, this is my first kiss since my husband died."

"No hell below us, above us only sky."

"Hell?" she echoed.

Of course she wouldn't be on his wavelength.

Her question had been a good one, though: What else would he do, if dared? He was male. Anything, he thought, though such an answer might have been self-serving, an expedient epiphany. He *did* believe that if you didn't keep on top of things, things would keep on top of you until you were smothered under the weight. That had almost happened to him in New York, but he'd slid out from underneath, made his escape. One thing he remembered about LaVerdere was the way the man stayed in motion, never mistaking talk for action. No, he'd liked that catch-and-release of hypothetical thoughts; he'd liked the way some of them flashed as they quickly disappeared back into the water, with only a cut lip or a newfound understanding of the way the world worked, never to be hooked again.

He said goodbye in what he hoped was a friendly way. She still seemed totally taken aback. That was another thing: You could usually scare yourself more than anyone else could scare you.

In his car, it seemed to him that Arly had been the person in the shadows of his thinking, not LaVerdere. RM 816.

There'd been a package delivery in his absence. Meadow in a

Can, sent by Elin. It arrived so soon after she left, she must have ordered it in advance of her visit as a thank-you gift. She really was from a different generation. How bizarre to send such a thing. He quickly checked his computer—no unexpected dramas so far from the company he freelanced for in D.C.—opened a bottle, and poured a glass of wine, debating whether he should call Elin and get it over with, or delay and try to think of something more genuine he might say. It didn't seem to be a day when much of anything he said was right. He wasn't sure he could sound persuasively grateful. Meadow in a Can might be something Steve and Gin's daughter, Maude, would enjoy scattering on the lawn, though a child her age probably wouldn't grasp the concept, and the child was fastidious about her hands being clean, so maybe that wasn't such a good idea, after all.

A photograph showing a haze of pastel flowers was spread across the label, a depiction so bad, he wasn't sure if it was a blurred photograph or a painting by someone who'd learned the wrong lesson from the Impressionists.

He poured a second glass of wine. Compulsively checked his email again. Still no crisis at work, in spite of the fact that he'd ignored them all day. There was a brief message from Gerard, who was working as a chef, loving what he was doing, liking the Midwest, except that he'd developed a real fear of thunderstorms.

He'd heard from Rick that Arly had moved to Los Angeles, with no job to date, into a condo in Hollywood with a purported producer she'd broken up with twice years before. She was certainly not going to be growing peas on a trellis. He'd also heard that she'd auditioned for a few parts she hadn't gotten, that she'd started getting Botox—something women in L.A. did at her age.

So what had she been talking about, criticizing him for not being self-sufficient, since that had never been her goal? He'd hardly dropped off the grid, or tried to, when he'd first circled the map and looked at places within reasonable driving distance of the city. Moving there had never been synonymous with disappearing. And as for that, even Thoreau had lived in a house and walked to his beloved pond. Thinking about him in his house was one of the ways readers enjoyed looking down on Thoreau.

Ben sat down and quickly sent by attachment a report and a chart he'd created earlier, adjusting only one minor thing. Then he went outside, intending to unscrew the lid and scatter the seeds. There was no breeze to help him. The seeds looked like tiny dead insects in some confetti-like blue substance he supposed was intended to make them adhere to the ground. They smelled rubbery. He pulled out his cell, scrolled to Elin's name, but decided against it. An old-fashioned thank-you note—she'd prefer that.

He looked at his house, which appeared so different at different times of day. In the evening—though it was past that time, darker—its flaws were almost invisible. He'd been told that after a couple of years he'd need a new roof. Steve had a client who was a roofer, so leaving aside the expense, that would probably work out. In spite of kidding Steve as mercilessly as Steve kidded him, he'd come to rely on him for advice, or at least advice of a certain kind. Steve was the Ultimate Guy: lovely wife, beautiful daughter, a big house he could always find somebody to work on. No longer did you have to do the work yourself to be an Ultimate Guy—that only made you a chump. From Ben's lawn, you could hardly see Steve and Gin's house. That had been the point of buying a place with some acreage. Gin and her daughter liked to come over, making a game of pointing through the trees to where their house was, the kitchen, their bedrooms, Daddy's library.

A wide-winged raptor circled above a rabbit that ran under a bush.

He accidentally knocked a clump out of the can as he fumbled for his phone to call Steve. It went immediately to voicemail. Of course: They'd been going out for dinner. Steve had mentioned that. Maude had probably already been tucked in bed now by the perky babysitter whose father had won a MacArthur. It was dark. Not the time to sow his meadow, though it seemed to have escaped the can like an evil genie. Time to go cook some pasta with Parmesan and olive oil and a shake of pepper flakes. Damn! The last of the blue stuff tipped out of the can, lighter than a hairball. He bent to separate the clump, bits of it flying around in the wind. Wind! Perfect timing. He tipped the can so the last of it would fly loose. Another spongy clot, the last one, rolled away like tumbleweed. He continued toward the house, fingering the last tiny bits out of the can to drift away.

"Dust to dust, ashes to ashes, Technicolor tumbleweed to the lawn," he said. He was out in the dark, talking to himself. Of course he didn't believe there was going to be a meadow, but if he called Elin he could say he'd already made use of her present. How stupid was he, though? He finally got it. After his father was cremated, she'd asked if he wanted some of his ashes. No, he hadn't. So now the concept of scattering ashes had been displaced onto Meadow in a Can, even if that had been her subconscious motive. There he stood, ironically playing his part, after all.

Sixteen

teve called to say he'd have to put off their tennis game, but that he'd rebook the court. "Our friend Claire called. What exactly happened when you ran into her? Not that it's any of my business," Steve said.

"She caught me on a bad night. You know how it is, sometimes, when everything you say comes out wrong? Maybe proof of what you say about my living too much inside my head."

"She told Gin you kissed her."

"She asked me to kiss her."

"Excuse me? Let me get this straight, Claire asked you to kiss her. Why would she do that?"

"I think I said something about being flustered. I couldn't remember who she was."

"She said you were very—however she put it—anxious. She thought maybe you were off your meds. Direct quote. Gin really doesn't know what to think."

Ben closed his eyes.

"You just stop responding when you don't want to answer," Steve said. "In a way, I've got to admire that."

"Look, Steve, promise Gin I'll never do such a thing again, if a woman asks me. Tell her she should be really afraid of me, personally. I jump out of bushes with my lips puckered. I'm a huge threat."

"Can we stop talking about this shit? Weren't you going to come over and help me get the TV on the wall?"

"Oh, shit. I forgot. I've got company coming, Steve." At least that had been the real reason for Steve's call, not this (as Steve rightly called it) "shit."

"Hot date?"

"Feeling the need to live vicariously?" Ben asked.

"Tell me who it is. Is it somebody I know?"

"You're really ridiculous, Steve. That's no way to ask a serious question, if it is at all serious."

"Oh, Jesus, Arly's not back, is she?"

"No," Ben said immediately. "It's somebody I went to school with. And her girlfriend. They've been here before."

"Two friends are visiting, so I become dog shit and you can't help me hang my TV?"

"Right. If you want to put it that way. You know, everybody doesn't appreciate your bluntness."

"Yeah, I've sort of noticed that from my father and my old boss and my new boss and from Gin, when I'm telling her something she doesn't want to hear, and she makes her arms go limp like she's gonna collapse. Well, have a great evening. Don't take any wooden nickels, as my grandfather used to say, and you already know what

I advise you to do. Which is to stay away from Claire at least until she pulls herself together."

"What else would you do if you were dared?" Had she been that deeply conventional, Claire Morris? He'd dived off a rock ledge where his father had forbidden him to swim. Almost everything Arly thought up was a dare, those times it wasn't mere provocation. That was true, actually. He'd never realized that, but now it seemed so obvious. Then there'd been the guy in the poem, the one LaVerdere had shaken his head over: "The required curriculum of Bailey Academy, drawn up by The Powers That Be, asks us, today, to consider what is often regarded as a seminal poem of the twentieth century. 'Do I dare to eat a peach?'" Phillip Collins had snickered. "Thank you, Mr. Collins, for your suggestion that we move on to a slightly more complex matter, 'The Waste Land.' Ladies and gentlemen, prepare to accept each asterisk as your personal savior, each footnote as the sound of Gabriel's trumpet."

Sometimes Steve could really get under his skin. It seemed almost impossible that he'd once seen Steve with no defenses, Steve when he was real: Ginny, well into her fourth month of pregnancy, had suddenly started to bleed. Ben was next door, as much as a house with significant acreage between it and the neighbor's could be thought of as "next door," playing solitaire—nothing could be more mundane.

It had been such a cold day. He'd finally finished a report that was overdue and relayed it to the guys in Washington. He hadn't been sitting there jerking off, so why was he *so* startled when his back door swung open? Steve had raced in with Maude in his arms and thrust her forward, in a panic. Ben had assumed—to the extent that he reached any conclusion; really, he'd only reacted—that the blood on Steve's shirt emanated from Steve's chest. Then he'd thought, My god, no, it's Maude. He couldn't unscramble Steve's hysterical words. Then, Maude wailing mightily, Steve had toppled a pitcher and knocked the photograph of Mama Cass off the wall as he'd run out, the car idling in his driveway.

How had Ben quieted the two-year-old? It might be good to know, for future reference. As the sky brightened to its seasonal, yellowish white that portended pastel colors at twilight (*twilight!*), Ben had tried to jolly Maude into a smile, and then, trying another approach entirely, carried her down the path that always revealed something new. He'd found himself outside, clad sensibly in his ski parka, with the afghan Elin had made him for Christmas swirled around Maude (he'd gone into the living room, rather than grabbing Maude's little red jacket that had fallen out of Steve's arms?). That was what he'd done: He'd unzipped his own jacket and pulled one side of it over the already-well-bundled Maude, they'd waved goodbye to Tommy Turtle, and walked the mercifully distracting path. The farther he went from the house, the worse the phone reception became.

He had no idea of what he might do besides walk and talk, and they had eventually come upon the much-discussed tree, where a squirrel eating a nut sat on a low branch, poised to run. He'd echoed Gin's "Here we are at the Story Book Tree" as reassuringly as he could, and finally the confused child had lit up with a bright smile, as if he'd performed a miracle. He'd probably jiggled her in his arms, pulled the blanket around her in a less haphazard fashion . . . Whatever he'd done, it had distracted and soothed her.

He and LouLou took walks down that same path when she and Dale came to visit, though Dale didn't accompany them. Dale disliked even conventional pets, like cats and dogs. Birds? She never wanted to see anything in its so-called natural habitat. She swatted away butterflies. He had neither a cat nor a dog, though he'd been enough of a good citizen to take a kitten he'd found wandering alongside the highway to the SPCA. He wouldn't even have a rabbit going hippity-hop in the front yard anymore, he imagined—though of course you never "had" a wild animal, any more than you had a special bond with whatever raptor spread its wings. Only in *The Peaceable Kingdom* did the animals coexist without bloodshed—a romanticized ideal of equality, in the same paintings that featured in the background small figures depicting the first settlers negotiating their contract with Native Americans. What a joke. Walt Disney couldn't have done better. In a way, Hicks had been the Walt Disney of his day. When Ben bought the house, there'd been an assortment of small lawn statuary tucked here and there, in various states of decay. He'd kept only the cement turtle with its eroded hump that LouLou called Quasimodo.

LouLou's getting back in touch had allowed him to admit he'd been a little too solitary. How flattering that she told him how much she'd cared for him. LouLou had thought about it and decided that Bailey hadn't been the experience they'd once thought. Away from school, she'd consistently realized the place had fostered distance between them at the same time it provided opportunities for them to get together. But everything had been so contrived! Why have a required weekly event and pass it off as a "social"? LaVerdere didn't just teach there, he was the unacknowledged force behind the place. Who else had an on-campus apartment, as well as a house? Why were The Brains, the math students, kept separate from them? And 9/11 had been handled so badly, even before the parents dive-bombed, lifting off Akemi,

Darius. LaVerdere, she said, was the fox brought in to guard the henhouse—okay; an unfortunate analogy, because except for The Brains, who comprised the minority of the school, there'd been as many females as males at Bailey.

Jasper, on the phone, basically said the same thing, even though Ben never discussed LouLou's thoughts with him. In a paper Ben could still remember, which Jasper had been asked to read aloud for a philosophy course, Jasper had written about the trees on Bailey's campus, comparing them to equally enormous trees at the crossroads of the nearest town, where the post office was at the back of the general store and the used-car lot rarely sold anything. It was a place where people couldn't afford to have their trees pruned, or cut down when they'd been uprooted or broken by wind. LaVerdere's appreciation of Jasper's addressing the class system in this way had been palpable. It was also something Jasper never forgave LaVerdere for. He still insisted that he'd conjured up what he knew LaVerdere would most like to hear. He'd deliberately created a bruise—exactly what someone like LaVerdere would get off on rubbing, its soreness attracting your attention, your attention making the sore spot sorer.

LouLou and Dale planned to arrive in time for dinner, but if they were late, he'd been told not to wait for them. It was touching that they assumed that in the absence of company, he'd still be preparing dinner. Hadn't they heard of microwave burritos and takeout chicken? But yes, he'd probably be drinking wine, anyway. A linen napkin to wipe your fingers also helped. He'd cooked dinner recently for Steve and Ginny (linguine with artichoke sauce, and a side of broccoli rabe; no dessert, as per Gin's instructions), who probably also thought he prepared solo meals. That is, if married couples had any fantasies about single men at all. Gin hadn't disliked Arly as much as Steve had, or she'd tried to act as though she didn't. "So beautiful!" was always what Gin exclaimed. Weren't women not supposed to assess other women by their looks? But she'd never volunteered anything more substantive.

Traffic was bad on Fridays, and a long stretch of highway was under construction. LouLou had been certain she couldn't duck out of her job early. She'd also said that they were both tired, so they'd prefer not to go out: no to the antique show at the church; no interest, really, even in watching an old movie. As irony would have it, her girlfriend Dale was a writer, as LouLou had announced herself to be, at Bailey—LouLou the novelist, whose writing existed so that she could renounce writing. Dale's memoir was about growing up as a zookeeper's daughter (the Florida zoo was gone, though a photograph of its elephant house, taken from a postcard, appeared on the cover). When the iron gates closed and the assistants went home, Dale's mother—a vet's assistant who'd become the zookeeper when the director ran off with José, from the Reptile House—dressed in home-sewn animal costumes. She sat at the kitchen table and verbalized the animals' thoughts into a Dictaphone, using a variety of voices. She believed she could read their minds.

For years Dale did her homework supervised by a costumed water buffalo or Bengal tiger seated across from her, as her mother expressed the animal's innermost feelings of shame, frustration, and anger, pounding her paws on the table, channeling the sad accounts of their former lives, all of them trapped in the zoo because of previous transgressions: the leopard who'd once been a stylish, politically incorrect Fifth Avenue rich man's wife, attired in her trademark fashionable hats; a group of greedy landlords, returned as vipers. (Unclear who the bear had formerly been—the bear that finally killed her.)

He put on old Dylan: "You're a Big Girl Now."

How really unexpected that when LouLou got over her fascination with older men, she'd proceeded directly to women. How lucky, though, that she had been the one who'd gotten back in touch.

His thoughts were interrupted by the sound of a car bumping up his driveway. If it was Dale and LouLou, it was hours earlier than they'd said. He dropped the linen napkins (a gift from Elin that he'd come to like) and cutlery on the table and went to greet them, happy they'd arrived. Behind their car, a deer jumped across the path and disappeared into the woods.

Dale was the first one out of the rented Toyota. Dale's hair was cut very short, only the sideburns long enough to curl into tendrils. She had thick hair, chestnut brown, but no one had hair as lovely as LouLou's.

He walked around to the driver's side and gave her a one-armed hug and asked if the construction on the Taconic had slowed them down. He didn't quite hear her answer, distracted by the sight of LouLou, emerging from the other side with a box of blooming orchids. He ran around to help her. "They gave them to Mavis. She's retiring. She traded them to me for my *Mastering the Art of French Cooking*," LouLou said, thrusting the box at him. "What's a Victorian manse without orchids?"

"Thank you, but are you under the impression this is a Victorian?"

"It isn't?"

"No—1925."

"Oh. Well, they'll look good. Last year it was chic to group them together, but this year everybody's lining them up with exact spacing."

"Her most profound thoughts come from *Elle Decor*," Dale said.

"I thought you said you couldn't get off early," he said to LouLou.

"They ended up having the going-away party yesterday, so today I worked through lunch. I'm a Hertz Gold member."

"You get away as fast as a bank robber," Dale said.

"Thank you for such an unexpected gift," he said.

LouLou wore jeans, with a brightly colored shirt and sweater. Dale wore black with black. The thin yellow stitching around her low boots was a radical statement. Even her tattoo—at least, the only one visible—was chiaroscuro.

LouLou stood just inside the door, debating where to put the orchids. He remembered Elin, standing in the same place, holding the oversize box from the bakery that contained his birthday cheesecake. Delicious stuff, though it had become a joke, like merlot. The same bottle that sat on his counter. Dale saw the wine, raced forward as if she were seeing her favorite movie star, poured a few inches, held out a glass to LouLou, with a flourish. "Wine, hon?"

"I did the wrong thing, bringing orchids," LouLou said, ignoring the glass of wine poked in her direction. Dale shrugged and took a sip. "They're for lofts in TriBeCa and trendy restaurants."

"She gets more insecure by the day," Dale said.

"They're beautiful. Really. I'll read up on how to care for them."

"Also, you're supposed to bring a brand-new gift to your host. It's tainted if it's barter."

She was being a little exasperating. He took the box from her and put it under the window. When his friend Peter came to visit, his German shepherd, Princess, who'd been raised by monks and then spent months of her life learning from other German shepherds, had jumped up on the cushioned windowsill to bask in the sunlight. The dog didn't check out the house the way dogs usually did; she just walked into the kitchen, jumped onto the built-in bench below the windowsill, then made a final jump before curling up to survey everything from the highest perch. Peter had told him that dogs raised by the monks had been used to sniff through rubble at the World Trade Center.

Dale poured wine again for LouLou, who accepted this time. She sat in the chair where Dale had draped her coat, though she miscalculated and sat too close to the edge of the seat, splashing wine onto the jacket. LouLou quickly wiped it off. "'All the perfumes of Arabia,'" she said, licking the wine off her fingers.

"Allusions night," Ben said fondly.

"Perfumes?" Dale asked.

To his dismay, LouLou had started to cry.

"What?" he said, stricken.

"Don't look at me. I'm a mess," LouLou said.

"Oh, hon, take it easy," Dale said, shooting her hand across the table, looking helpless.

"What's the matter?" Ben said.

"Does he know . . . do you know what I'm going to say?" LouLou said, running the back of her hand over her cheek. Everything about her looked pinker. Pinker and sadder. Could she possibly be this upset because she didn't think what she'd brought was a nice enough gift?

"I don't talk about you behind your back," Dale said. "I don't," she repeated to Ben.

"LouLou, Dale, tell me what's wrong!" he said.

So that was the question that LouLou addressed until she couldn't say anything more. Just like that, as he stood hovering beside her in his kitchen, LouLou blurted out that they wanted him to be the sperm donor for their child. "I know you're going to say no, I did this all wrong, now you think I'm crazy," LouLou said, getting up and collapsing in Dale's arms. In Dale's arms, not his. He could hardly believe what he'd just heard. A child? She wanted him to father her—their—child? Why would she want a baby? What about her job—she'd just made plans to leave the job she had for a new one. On the last visit, she'd been so excited about that. The Obamas were in the White House, and all was right with the world. Could she really have said—but yes, she had; she'd spoken quite clearly before she was unable to speak any longer. Maude in his arms was one thing, but a child of his own? He'd never considered it. He wouldn't consider it now. He tried to speak as calmly as he could.

"I never even considered it. Fatherhood. I'm in no position . . . Of course, nobody's ever asked me anything like this. I mean, of course they haven't. LouLou—as much as I care for you, *both of you*"—he quickly corrected himself—"I just can't do that."

"There'd be absolutely no responsibility," Dale said. "Isn't that right, hon? Unless he wanted it?"

"You can't imagine," LouLou said. "Being in some doctor's office, being handed a piece of paper. A printed-out form with an option to write a little essay later, where you're supposed to check off your fairy-tale sperm donor, like I'm supposed to say, 'Oh, I want to make sure the father's from a very liberal New England family, he should have curly hair and be really great at sports, Oh, and also a millionaire who plays the oboe, he has to have a good sense of humor—men always have to have a good fucking sense of humor, we all know that. And he has to be six feet tall. Seven!'"

He felt tears well in his eyes. Was this really something she had to think about now, at her age, just starting her career? Had it been more Dale's idea? Because his father had died, had that made him think that being a father would force him to acknowledge, or might it even hasten, his own mortality? He and his father hadn't gotten along so well in the years before his father met Elin, though he'd never been under any illusions that if he were a father he'd do any better with his own son.

Okay, Steve, he thought: This was my hot date. LouLou wants a kid, and basically—except for the oboe—the ideal father turns out to be you.

Seventeen

After they left, he took a nap and had a dream. He was walking in an unfamiliar place, though certain landmarks were the same, such as the tree with its lightning-cracked trunk. Tommy Turtle, a.k.a. Quasimodo, appeared. (The tortoise can retract its head; the sea turtle cannot.) Then the dream turned into a version of *The Wizard of Oz*. The sci-fi creature walking next to him was the Tin Man, except that he—he, Ben—was the same person, talking, though no one could hear him, including the little girl he felt responsible for... Maude? LouLou, as a child? She kept running; he couldn't see her face. No, Judy Garland's in that movie, he thought, as, confused, he awakened.

Fatherhood? No thanks. Dale, whom he cared for so much, had been excruciatingly clear that everything would be done with the advice of a lawyer, that he'd have to assume no responsibility, unless of course he wished to. His participation would never be disclosed, if that was his desire. Who believed such a thing? (Oh, this breed never bites! as his father used to say sarcastically.) He sent an email to LouLou after the dream—only later did he realize that it was insensitive to forget to include Dale in the message— saying that while he hugely valued their friendship, he really had to be sure that she understood that this . . . what word had he found to replace "impossibility"?—that the idea of being a father, even without obligation or responsibilities, struck terror into his heart.

Maybe Arly had had a point, though; maybe he did introspect too much. What the hell had Bailey been, except daily training in that? He sent another message to both LouLou and Dale, say- ing that while it was none of his business, he certainly cared for them deeply. Had they really thought out whether this was the moment to have a child? Only Dale replied. "She's got endometri- osis, so the earlier she gets pregnant, the better. Google it. While we didn't go about it right, for which I apologize, pls give it a few mins more of serious thought." He looked up *endometriosis*, which, like all such medical terms he researched, was clearly not a good thing to have. In this case, he wouldn't have to worry about it— though there was still the problem of having to shave every day.

Ben went into the kitchen and put water on to boil. Mama Cass was hung above the tea canisters, the frame still missing the glass. Recently, Maude had asked to be lifted so she could give Mama a present: a "horsie" to sit on her shoulder. Her aim had been off; the glittering unicorn decal looked more like a jaunty hat with a too- large feather.

Damn it: LouLou had planted an idea. No different than an acorn rooting. A seedling sprouting beneath a tree. It was there, as if it could be touched. Worse, as if it demanded tactile contact. He told himself to forget the dream, to eat something, to try to distract himself. It wasn't even a conscious attempt at repression, it was that survival strategy of taking one step after another, continuing forward. How babies learned to walk. Babies. The kitten he'd found wandering at the side of the road that he'd dropped at the shelter, he hoped, had been cute enough for someone to adopt, because it could settle softly in the palm of their hand, *so cute.* Good looks could save you. At least, they could if you stayed off the highway.

Okay. It was Saturday evening, and LouLou and Dale were back in the city—he agreed that there seemed just too much tension in the air for them to stay longer, even if they all wanted things to be otherwise—and he was going to proceed with his life and help Steve put up a TV. Ordinary life seemed a blessing.

He'd gone to Steve's before realizing he'd forgotten to take tools Steve might not have—the guy certainly wasn't Mr. Fixit; his usual go-to product was Gorilla Glue. Somehow, they'd wrestle the thing up on the wall.

He couldn't stop thinking about LouLou. Her hysteria had only made him feel sorrier for her. He was confused, though; Dale had told him at breakfast that at first they weren't going to try until the following year, especially if LouLou definitely decided to take the new job. If this was what life was like now, what were things going to be like when he was fifty, Steve's age?

"What kind of a father do you think I'd be?" he asked Steve, pushing open the back door, entering without knocking, though Steve was incapable of being taught an implicit lesson silently. Steve had been trying to uncrate the TV alone, with no success. He, too, had been drinking a glass of wine.

"You? Okay, I guess. Why? Did you get somebody pregnant?"

Yeah, Claire Morris, he was tempted to say. He looked around.

The ugly plaid chairs faced each other in the cavernous kitchen like mirror images.

"In answer to your question, Gin and Maude are at a reeeeally grown-up, *nighttime* birthday party, where all the kids get to feel super-special. Some friend of Ginny's whose husband walked out, who sleeps until noon now and throws a party for herself at dinnertime on Saturday night, when she knows nobody can get a babysitter, then guilt-trips anybody who doesn't show up. She actually asked Gin to sit in on her therapy group and offer her perspective about why people could so rarely come through for their friends."

"Oh. That is a fucking huge shipping container, Steve."

"Maybe I should put it aside so she won't have to buy me a casket."

They came up with a plan to grip the box with their feet while pulling up the molded Styrofoam. It turned out to be next to impossible to get a good grip because everything was so smooth, though they tried with hernia-inducing intensity. Styrofoam cracked from the corners as the iceberg rose enough to give them a better grip. Pieces fell on the rug like clumps of snow. "Easy," Ben said, sweating, his legs widely spread. Somebody had to say "Easy." It was guy talk. Talk that cut across class, that expressed not real caution so much as buddy bonding.

His father had made him bond by standing on the roof in the snow, looking for the source of a leak. No, his father hadn't been trying to kill him, he'd just been an idiot. He'd also been an idiot when he'd said a wasps' nest was dormant and insisted they go on scraping the top of the chimney. His father had gotten the worst of it, ending up in the ER like an inflatable Santa Claus pumped up to occupy half the lawn. In any generation, who had fathers who weren't like that? Jasper said that The Man had once thrown a horseshoe through their picture window, breaking the front door of his mother's china cabinet. It was funny if you saw that stuff in the cartoons, but not at all funny if you had a father whose best thoughts had to do with how the front lawn, before it became *a potato field*, could be used as a "family amusement center." They were better than any sitcom character, all of them. Absolutely: Why should The Man spend his weekends mowing grass? That was a typical question, representative of those fathers. Anybody at Bailey could have topped it with his or her own story. No wonder LaVerdere had seemed so unusual, so focused, yet bemused. He'd never sent one of them to the roof in a snowstorm. When he fell up there, Ben's shin had been skinned like an opened can of sardines. His sister had thought he'd bleed to death.

"So here we have a TV on which we'll soon see Big Bird early, way too early in the morning. Which a very special little girl can watch while Daddy and Mommy do unimaginable things in the bedroom."

Ben snorted.

"Seriously," Steve said. "Did you knock somebody up?"

"Why would you think that—just because I asked your opinion?"

"I'm the only Jew here. You don't get to answer questions with questions."

"You're stereotyping, condescending, being too blunt in the guise of being funny, and generally acting in a way that would get you in big trouble with Gin. What's your answer?"

"What the fuck, Ben. Did you just get out of some consciousness-raising session?"

"Can I tell you something confidentially?"

"You're gay, but you're trying to pass by having a house full of women and by whipping my ass at tennis?"

"Can you talk seriously for one minute?" It bothered him that the only time he could be sure Steve was entirely serious was when they were playing tennis, and it was Steve's turn to serve.

"Shoot," Steve said.

"Well, it was a very weird visit. I mean, as close as we are, I don't really feel like I understand LouLou."

"Gay chicks are different," Steve said. "That come as news?"

"Steve, that's more of your stereotyping. It's not a factor that she's gay."

"You're here to reform my thinking? What, exactly, do you wanna tell me?"

He decided to say nothing about the drama that had just unfolded. It was good that Steve talked so much, because it gave him time to think. "She and her partner intend to have a family," he said instead.

"Oh, yeah? The full catastrophe? Have I met the girlfriend?"

"Sure. Dale. You met them the first time they came to the house. The one whose mother dressed up like a lion and roared all night."

"Oh, *that* woman! I read an excerpt online. I ordered the book."

"You did?"

"Well, yeah. What a story! I heard her on the radio the other day. Leave it to you to move to the middle of nowhere and still be on the cutting edge of who to hang out with. Sounds like she lived through an amazing amount of shit until the bear put an end to it."

"I can't bring myself to read it," he said. "Somehow, having Dale tell me about it has been more than enough." What he didn't say was that he'd been reading volume two of Proust. No need to give Steve ammunition to prove that he was not of this world.

Though if Steve thought it was the same town it had been when they moved in, he was just plain wrong. A brokerage house had opened where the toy shop used to be. The owner had sold out and moved to Florida to be near her son and family. In the back of the florist's, there was now a six-table restaurant that had really delighted Elin. They took reservations for "high tea."

"You heard her on the radio?" Ben asked.

"WNYC. The guy who does the interviews."

"What did he ask?"

"What she thought of Halloween. I'm not kidding. He did come out with that, and she burst into laughter and sort of embarrassed him, I think. You're stalling for time so you don't have to lift your side of the TV."

"Absolutely."

"I've got a wonky shoulder and I shouldn't be doing this," Steve said. "Also, it makes my balls ache, and I hate to be conscious of my balls."

"Tough shit. I can't possibly support the entire weight. Where's it going?"

"She thinks the den, but I'd say the living room."

"Can you decide, so I can go home?"

"Let's leave it on the floor. I'll talk to Gin when she gets back. Get out. Thanks for coming over," Steve said. "What I'm really thinking, to be perfectly honest? That she'll realize this TV is interchangeable with the other one, and we can put this in the bedroom. Watch porn on a bigger screen."

"Is that right? Do you do that?"

"No," Steve said. "I think you don't get my jokes because of the age gap. But then, how do I know what assumptions you have? Some days you act like I'm a monster, like all of America hates everything I stand for. The financial crisis is over, but you bring it up all the time. Then I remind myself: We're from different generations."

"So if you were to say one thing that strikes you as young about me—you know what I mean; you're the one who's obsessed with the fact that I'm younger—what would it be?"

"That you're hopeful," Steve said. "I admire optimism."

"Really? I didn't expect any sort of compliment. Thank you."

"Uh-huh. I didn't expect it of myself, after that crack you made about how I'm pussy-whipped."

"I didn't say that."

"You all but said it when I told you my plan about leaving the other TV in place. Go on, go home. Aw, shit, it sounds like I'm talking to a dog. Anyway, come back and watch Big Bird. Or send your friend. With her background, somebody shedding feathers and talking shit, bouncing around pretending to be a bird, or whatever the hell, has got to be just another day. You know, I never imagined living next to somebody like you, but I've got to say— *Arly?* Now it's interesting that you've probably got this ménage-à-trois thing going on, and you're just not telling me."

On the quick drive home, no deer crossed his path, though he drove slowly. He hated people who hunted deer for sport when they didn't even eat venison. Some did need the meat. People who lived not far away. Sure, because of the huge deer population a lot of gardens had been gnawed like ragged cuticles, but couldn't people just go to the farmers' markets and buy what they'd lost? Pride stopped them; they wanted to grow their *own* food; it wasn't enough to support some hardworking farmer. With every fucking sprouting radish, you were staking a claim to what was rightfully yours. It was a form of vanity to think you were obliged to be self-sufficient.

Eighteen

Six weeks later, LouLou and Dale were coming to visit again. He'd felt like he was in exile in his own house. Finally Lou-Lou had called and admitted that she'd just been too embarrassed to communicate with him—that was why she hadn't responded to his messages. Dale had texted a few times, first saying that she hoped his silence meant he might be reconsidering, then apologizing for sending the message, then inviting themselves for the weekend, then apologizing for being so bold, then leaving a voice message that she meant to be funny, saying that if he'd like to come stay with them in Brooklyn, that would be fine, and she'd even make her specialty, grilled cheese sandwiches. "You bring the wine," she'd said.

They were embarrassed. He was, too. He couldn't let things stay that way. He could still remember how bad he'd felt at Bailey, when LouLou wouldn't speak to him for days after their stupid attempt to get to Vermont.

He'd written back, apologizing, then apologizing for apologizing. In her reply, Dale said that they'd be there Friday night, "as usual." He'd written back that there was another, bigger antique show. Would they be interested in that? Her response: DOES THE CHESHIRE CAT SMILE?

Now they were coming.

He took the roast out to get it to room temperature before seasoning it, a pork loin he thought he might slice into cutlets and cook outside on the Weber. He started assembling bottles. A health food store had recently opened, and one of the clerks had been so enthusiastic, he'd bought too many unwanted spices. Tunisian braising spice? He'd learned to avoid turmeric, since it stained anything it came in contact with. Pink peppercorns, which he'd found out were not peppercorns (as a shooting star was not a star), had been a happy surprise, though. White pepper. How was white pepper different from, and sometimes preferable to, black pepper? The clerk had really run with that.

When he heard the car in the driveway, he felt relieved—and then was relieved that he felt that way. He went out to greet them. No pretending he hadn't heard the car, no standing his territory. Dale fumbled in the car, probably intentionally, to delay getting out. Once again he had LouLou in his arms.

"We're going to the antique thing tonight?" LouLou asked, almost inaudibly, nuzzling his chest.

"Yeah, I got tickets to the preview." He rocked her back and forth a little. "I told you that, right?"

"Mmm," she said, not letting go of him. Dale got out of the car and hugged LouLou's back. "If the three of us fall, we go down like dominoes," Dale said.

The awkwardness was over. A weight was lifted.

They followed him into the kitchen. Dale examined the roast from a distance. "At first I thought you might have gotten a pet," she said. It was a rather large roast.

"Why don't we go now? Can we, Ben, before dinner? I feel like if I have a drink and sit down, I'll start apologizing and I won't be able to stop myself."

"Hon, do you remember in the car that you told me over and over *not to mention it*?" Dale said.

"We can do that, if you want," Ben said. This was the old Lou-Lou, the one who was always on the run. "But are you tired from driving, Dale? Need a few minutes?"

"You drive—I don't care," Dale said. "I'll even sit in the back-seat."

He took his key ring from the nail by the door.

"It's really such a beautiful spot you live in," Dale said.

"Yeah," he said. He was feeling better about everything. Dale did get in the backseat. LouLou sat beside him. She stepped on something and leaned over to pick it up. "You'd be in trouble if I was your wife and I found this lipstick," she said.

He took it from her hand. Whether she was joking or not, that wasn't what it was. It was saffron, inside a narrow tube. It had fallen out of the grocery bag.

"Hey, tell him who you heard from," Dale said, poking Lou-Lou's shoulder.

"Oh, yeah. I asked her to remind me. Aqua. She's in L.A., working for ICM—can you believe that? They gave her an AmEx Gold Card and an expense account. She met Tom Cruise—watch out, if he's looking for the next wife—and she sent a selfie with that comic, the English guy who cross-dresses. She met him at a comedy club near the Chateau Marmont."

"I hate it that John Belushi's dead," Dale said. "'Cheeseburger, cheeseburger.'"

"That's cool. How long has she been out there?"

What was this sudden exodus to L.A.? What was that about?

LouLou shrugged. "She's back to being called Aquinnah. She's sharing a tiny place in Venice with her sister's ex. It's that reverse-snobbery California thing, you know? Like your space is the tee-niest, tiniest, couldn't be any smaller or you couldn't stand up in it, but meanwhile it's got light-sensitive shades, central air, and a view of the water. The sister's ex-boyfriend was in rehab and didn't ask Aqua to leave when he got home. He came back in a limo that was probably bigger than the space they lived in, though she forgot to say that. She wouldn't tell me who he was, but she said I'd recognize his name."

Arly, he thought. Somewhere in California was Arly.

"I remember her sister. She came to graduation and had a flower on her collar that squirted water."

"You were so lucky," Dale said. "At my school I was known by my Social Security number. I had to ride a bus an hour each way. A bully who knew my mother hosed animal shit out of cages would bring plastic baggies filled with dog poop onto the bus and send them around, saying it was my mother's homemade fudge."

"That's horrible," he said.

LouLou said, as if she hadn't been listening, "I want one of those golden oak coat racks with an oval mirror. I envision it in the hallway of our country house. I've already ordered the per-fect runner on eBay. Caucasians are as cheap as golden oak now; they're the Diet Pepsi of rugs."

Country house? They lived in a one-bedroom in Park Slope, where someone had removed one of the bedroom windows to install an aquarium empty of fish. Air leaked in around it. Plastic seaweed and an unattractive gray castle sat nestled in faded pink stones. "As for me," Dale said, "I'm looking for a claw-foot bathtub. We can store it in our detached studio until the renovation gets finished."

"There was one other person I got a message from," LouLou said. "LaVerdere. He was in Key West, renting a house that once belonged to Tom McGuane."

"Who's Tom McGuane?" Dale asked.

"A writer," LouLou said. "I used to go out with a guy who thought *Ninety-two in the Shade* was the best American novel since *Gatsby*."

"What does he say he's doing?" Ben asked.

"I'll tell you," she said, checking her cell phone, and scrolling. It took her a minute. "Okay," she said. "He's convinced watching the sun go down and waiting for the green flash is like looking into the bottom of an empty glass and expecting to see pixie dust. Pure LaVerdere." She turned off her phone and dropped it into her bag.

"After all I've heard about this guy, I still never find him a million laughs," Dale said.

"Is he still at Bailey?" Ben asked.

"He left. He's teaching philosophy at The New School."

"Really?" he said. He was still having trouble imagining La-Verdere in the tropics.

"Yeah. You never hear from him?"

He didn't, though he'd thought of him recently when he'd re-read an essay by Flannery O'Connor. It was one LaVerdere had particularly admired (for a long time, Ben had thought Flannery O'Connor was a man)—something to the effect that when writers succeed, it's because their conscious mind, alone, hasn't been the most significant factor. To the extent that LaVerdere could be called mystical (he wouldn't have liked that word), he did seem to believe, as O'Connor did, that there were enormous realms— pre-existing realms, like as-yet-unseen galaxies—that contextualized for you. That was why writers were so often quoted as being paradoxically relieved to be surprised. At Cornell, when he wasn't busy learning how to code, Ben had briefly joined the debate team, but at Bailey he'd distrusted his ability to talk almost in proportion to how successful he'd been. Now, he took pleasure in silence. A day would pass when he'd forgotten to put on music.

He'd begun to envision the rest of the evening, which was probably going to be fine. His thoughts returned to Aqua, to how annoying she could be. "That girl kissed me on the lips!" his father had exclaimed at graduation. "I always tell you you're attractive," Elin had replied. Women were never as jealous as men thought. It was the only time Elin had been to Bailey, except for the time she and his father had dropped him off. Still, she'd looked at colleges with Ben, which was more than his father had done. She'd been the one who urged him to rethink Cornell. It was due to her generosity that he had the house he was living in. And his father had hit her. Once.

They saw a fox, though it had a thin tail and pronounced ribs. Darius Beltz, he thought, as they turned in to the parking lot. People emerging from their cars looked fashionable, a totally different crowd from the regulars at Rick's.

There'd been another recent exodus from New York City here, as well as to other towns nearby. Of course: Rents never stopped increasing in the city; people burned out; more people were working from home. In the last six months he'd observed many fortyish women—the Claire woman among them—in stiletto-heeled boots. LouLou had never worn heels. Only boots or flats. She'd always been her own person. She'd never changed the way she wore her hair. It remained long, eye-catching. Now she didn't bother with contacts, though, so she conveyed a different message with the seal-slick hair; the sexy Prada geek glasses; lip gloss, no lipstick. She resembled the young Susan Sontag, as photographed by Thomas Victor. Sontag had been one of the first people to write an eminently sensible thing after 9/11, asking people to think seriously whether there might not be reasons for our enemies to hate us.

When they walked into the drafty grange hall, things were still being unpacked at some of the booths. A long table had been set up in the entranceway, with organic popcorn in small brown bags and shakers that offered a choice of Indian spices or Parmesan cheese. A photograph of Barack Obama was hung above the table. Obama was wearing a red tie and smiling. Middle school kids, dressed in party dresses and suits, giggled as they took tickets. Locals were lucky to get peanuts at Rick's, watching *Homeland*. It did not augur well for what the dealers would be asking, though Steve had informed him that "Grandma's attic shit" was already being bulldozed into landfills. Steve was always aware of how the world was changing around him, adjusting his attention toward what he could get, rather than being sentimental about what was vanishing. Ben had paid attention when Steve recommended a stock. He'd done well. Steve's father owned stock in the same fund. "Stock is like a marriage. At some point, you opt for it or you opt out, but if you buy in, it's better to hold," as the old man put it.

"Let's meet every half hour at the front if we get separated," LouLou said.

"I'm sticking close. I'm worried you might act on your country house fantasy," Dale said. To Ben, she said, "If we ever get one, it'll be in Red Hook."

Very little he saw at antique sales (he'd been to several, one with his real estate agent, though that potential friendship had never taken off) made him nostalgic for his youth. His mother had loved hand-painted porcelain vases. Though he'd tried to remember, he could bring to mind very little of what his childhood environment had looked like. At Cornell, he'd seen a psychiatrist, who'd observed that he was quite critical of himself for not having a good visual memory. "You've got an amazing ability to recall what music was playing at a certain time, for literature, for doing mathematical computations in your head. Many people might think you were being a little hard on yourself."

Wasn't he supposed to remember what everything looked like? He always got in trouble when he didn't recognize someone, though he got into almost as much trouble when he complimented a jacket the person had worn for years, or didn't know what they liked to drink. What did they think—that he was the bartender on *Cheers*? People could tell you in excruciating detail how horrible the fabrics had been in their childhood bedrooms, how ugly the wallpaper looked, how pathetic the furniture their parents had inherited was, with feeble chair legs and broken springs, sofas draped in bedspreads.

"Why do you find this upsetting?" Dr. Minetti had asked. She must have thought she was dealing with a crazed interior decorator.

He saw few Victorian pieces around him as he walked down the wide center aisle. Maybe Steve was right, and a meteor had killed it all. What he saw was modern, along with Italian furniture, the primary features of which were length and proximity to the floor.

More seriously, what he'd meant to say to the shrink, which he'd expressed all wrong, involved his anger over his father's generation's ostensible love of hand-me-downs, when really it was that the stuff came free, which made his sanctimonious father not so different from the hippies he dismissed as "scum." But complaining about your parents—wasn't that too much of a cliché? He'd seen the doctor only three or four times.

Two booths down, he saw a cluster of weathervanes. One was of a swooping bird that reminded him of the rabbit chased by the bird of prey.

"Ben!" a tall, familiar-looking man said. "Finding any bargains?"

"Hi," Ben said.

"Ed Moulton. Guy you bought the tires from," the man said, extending his hand.

"Right. Of course. How's it going?"

"My wife made me come. At least there's free popcorn."

"Right," Ben said.

"Car riding good?"

"Very well. Your advice was good, Ed. Smoother ride."

"Safer," Ed said.

"That, too," Ben said, plotting his escape. He put the postcard of Kansas that he'd been examining back in the box—even if he bought it, he'd forget to ever mail it to Gerard—and nodded to Ed to signal goodbye. Ed stuck out his hand. Ben shook it. A firm grip with soft skin, like a pillow-top bed at an expensive hotel.

When Dale came up behind him, he'd been examining images from New Hampshire, hoping to find some old colorized cards—if

not of the school, of the Episcopal church, or the farmland sur-
rounding Bailey's grounds, many of which, including the or-
chards, had now been developed.

LaVerdere's house had been the ideal he'd had in mind when
he'd spoken to Dr. Minetti. LaVerdere had a small, high-ceilinged
place on campus on the second floor of an 1880s building that also
housed the registrar's office, as well as his off-campus house,
whose existence was shrouded in mystery. When Ben had first
gone to Bailey, he'd heard rumors that LaVerdere's wife—the
same one who was rumored to have died in England—was a re-
cluse in the house (it was obvious what novel everyone had been
reading). Sometimes rumors circulated that one of them had been
invited there, but it never turned out to be true. Its exact location
was also contested, and though Ben himself was rumored to have
gone there more than once, all he'd seen—Honor Society students had all seen it—was LaVerdere's apartment, where he'd had
skylights installed. The floors sanded. Over a series of weekends,
LaVerdere and Darius had filled the cracks in the plaster and
whitewashed the walls.

Framed and hung on the highest wall, where there was still a
fireplace but no chimney, was a black-and-white Avedon photograph of Marilyn Monroe in a low-cut evening dress, eyes down-
cast. The ultimate proof that you could blink and not ruin the
shot. Spotlighted, it was the single piece of art. Only someone
clueless would have assumed LaVerdere cared about Marilyn.
What had they discussed when Ben went alone for tea at LaVerdere's? He'd understood that Dr. Minetti expected to hear some
sad, repressed, halting account of his seduction, though that had
never happened, there or anywhere.

That afternoon in LaVerdere's apartment, he'd had his first

taste of lapsang souchong tea, as potent as alcohol, though more like drinking liquid charcoal. Their discussion had been about a play he'd read for class, *Hotel in Amsterdam*. They'd disagreed about a character's motivation. He'd felt that he was letting LaVerdere down by failing to understand nuance. You didn't talk about literature to LaVerdere without realizing your own deficiencies. What LaVerdere wanted wasn't sexual. Something about the way Ben thought had at first impressed, then disappointed, his teacher: Unless it was as part of the debate team, Ben wouldn't develop a point. Also, Ben never stood by his interpretations, especially of anything off the page, only understood through inference— though there'd been little LaVerdere disliked more than a person's simply falling silent. "Venture something, ladies and gentlemen," LaVerdere often said. "If your knowledge is insufficient, rely on your intuition. How could Shakespeare's plays be considered great, if the audience wasn't expected to rely on intuition?"

LouLou, browsing at the booth behind Ben, was listening to the elderly salesperson, who told her—as she wrapped LouLou's four soufflé dishes—that she could remember when everyone thought electric mixers would replace whisks, though eventually women realized that whisks had their place and required little cleaning.

"They did sort of have my bathtub, but ugh! The thing had been painted pastel blue, so I'm going to keep my seven hundred bucks," Dale said, when they met her at the front door. "Tonight I'm going to really enjoy soaking in your tub. Do you have anything girly, like bath salts? I mean, that somebody might have left behind?"

He did not. Had that been a leading question? At her request, they stopped at the drugstore and bought a funny Cinderella container of bubble bath that Dale couldn't stop admiring. She looked at it lovingly, as if she'd been given an Oscar. LouLou had stayed behind in the car, texting.

"I'm starving," LouLou said. "But thank you for taking us."

"There's a good bottle of wine at the house," he said. "Dinner might take a while to cook, though."

It had been in the back of his mind that he might bring up his father's suicide, the surprising telephone call his sister had had with Elin. Like imagining he'd been on the bus with Jasper, he sometimes now felt like he'd been with Elin when she'd sat in the car, conflicted, not turning on the ignition. For no reason that he understood, his father's death had been on his mind for days.

"Ben," LouLou said. "I want to ask you something serious."

"That sounds ominous."

"Don't shut me up when I need to say something important. You don't realize how much your mood's affected by Steve and his wife, Ben. Every time we talk, you've got something going on with them. It's great you're neighborly, and I've met Steve—he's interesting, even if he does give off vibes like he's the most important person in the room. But do you realize how much you bring them up, how often you're taking a walk with her, or how preoccupied you are with the next time you'll play tennis?"

"I've been helping him out with his father's foundation. You know about that."

"Yeah, sure, you've got this job that you also do for Steve, so his father can save the world before he keels over. It's totally entangled: work, money, the neighbors. You bring Steve's kid into conversation like she's your own, how cute she is, how much time you spend with Steve's daughter and Mommy."

"There's something wrong with that?"

"Yeah. You're not a member of their family."

"LouLou. You're jealous."

"I'm worried."

"Just stop worrying," Dale said, running her hand through her hair. "Or go ahead, worry—what do I care? But if Ben mistakes criticism for caring about him, he's nuts."

The trees were dark shapes that could have been made with enormous cookie cutters. It was Friday, a day that used to seem significant, that now seemed like every other day. Gin's miscarriage, the little girl thrust into his arms . . . anyone would understand why he'd bonded with them afterward. But that wasn't what was bothering her. She was really only interested in Ginny.

"Don't you think my relationship with the neighbors might be a smokescreen, in terms of your own unhappiness right now, LouLou?"

"He's a fucking Republican!"

"What?" he said.

"And I'm sure his cheerleader wife shares every belief he has."

"Steve? Are you talking about Steve? He wrote a check for five thousand bucks to the Democratic campaign!"

"He can't have. He believes in school vouchers and in never withdrawing our troops from anywhere."

"That's insane, LouLou. Wait . . . am I being punked, or something?"

"I'm looking forward to having that wine when we get home," Dale said. "A relaxing evening, no contention. A warm bath with bubbles popping around me."

"Women just love Ben," LouLou said. "Not the way you and I love him, Dale. Half the women at Bailey had a crush on him."

"The smoke's getting thicker," he said.

"You think so? You're that intent on not talking about your feelings for her?"

"I thought Gin might die. It made me re-evaluate every stupid thing we'd done or talked about. It happens to have been a very bad situation."

"Okay, we're circling the truth, but we're still not looking at it directly."

"I'm not in love with Steve's wife, if that's what you're thinking."

"You aren't?"

"What is *with* her?" Ben asked Dale.

"Can we talk about Ben's neighbors tomorrow?" Dale asked.

"Yeah, why is this your call, LouLou?" he asked, parking and getting out.

"Do you know?" LouLou said, in a gentler tone of voice, as they went through the door into the kitchen. "Do you know what I'm going to tell you, because you can read my mind and because nobody on Earth is more attuned to what's going on with me? You know, don't you?"

"I don't know what you're going to say," he said. "But I strongly suspect I'm not going to want to hear it."

"Going to bed!" Dale said. "Good night to everyone."

"It's so fucking *predictable*," LouLou said, collapsing into a kitchen chair. "LaVerdere. He had an affair with Elin."

He blinked. It wasn't a blink, but a spasm. His eye had gone out of control, a thing that rarely happened, usually only when he'd played too much tennis, or lifted too heavy a weight. Had this happened when his father was alive?

"Does this come as no surprise?"

"An extreme surprise. He thought it was a good idea to tell you? Why?"

"I'm sorry. I should have found a better way to say it. But he's had, or he's having, an affair with her. I didn't know that in the beginning."

He sat across from her. He said nothing for a long time. Then he said, "What beginning?"

"When he agreed to be the sperm donor."

"Now you're kidding. You're definitely kidding."

"We planned to do it through the center. Dale and I, I mean. I wanted it to all be aboveboard, meaning hidden."

He had no desire to hear more.

"As you know, I wanted you," LouLou said, her voice softening. "But your saying no, I can totally understand. I can imagine what this sounds like, but he and I talked, and since you said you didn't want to, I thought maybe he'd donate. It would be the turkey baster . . . you know what I'm going to say, right? But he did have a point about technology being the least reliable part. Listen, Ben, I said no. But now we're both really determined, I mean Dale and I are. It made me super-aware of my bullshit list, how ridiculous it was to pretend that I could make sure what kind of kid we'd get." Her hands flew apart. "So now the thing is, he's gone back to Elin."

"I can't take this in."

"Please say something to help," LouLou said. "Don't make me feel like a creep."

"So let me understand this: He offered to fuck you, but he also mentioned that he'd been having, or was having, an affair with my stepmother? Is that right?"

"In the past," Dale said, as she walked down the hallway. "They're not still involved. When she gets like this, chronology goes out the window."

"And have you given any thought to why he might have agreed, in the first place?" he asked LouLou.

"Of course! Do you think I'm stupid? Because of male pride. Or one-upmanship. He's invested in *screwing you*. He'd be screwing you whether his semen got squirted into me with a turkey baster or if he jumped on top. I totally get that."

"Which is what he proposed to do."

"It did seem to make more sense. Look, I'm in love with Dale. He's not under any illusions."

"Excuse me while I go drown myself," Dale said. "I don't think you gave the best possible thought to the way you gave Ben this information, LouLou."

"Wow," he said. "And I thought you were just being irrational about my friendship with Gin and Steve."

LouLou pushed her knuckles into her lips. Dale walked on, carrying the absurd bubble-bath container held high like a torch, her wineglass in the other hand. He waited to hear the bathroom door latch. He waited for water to start running. The house remained silent.

"Ginny looks like me. She could be my sister," LouLou said.

"Oh, please, let's not make this about me and Ginny," he said. "That's nothing but an attempt to deflect attention from how out of control you are. I can live without Ginny very easily, with her insecurity and her covert demands, and her precious Santa Maria Novella perfume and her secret nips of vodka. But you and me— haven't we always shared something real? People can live without a friend, though. Because if you thought I'd like to step in where LaVerdere left off? I wouldn't. I'm not standing on the sidelines, waiting for the next dance." He gestured. No one stood on the sidelines except the radiator.

It gave him an idea. He walked away and turned on the radio that he'd taken from his father's study after he died. He'd liked the fact that it turned on with a dial that rotated only between "off" and "on." There was a sea lion sticker on the front from one of Maude's decorating fits, running through his house, marking things as if they were going to be in a yard sale. The music was from some Motown group he'd forgotten the name of—not a particularly danceable tune, but he was already doing his best, his hands climbing an invisible ladder, doing fancy footwork.

He wiped his forehead with his forearm and, crossing the kitchen again without looking at LouLou, picked up the roasting pan and shoved the meat back into the refrigerator. Cook for her? Had he once cared what she'd have for dinner? He took down a small glass he often poured his morning orange juice into, one of several that had been left in the cabinet when he moved in. He poured the last of the wine. He said, "We're still friends, LouLou." He placed his hand over hers, as she'd done, earlier. "Just not the friends we used to be."

He slipped off his shoes, turned up the volume, and continued dancing the slow dance he might have had with her if she'd been straight.

Eventually, because she could think of nothing else to do, she got up and moved into his arms to dance.

Nineteen

He reluctantly agreed he would go to the movies the following weekend with Steve, along with Ginny and
Hannah. He'd met Hannah before, and a second meeting with Hannah wasn't going to get anything going. He and she
didn't have much in common except that they were both good-
natured about Steve's kidding. Ginny's younger sister was definitely second best.

Meanwhile, he went to the gym for the first time in weeks.
The new person behind the desk asked him to scan his card, then
was flustered when his membership turned out to be valid. He'd
said hello to a guy doing free weights who'd helped him the winter before by attaching jumper cables when the battery died in the
parking lot. "Hey," was all the man had to say, sweat dripping off
his face in spite of a bandanna wrapped tightly around his forehead. After using the stair-stepper, lifting weights, riding the

stationary bike, and doing three sets of pull-downs, he'd left, confused about whether he was exhausted or energized.

He stopped on the way back for a haircut, though he hesitated because he was so sweaty. It was a unisex salon that cost more than it should, where he disappointed them by never wanting a manicure and never buying any products. The magazine selection tended to be unisex, too: *The American Scholar* (the owner's husband taught at Bard), *The Week*. When Amy finished his haircut, she untied the black cape from around his neck, brushing his shoulders with a brush so light, it felt like a thrilling little breeze passing over his neck.

"You stayed away too long," she chided. She introduced him to her sister, Kayla, who'd been curled in a chair in the waiting area, reading a magazine. He'd assumed she was a client. He stayed for a San Pellegrino and chatted. It was the first time he'd heard Amy's pronouncement on Arly (who'd loved the salon): "One of those women who thinks she's complicated just because she complicates other people's lives."

Leaving, he tried to remember the last time he'd felt any sexual desire. He wouldn't pretend the little internal fizzle that sometimes tickled his ribs when LouLou appeared didn't surprise him, but it wasn't because he wanted to sleep with her. He especially didn't want to do that now, though her name detonated a brief, tiny spark. He'd checked some photographs on his cell phone. He didn't agree that LouLou looked like Ginny. LouLou radiated sleekness; Ginny only seemed skinny. LouLou's hair was a deep, magnificent brown, Ginny's was ordinary, though highlighted, as if an invisible light shone from within. They did not have the same nose, even if they had similarly intense eyes.

The day before he was supposed to go to the movie with his neighbors—since LouLou's objection to his purported infatuation, he'd tried to think of Ginny and Steve as his neighbors—he called and lied. "I screwed up, Gin; I'd already bought tickets to a concert," he told her. Of course they could do it another time, she said. Hannah had a cold and wouldn't be coming anyway.

He'd made an alternate plan: He'd be driving to Rhinebeck to get together with Kayla. Her husband had left her and their fourteen-month-old son for another man. That had come up in conversation. Seeing Amy's sister made a lot more sense than screwing Steve's sister-in-law. Despite what LouLou believed, he didn't want to be more involved with Steve's family. The more he thought about it, the less he thought LouLou got him. She took his friendship for granted. She rarely spent time with him anymore. Before she wanted something from him, she'd fixated on how elusive he was, denying that she—with her ten-hour workdays and her girlfriend—was the one who was withholding.

That Saturday he bought a bag of Tate's chocolate-chip cookies (opting for gluten-free just to be safe), a bottle of Perrier (bringing wine was such a cliché), and Winky Walrus, a bug-eyed toy with exceedingly long eyelashes he'd gotten from the pharmacy. It ran on four AAA batteries. He opened a small flap and clicked them into Winky's gray plastic ass, watched with interest as it crawled and batted its black plastic lashes. He replaced it in the box.

Since college, he'd slept with Rita, Callie, Irina (that had been a mistake), Catherine, Doreen, Gina, Alissa, Lonni, Kathy (the real estate agent Kathy; there'd also been Kathy2), Deirdre, and Kendra. Lonni he'd been pretty crazy about, but she'd decamped for Hawaii. He'd been fascinated by Deirdre's inverted nipples—

an actress working as a waitress—but her shrink advised her to drop him, and after a few dates she had. Who'd want to be with anybody who'd do that? He'd never returned to the pretentious Les Quatre Cornichons, where he'd gone with Steve the night he met her, when she waited on their table. Damn! That had been the *other* time he'd met the tire salesman, Ed, from the antique show. Ed and the guy's redheaded wife. Steve had liked Deidre, though she hadn't taken Steve seriously. "Your friend the comedian," she'd later called him, "and his really nice wife."

On the way to Rhinebeck, Tory (he'd mistakenly left her off the list) came to mind. She'd gone to his house to have sex on the second date, her LeSportsac a Trojan Horse of condom packets. He'd hurt her feelings by laughing when she unzipped the bag. Later, she'd called a girlfriend to pick her up in the middle of the night—she hadn't even asked him to give her a ride, though of course he would have. The sex had been good; they hadn't had a fight, afterward they'd watched Colbert, he'd found a bag of mint Milanos. How was he supposed to know she had diabetes? He'd forgotten to include her on his list because he felt guilty, he supposed. Well, at least he didn't have to write a response paper about any of that. And when you got to a certain age, it wasn't that you couldn't say what was funny, it was that if you had to explain, you were with the wrong person.

He'd been drawn to Tory the minute he met her. She was what Elin would have called "plucky," which made him think, for some reason, of a duck, which in turn made her a bit amusing to him, though she never knew why. Once they'd discussed his perceptions about trusting your instincts about what you were doing, taking a break from driving south at a service area, where they'd used the bathrooms and bought Starbucks. For half an hour, Tory had sat across from him on a picnic bench outside and insisted, with barely contained anger, that he wasn't like other men. (Should that have been what he aspired to?) He was too verbal, too inquisitive, as interested in words, which plenty of women would find intimidating (she did not) as he was in sex, and as for that, the vibes he gave off were relentless. Okay: He'd been honest; he didn't think he was interested in marriage.

"Is that it? You can have whatever you want, so with hookups and one-night stands, you're never going to get serious? Even if you've convinced yourself, which I'm not so sure of, what's wrong with being *realistic*? Let's just talk about a long-term relationship— we don't have to cover the scary shit, like marriage. You've got two modes: on and off. Mostly you prefer on, but sometimes, even in the middle of a conversation, you flip the switch and the person you're talking to goes dark. If that's out of your control, if you don't recognize what I'm talking about, you should—what's the euphemism—'get help.' And also, also, if you think I'm discussing this anymore when we get back on the highway, Ben? Keep your fingers off the radio dial, with your supernatural ability to find spooky songs that speak to the sexual subtext of whatever you're talking about. You send out pheromones like skunk spray."

The chai latte he'd bought her had certainly not soothed her like mother's milk. He was happy to have ordered two double espressos. ("I'm sorry. There's no such thing as four shots in a Tall.")

Dale had once asked him, after saying it was none of her business, if he knew how many women he'd slept with.

"You go first," he'd said.

"It's embarrassing," she'd replied. "Two men and three women."

"Going back to the beginning?"

"Yeah. Just like the Bible," she'd replied.

He'd thought for a minute, then told her maybe ten. Corrected that to a dozen. In his mental list just now, he'd failed to count. He resisted being a glorified accountant. That was all he was, even if he could write programs. Sex with Arly had begun in college, so it hadn't counted, even though he'd been hooked on her for years. Up to a point, he'd had sex with few women, but then it became like running downhill. It became whatever number it became. He'd thought he'd always remember the number of Arly's hotel room, but he'd forgotten. It didn't come back. Of course, neither did she. (He was as fast-thinking as Colbert, he decided—just as good with a quick comeback, even if, like LaVerdere, his ideal audience was himself.) Guys were disgusting if they kept lists, even mentally. Putting down names in code, or drawing four parallel lines, with the fifth fallen female the line on the diagonal . . . that was the worst, smarmy, like cutting yourself in a pattern, instead of just slashing. His father had shown him marks scratched with a paper clip inside his desk drawer: the number of times he'd had sex with Elin. There: proof positive the guy was a pig.

It was slightly embarrassing, but he'd been trying ever since he remembered her name to remember anything about Kathy2 except that she was the woman whose earrings weighed down her earlobes, dark-haired, anxious. Kendra—cool Kendra—had made an unusual request. She'd have sex with him only if he kept saying, "You're not Kendra, You're not Kendra." He had to say it that way; he couldn't say, "You're not her."

He listened to what turned out to be Dave Brubeck on the radio. Jazz wasn't his thing, though it had been his father's favorite music. He thought, as the piece progressed, that it sounded like the soundtrack that accompanied the downing of a shot elephant, one that tried over and over to rise but was damned by its injuries and its weight.

Her house was huge. If he turned in to the driveway, he'd block in the Lexus she'd parked outside the garage door, though there were three carports. *Joanne.* He'd almost forgotten Joanne. They'd smoked a joint and gone skinny-dipping in the pool behind an empty house, though when they dived in the motion detector went off, and a cop car had arrived in minutes; fortunately, the cop and his partner had been amused by the freaked-out naked woman, and totally believed Ben's story.

He parked at the curb. Even the concrete was embedded with something that sparkled. He'd soon be crossing an invisible line of demarcation. It would be like your *best* birthday party, though you could only know that in retrospect, or—grimmer—a news image on TV you'd never shake, which also brought in a whole new way of living.

He picked up his gift bags and walked toward the door. What would it be like to have your husband leave you for a guy? It probably happened all the time, though that wouldn't make it any easier. People were audited by the IRS all the time, too. If the guy hadn't left his wife, well, the lovely lady he was about to see wouldn't have been at the salon crying on her sister's shoulder, and he wouldn't be taking his long walk up the path. He'd tucked a condom in his wallet, pushing it behind a small, faded photograph of himself as a child, his chubby face jammed against his father's cheek in the photo booth. ("Carry this. It will make girls love you if they see it," Elin had told him years before, removing the little square from the album and handing it to him like a sacred wafer.)

Elin and LaVerdere. It boggled the mind. What business was it of his? What was he doing approaching a near-stranger's house with some toy her kid could bang on its head and break, with not even a bottle of wine for fortification? Only a jerk would bring bottled water. She'd think he was an alcoholic.

"Hi," she said, already opening the door, her son in her arms.

"Hi," he said.

There was an initial awkward moment. Then he stepped forward and hugged her—not that easy to get close, with the baby welded to her—the boy in his blue onesie turning away with whiplash force, burying his face in his mother's neck. The child also had hiccoughs.

"This is Lacey," she said, gesturing into the huge living room, where a young girl in particularly large Doc Martens sat, wearing a bright-purple sweater and bulging camouflage shorts over tights. "Lacey's babysitting tonight, while Mommy makes dinner, which Mommy really appreciates. They're going to watch a movie about dolphins."

"Nice, Kayla," he said. Dinner. What kind of a jerk was he, not to bring wine?

"My mother informs me I can't take any calls when I'm providing child care? So I'm just asking. In case you want to text me, or something?"

"Oh, I don't have any policy about turning off your phone. Tell your mother I said it was fine."

"It's not like I'm going to be chatting up some nonexistent boyfriend while Henry's sinking in the bathtub."

"Well, *I hope not*! But you don't have to bathe him. He'll be fine. You two have your pizza and—"

"She is *so* great!" Lacey exploded. "My mom told me I'd like to babysit here. I mean, provide child care."

"Her mother is my acupuncturist," Kayla said to Ben.

"Ah," he said.

With no protest, the hiccuping Henry was peeled from his mother's chest as Lacey asked, "Want to walk, Big Boy, or want a carry?"

The child started off, taking rubbery-kneed goose steps across the enormous Oriental rug that looked like a reef improbably crushed under a microscope lens. Lacey trailed him as he stopped and started, stopped and continued into the depths of the house.

"It was thoughtful of you to get a sitter," he said.

"It saves my sanity. What's left of it."

"I had no idea you'd live in a house like this, to tell you the truth."

"It looks like a court jester's hat on Google Earth," she said. "My lawyer pointed that out."

He followed her into the kitchen. Granite counters on the kitchen island. The floor was so shiny, he could have brought ice skates. A ceramic pink pig sat atop the refrigerator. "From a friend in San Francisco," she said, noticing him eyeing it. "I think there's vodka and scotch. There's wine. I hope you don't drink beer."

"Why do you hope that?"

"Because I don't have any."

"I'm not a beer drinker. Maybe a glass of red?"

"Cabernet?"

"Sounds good. Want me to open it?" He remembered the cork that had sunk into the bottle of wine he'd opened in the middle of the afternoon, as soon as LouLou and Dale had driven off, after their most recent intense visit, filled with their intense desires—the way a slight dusting of cork had repulsed him as it floated on the surface of the wine in his glass. What was LouLou thinking, considering having LaVerdere's child? Didn't she understand the way the man mind-fucked people? Did she not believe in genetic heritability?

"It's easier if I do it. Nobody can ever figure this out," Kayla said. She lifted an enormous wine opener from a stainless-steel stand. Her biceps were well defined, her arms lissome (lissome!), her hands delicate, her long, polished fingernails squared. The house was overheated. He could understand why she wore a sleeveless silk blouse with her jeans. With a sound like a chainsaw starting up, she extracted the cork. She sniffed it and handed it to him. Who was she? Who had she been married to? Such moments of speculative detachment were never good, because they implied an underlying reservation, like questions posed when you already had the answer.

("Ladies and gentlemen, there may be no real debate at all about certain matters, but to assert power, an issue must be invented. How, then, do we best fabricate a debate that is not instantly recognized as specious? By admitting to our own ostensible confusion, our unwillingness to accept what our society would term foregone conclusions."—LaVerdere)

Her refrigerator gleamed in the absence of photographs: other people's Christmas cards; dogs with red eyes; oldsters in their impeccable suits and timeless dresses—the food smudge the result of an indifferent observer's sticky fingers. Those pictures were clamped with magnets to Steve and Ginny's refrigerator. You inevitably knocked some bride to the floor, reaching in for ice.

"Great kitchen," he said. His kitchen, hardly updated, had been a good bargaining point. As had the lack of insulation, which had been easy enough to get blown into the attic. His real estate agent Zippy's brother—maybe his brother, Doo-Dah—no, the guy's name had been Peter or Paul, one of the Apostles—he'd never seen the guy again—but he'd insulated houses. Old people would put up with drafty houses, but no one younger would. He pulled out a stool.

"If it wouldn't seem too controlling, I think we might be more comfortable in the other room," she said.

He hopped down. The wineglass looked like a goldfish bowl atop a stem. If Dale had filled this one, it would have drained the bottle.

"So you probably know more about me than I realize, because you and my sister talk, right? But I mean, what *do* you know?"

"Very little," he said. "Last time I talked to Amy was with you. Amy was one of the first people I met after I moved in."

"She said she was surprised when you went back to her shop. She thought maybe she'd said something that offended you."

"I'm used to that. That wouldn't be a factor."

"Ooh. Did I hit a nerve?"

"Just being honest," he said.

"You know my husband left me, right?"

"Yes. That came up when we were talking before. You said that it was another man."

"It's somebody famous. I'm under a gag order."

"No kidding."

"Only because I want the best settlement I can get."

"Then I shouldn't ask who it is."

"No," she said, sipping wine. "Umm. Do you like it? What are those?" She pointed to the bags he'd carried into the living room and put at his feet. He could hear footsteps on the second floor.

"Oh!" he said. "I've been carrying them around like my lapdog, or something. I must be more nervous than I realized. It's a toy for Henry and a bottle of Perrier."

"You brought Henry water?"

"No. I brought us water."

"I was kidding."

She slipped out of her high-heeled, pointed-toed mules. One lay on its side. The shoes had red soles. Living in a house heated to this temperature, you could easily pretend winter was summer.

"Do you know who my father is?" she asked.

"No."

"He invented the operating tables that are used in almost every hospital in America."

"Really? So is he a designer, or—"

"An engineer."

"Interesting. What's his name?"

"Craig," she said. "Amy's my half-sister. We have the same mom. Daddy's generous with both of us. Amy's got a thing, though, about not taking any more money than she needs. To me, that's just silly. She could close the shop and go to people's houses to cut their hair, you know? Have her own schedule." Her eyes were an unusual gray-blue that reminded him slightly, only slightly, of Tory's.

"I don't like to snack before dinner," she said. "It raises your blood sugar so you eat too much. But help yourself to cashews."

"Wine's perfect," he said, raising his glass. In his whole life, had he ever offered a sincere toast?

"So how long have you been out of the city, Ben?"

"Five years. Something like that."

"What did you do? I mean, what's your job?"

Hadn't he asked something similar, years ago, and been put

down by LaVerdere? Elin, too, had told him that it was best to ask that question indirectly. There seemed no point in trying to describe his attempts to draw up a better financial plan for Steve's father's organization, though the work he'd put into that had taken more time than his real job.

"I was a sort of glorified accountant. The company I was working for split off from the parent company, and I ended up getting an offer from the competition. They've moved to D.C. I mostly design new software programs for them and provide them with charts and graphics. Makes it easy to work from home." Tory had worked for the same company before they relocated to D.C. and had sometimes given him a ride to Washington. During the time Arly had lived with him, she'd been jealous of their infrequent road trips. He missed them now more than he missed either woman. Tory had rented a house one town north, though her goal had always been to move to the Northeast Kingdom. By now, there was every chance she'd done that. She'd vanished from social media. When he'd asked a mutual friend at the company if she'd done a complete disappearing act, the response had been, "Sorry. She asked me not to talk about it." Did that mean not talk to him, or not tell anyone? That, he hadn't asked.

"Your area's changing fast. Rhinebeck, too. We came here because it was quiet and we liked the house. Well, I was so young— I would have liked a yurt, if that's what he'd decided we should move into. I was way too young to be living with anybody, really. And I don't think he liked it here. Randy preferred the West Coast. I thought eventually we'd move there, but I kept quiet because he always had to be the one who had all the good ideas. I was pregnant when he told me who he was in love with, but I had an abortion."

"Difficult," he said. In his experience, there'd been a time when women rushed to tell you about their abortions, but in recent years, no one mentioned them. They'd gone back to being secrets.

There was no longer any indication that the sitter and Henry were in the house. He took the animal out of the box and went to show it to her. He pushed the button. It sounded like a muffled alarm as it squirmed in his hand. It was ridiculous. You had to sympathize with Chinese workers. He placed it on the floor. After every few noisy steps, it slowed down, tilted its head back, blinked repeatedly, and screeched like a tropical bird. After the third screech, he turned it off.

"He's going to like it. Thank you," she said.

He scooped up the toy and stood it on a side table. "And Tate's cookies," he said, pulling the last thing from the bag. "Have you had them?"

"It's like you thought you were coming to a picnic!" she said. "I've been known to binge after midnight."

The bottle sat on the table with the toy, which seemed smaller when it was still. Which of these bucking, noisy toys would make it into a time capsule? He lifted the wine bottle from an absorbent coaster. "You wouldn't want to take a walk before dinner?" he asked.

"You didn't seem nervous before. What made you nervous?"

"I'm not good at small talk."

"Who'd want to be?"

Was this his cue for moving in? He got no feeling that it was.

"You know what?" she said. "Let's do it. I changed my mind."

He raised his glass with its one remaining sip glistening in the bottom. He remembered Elin saying, "This is the point at which you refill a glass, not after you swallow the last bit."

"We ordered a case of that," she said. "I see you approve. If the pollen starts to kill my eyes, we can turn back. The steps behind the yard lead to a path that runs down to the center of town."

"Okay," he said.

"Unless you'd rather just drink."

"No. I'd like to get out for a while before dark."

"To enjoy nature?"

There it was: that little blip indicating amusement, though he didn't understand why. He couldn't say he'd never been awkward with women, but he felt disempowered by Kayla, by her surroundings—not so much because of what he was doing, but because of what he wasn't doing. Maybe the idea behind houses like this one was to get lost in them.

Standing, she slipped into her pretty shoes long enough to walk to the back door, where she put a hand on his shoulder as she pulled on running shoes.

"So where did you go to college?" she asked.

"Cornell."

"I'll bet you got a free ride, right?"

"My father had to cover some expenses. A little of both." Who talked about college anymore? "Too cold?" he asked, as they put on their coats and he opened the door. Too late, he remembered that Dale had informed him to ask a woman if she wanted you to hold the door, and if you opened it, ask whether she wanted to precede you. The wind was blowing so hard he almost lost hold of the doorknob.

"Hold hands so we don't get blown away," she said, slipping her hand into his. "It's really sweet that you brought cookies and water. I have to ask, though: Are you disappointed I'm thirty-five?"

"Of course not," he said, though he'd assumed she was younger.

"In two weeks I'll be thirty-six."

"Well, that changes everything."

"Those are almost the exact words my husband used when he told me: 'What I've got to say is going to change everything.' And there I was, thinking, Well, whatever you've got to say, I've got the trump card, because, surprise! We're going to have another kid.'"

An image of Ginny holding Maude came to him. She'd come to his door to ask if Maude might have dropped her toy there. As Ginny carried Maude, they'd walked through the first floor, looking for Beanie Baby Bartleby—the tongue-twister toy that would always prefer not to be squeezed, let alone lost. His friend Daphne Randolph, who took pride in never going to college but owning a lucrative business (the secondhand-clothing store in town), had once, at her snarkiest, asked him if he thought Ginny's unannounced visits to his house were planned—whether she might not have tossed a toy here or there so that she'd have an excuse to visit more than once in the same day. Ginny didn't shop at her store; that was one thing that made Daphne suspicious of her. Her question had been paranoid, though, something LouLou might also have said, if he'd told her about the number of dropped toys.

"You and Amy—you're the only kids in your family?"

"Right. No secret brother who's a monk or a heroin addict. You?"

"I have a sister, Brenda. She's a college professor. She got hired at the same place she went to school. We're fond of each other, but we don't talk that much. My mother died when I was young. My father's dead, too. I think he killed himself."

"You think?"

"Well, he had cancer, and chemo, and he wasn't looking forward to the next round."

"I'm sorry."

"I don't think he ever recovered from my mother's death. That's what my sister thinks, anyway, but she's got something invested in believing that."

"I was actually happy when I had amnio and found out I was pregnant with a boy. By the way, I'm already thirty-six. But that's all I've lied about. Now you know I'm a liar. What's your secret?"

"I don't know," he said. "I'm sure I lie. Doesn't everybody, sometimes?"

"That's all you can come up with, sometimes you lie?"

Was *this* a cue? He said, "I'll try to come up with something worse."

"We've been talking around some subject, Ben. I just don't know what it is."

It raised the possibility that she was up for something more genuine. Good. Though they were sheltered by the trees from much of the wind, he continued to hold her hand. The path wasn't steep. When his father did what he did . . . when he got up in the middle of the night, so weak and ill, who'd gone with him? He hadn't been well enough to drive himself to the state park. Who'd agreed that such a plan made any sense? An airplane flew over. For his parents' generation, the question was always, Where were you when Kennedy was shot? Now, it was, What were you doing on 9/11? Jasper had been on a bus. He himself had been asleep, then crowded into a room where the students and teachers sat in front of the TV, watching the world change. Jasper's loss had been so much greater than his own. Odd, that they'd more or less fallen out of contact. He shouldn't have let that happen.

"Give me a hint about what's wrong. Something about a

woman?" she said. "Guys never get bent out of shape about other guys."

"A sort of complicated situation with an old friend, who's gay. I'm close to her and her girlfriend."

"They want you to father their child."

"That is what she wanted," he said. "How amazing you'd say that."

"I'm good at guessing. But apparently not good enough."

A birdhouse sat wedged between a tree's trunk and a sturdy branch. No sign of an occupant, but the little structure seemed to be in good shape, welcoming. Maybe it was part of some child's personal kingdom. Until it deteriorated enough to become dangerous, he'd played in a tree house a long walk from his father's summer place, never knowing who'd built it, but imagining the lives that had preceded him. He felt like he'd been rewarded for something when he'd found it. Sometimes he sat there with binoculars, hoping to see deer. Deer browsed on pine, hemlock, maple, and swamp maple in the winter. He'd been a lonely kid, private.

"It's okay that we left without saying anything to the sitter?"

"She's super-reliable. I'd have messed up their dynamic if I'd intruded."

"Good to have someone you can be sure of."

"Meaning that I shouldn't be?"

"No. Meaning just what I said."

"And your friend, she used to be your girlfriend?"

"LouLou."

"LouLou. You didn't answer me."

(LaVerdere: "A question is a proposition. Which you might waste time by addressing directly.")

"People don't have to be couples to be close."

"Absolutely. I wish my husband had just remained my friend. Or better yet, my enemy. Then none of this would have happened."

"You'll come out of it okay."

"LouLou," she said again. "Actually, I don't want to hear about her. Guys assume women are so curious. You know what? I'm over curiosity."

"That was the one thing I was *required* to be. The school I went to was for bright, screwed-up kids. I never understood why my father sent me there, since I wasn't a troublemaker."

"I couldn't stand for Henry to go away."

"I didn't want to go to high school where my dad and step-mother lived. Nobody wanted to go to that school. Even if it had been great, who wants to live with his parents?"

"Was she an evil stepmother?"

"Elin? No. No, she was fine."

"I always wished I could live with Daddy," she said. "But Daddy was in constant motion. Daddy was busy. I left home when I was eighteen. I moved in with my ex, my soon-to-be ex, too young. I decided to when we were snorkeling off Virgin Gorda— isn't that perfect? I'd actually been a virgin when I met him. I mean, technically. But that's enough about me. Aren't there quite a few LouLous? Like Little Lulu."

He couldn't think what to say. Was she self-loathing, or was she angry at him? He'd felt sympathy for her when she'd said how much her son meant to her. Then she'd reverted to talking about LouLou.

"Hey," he said, trying to change the subject, "I haven't had a home-cooked dinner in a while. What are we having?"

"Tubby Tompkins," she answered, momentarily confusing him. "We're having ratatouille. Seared duck breast with porcini-mushroom sauce. Assuming you eat red meat."

"That sounds great."

"I couldn't stand to make one more phone call and ask one more person, 'Oh, are you vegetarian, and can you tolerate dairy, or should I get almond milk, and do you like bottled water, and if so, do you like it bubbly or still, and if the spring runs dry in France, is there any alternative?'"

"Good I brought my own."

"I had a women's lunch here to support breast cancer research, and somebody had her cook call ahead. 'I'm Manuel, the cook.' Then he started in about how the sodium content often isn't listed on the labels of imported water."

"It's too bad more of these things aren't funny in the moment."

"Right! That could be the motto of our age: 'This'll seem funny later.' You know what? I blew it by telling you we ordered wine by the case. Like we're people whose wine has to be special. Like nobody's got anything better to think about."

"That didn't occur to me, Kayla. I did notice that you keep speaking in terms of 'we,' though."

"Let's change the subject," she said. "You don't want to talk about LouLou, and I don't want to talk about my ex."

Something in her directness—a way of speaking that made it seem like she relied on talk that seemed confessional, at the same time giving him less of a sense of her, rather than more—reminded him of what it could be like to talk to LouLou. He decided to try his own digression, even if he hadn't had enough to drink to make that interesting.

"Where were you on 9/11?" he asked.

"Yoga," she said. "I'm sounding worse and worse."

"What's wrong with doing yoga?"

"I'm not sure I can tell when you're kidding."

"I just mean what I say."

"Refreshing." She stopped to rub dirt off her shoe. "On 9/11," she said, "we had a dinner reservation. I'd woken up with the sense he was going to ask me to marry him before I got too old."

"You obviously wanted that."

"Well, I wasn't controlling or anything. I just thought we might have been moving in that direction."

"Did I say something to suggest I thought you were controlling?"

"After he left, he told me that at weddings, straight weddings, there were invisible darts being sent out between men, sexual darts. That women didn't pick up on them; they were no-see-ums. Anyway, obviously that night we didn't go to dinner." She played with her hair. She said, "If you and I got married, do you think we could make it? Or do you think marriage is just impossible?"

"Excuse me?"

"Are you only attracted to girls who are bi?"

"You're teasing."

"No. I'm like you. I mean what I say."

"Really? So what's your sense of it? Should we get married?"

"We'd probably get along pretty well, but I'm not looking for another husband. I feel like I've already wasted half my life. Well, I mean, I really *have* almost wasted half my life! I mistook him for things he just wasn't. I thought his anxiety was energy, and I thought his lack of focus was because he had so many brilliant, conflicting ideas. He didn't want children. I felt the same way. Like we could just dodge the baby bullet. When he started to say maybe we should try, I thought that made him so vulnerable—it was rethinking him, more than rethinking motherhood. Henry's made me do that. I mean, I might not have loved him. I might have been one of those women who drove the baby into that lake." She gestured.

"That's somebody's swimming pool."

"Whatever it takes. A psychopath will find a way to get the car into the water."

"Now you're joking."

"Ben," she said. "Do you at least understand *LouLou*?"

Twenty

H e thought that he did. He remembered the person she'd been at school and missed her, and those days. He'd finally talked to Jasper—you had to text your friends to arrange a time to talk—though after the initial rush of relief upon hearing Jasper's voice, he'd found himself withholding. Petulant. Everything Jasper said was said dispassionately. After Stanford, where he'd given up the idea of being a doctor, he'd spent two years as an office manager at a sports store in San Diego before moving to Chicago to live with his neurologist-to-be girlfriend. He, too, now wrote software programs. Jasper was still running ("Why wouldn't I be?"), though his knees weren't in the best shape. One of his clients managed a gym with an indoor track. He went there for free three or four days a week. Jasper and his girlfriend had talked about marriage, but he was going to wait and see where she'd be doing her residency. Not that marrying hinged on that, but if he had to make a big change geographically, it seemed best to delay wedding plans. He'd move wherever she went ("Why wouldn't I?"). Her name was Yuna. She'd grown up in Santa Barbara, riding horses.

"Who do you see from the old days besides LouLou and her girlfriend?" Jasper had asked. He'd asked quietly, as if whatever Ben answered, they'd be sharing a confidence. Ben said he'd seen Eleanor Rule once, at her instigation. Benson Whitacre. Benson, whose name had been in the paper when Lehman Brothers went under. They'd spent hours at a bar on Tenth Avenue as he'd listened to Benson's self-justifying tale of woe.

The day Ben called Jasper, he'd intended to tell him that he had his father's hat. Not that it was the elephant in the room. It was more like Ben sensed an animal hovering silently at the edge of the forest, listening acutely. The Man was the only person Ben had personally known who'd died in the World Trade Center. Soon afterward, Jasper had been orphaned, his mother living only a few months longer than his father.

In Ben's town there were two men who were one hundred years old and who didn't speak to each other, and a Hungarian woman who cut silhouettes, age ninety-nine. He'd read about them in the local paper, the two men flanking the birthday sheet cake the newspaper editor had bought for them, one standing with a cane raised in triumph, the other leaning against a walker with balloons on the handles. The female artist was seated, mugging for the camera with a toothless smile.

He still hadn't called Elin to say that he knew about her and LaVerdere, though he'd found a way to decline her emailed requests that he visit. The news about Elin and LaVerdere was difficult to absorb. He thought it best to keep his distance. Elin sensed something was wrong, which for a while meant that she called more often; he'd gotten into the habit of looking more carefully at caller ID. Yet for all he knew, the affair began after his father died.

Kayla, he came to find out, had her off-moments, when she could hardly be engaged. She'd twice said she'd visit—she'd been the one to suggest it, but twice she'd canceled. They didn't see each other for two weeks after the dinner. No sex had followed the meal. The first time she called to say she couldn't visit, it was because the sitter got sick. The second time she and her ex-husband had to check out a Montessori school. For Henry's sake, they'd planned to have lunch afterward. Did people believe their own stories? Was she presenting it to him that way, or did she believe it herself? He'd asked, as gently as possible, why visiting a school would interfere with seeing him that night. The answer had been that, for Henry's sake, her soon-to-be-ex-husband and his mother would be spending the night at the house. Ben wondered whether the toy had vanished into the heap he'd caught sight of at the end of the evening, when he and Kayla peeked into the boy's room to see the babysitter asleep on the rug, her feet splayed in those Doc Martens, which looked like diving weights, one of Henry's old receiving blankets clutched over her chest, as if she were a soldier who'd been killed at the base of Toy Mountain.

The day after the dinner, he'd slept with Daphne Randolph. There was another name he'd omitted from the list. She'd called and asked if he could stop by to offer advice about dividing the changing area of her vintage clothing store into private dressing rooms. Guys had started to try on dresses, making her women customers uncomfortable. She ran the store out of her finished, above-ground basement, mannequins standing outside the door like sentries in drag, draped with boas and gowns shedding their sequins like snakes.

Amy, from the salon, stopped in to Daphne's store from time to time. Daphne knew to put aside any size-nine designer shoes so Amy could see them first. Hearing these things about women's fashion, he'd felt like a person who had briefly been intrigued by Kayla, who had herself been nothing but an animated mannequin. That mansion she lived in, her indifference to good causes she supported only because she was obliged to—that was part of buying into marriage, Rhinebeck, wine by the case, a babysitter even when you spent the evening at home.

He'd suggested, after taking some measurements and writing down the name of a carpenter who'd also helped him at his own house, that he and Daphne go upstairs. To his surprise, she'd instantly stretched out on the rug in the area they'd been considering partitioning, like an old-fashioned hinged toy that went wobbly when you pushed below the disc it stood on. She, at least, had a sense of humor. He'd rubbed his thumb over her mandala tattoo. If the tattoo artist wasn't good enough, something that complex could fail to convey at all: spaghetti on a plate; Spanish moss (which was usually filled with mites).

At Bailey, when he'd been a privileged, stupid young man, he'd gossiped along with everyone else about the school nurse's tattoo. Almost as surprising as the tattoo were Daphne's navy-blue toenails, bruised, prehensile claws. She'd done them herself and given the money she'd saved to the liquor store, she informed him. She'd proved it by bringing out a bottle of Jameson's after they'd had sex. He'd ordered a pizza, and paid the delivery guy, who'd all but gone on tiptoes, trying to look at the naked woman in the living room, then he and Daphne had watched TV: Anderson Cooper standing in some war zone, with his characteristic expression that bridged the gap between being reconciled to anything, while still being mildly concerned, wearing a multi-pocketed camouflage vest with neat, empty pockets. Explosions behind him drowned out his voice. It took Ben a while to realize that his cell's ringing was adding to the noise level. He didn't take the call, or look at the screen. Daphne, too, ignored it.

"I'm your townie. I'm your demimondaine," Daphne said. "Like that fancy word? I looked it up when I read it in a book."

"Not a Stephen King novel, I suspect."

"No. Some Southern writer who spent about a hundred pages going on about some guy on the eve of his wedding, whose car goes off the road and the local girl, the demimondaine who's not his fiancée, who was in the passenger seat, disappears into the forest. I was worried it was going to turn into another *Scarlet Letter,* or something."

"Does he find her?"

"The townie? Well, his fiancée makes him search for her, of all things, because they can't get married unless the other one's found, because she might be dead, or something. She does show up, yeah, but it's not so easy because her friends all want to protect her."

"I don't know that story," he said.

"Well, let's admit you haven't read everything," she said. "And let's also admit that except for my current beau, nobody'd be racing around looking for me if I disappeared. They'd think I'd gone to a flea market, or something. I don't have any women friends. *You're* my friend. Imagine that!"

His cell was ringing again. This time, he took it out and looked at it. It was Steve.

"Yeah, Steve. What's up?" he said.

"If I say to you, 'Texas,' what's the first thing that pops into your mind?"

"Lyndon Johnson."

"Really? Not all the vast stretches of land, not even horses?"

"Is there a right and wrong answer, Steve? Can we play this game later? I'm involved in something right now."

"What pops into my mind when you say 'involved in something' is sex," Steve replied. "We'll talk later."

But that discussion wasn't picked up again, though he saw Steve the next day. By then, Ben assumed he'd been given a clue, rather than really having been asked a question. Changing jobs had been much on Steve's mind. It seemed likely that he'd be going to Texas. And if Steve wanted to play a word-association game, rather than clarifying what he meant to say? That was pure Steve.

He called Kayla a few times, hoping to be invited back. He supposed he was doing that because she'd hurt his feelings by wanting nothing from him. On the phone, he made sure not to put pressure on her. He was relieved when she laughed at something he said—though he couldn't predict what would amuse her. All those years in the debate club, along with all the years afterward trying to forget what he'd learned so he could talk like a human being again. People he met seemed different, as if he'd been whirled around and let go, so that when he landed it took a minute to bring things into focus. The town itself had been whirled around, its land developed, people moving in, the florist out of business, the tombstones in the cemetery cleaned by a pressure washer to look like polished incisors. Some of the new people were witty, communicative. A dance group moved from one of the churches to the annex of the hardware store, which had been transformed to a performance facility, courtesy of an anonymous donor's money.

Women went to Rick's in groups and held impromptu arm-wrestling contests. Daphne certainly did whatever she wanted. He experienced the opposite of what was written in magazine articles about the dumbing-down of the culture, in which technology zombies communicated in internet shorthand, emojis having the last frown or smile, like Maude sticking the unicorn "horsie" on Mama. All his sister seemed to care about when she called now was how money could be used to grow more money. It was perplexing, since she had no clear idea about what she wanted to do with the accumulated money. He felt she might circle her pile as it got higher and higher, as in "Jack and the Beanstalk."

At Kayla's, and afterward, things had started to seem more like a warped fairy tale, less like life as he knew it, or even the life he'd fled to live in what had once been a slightly scruffy small town in New York State. He'd kicked it around with Steve—not the money part; how life had changed, more generally. Steve simply thought he was wrong and that people had always resisted progress.

"Look at your average tennis court," Steve had said to Ben in the coffee shop, after their most recent game. "The elite play tennis. Guys who've got an afternoon free because they're so fucking flexible, which is a euphemism for not getting a full-time job even if they're panting for it like dogs with their tongues hanging out, so they're able to grab free time, which is only possible if you've laid claim to your territory through hard work, sweat, and tears, or maybe tapped into your fucking trust fund—present company excepted—and you can stand outside in the sunshine in your white shorts, banging your catgut-strung racket against your thigh, and not be seen as a fucking faggot, but as a person of privilege, good luck ascendant. *Cars slow down to see who's on the courts.*"

Ben called Kayla one last time, but it wasn't lost on him that he alone instigated contact. Everything had been upbeat those few times they'd spoken, but he'd sensed her pulling back. She'd brought up marriage the first time he went to her house! She was going through what was conventionally called a difficult time. What did he have to offer? (Which had also been his question of Daphne, on the dressing room floor, when she'd asked him not to leave. She'd pretended it was a real question. She'd answered, "Pizza.") Okay: a large mozzarella with mushrooms was certainly easier than marriage, or even what Tory had mockingly termed "a long-term relationship," as if he'd find the idea incomprehensible, as if he'd already failed a test.

He threw himself into his work, and the guys in Washington were impressed. Ginny and Maude were visiting Ginny's parents in Mill Valley. He'd gotten tired of Steve's needling jokes, intended to level him like a duck brought down with buckshot. Maybe if they stopped playing tennis—if he stopped winning and let Steve cool off—things would improve. Ben decided to pretend to have an injured ankle.

Twenty-one

TRINITY came up on Ben's phone. He took the call, having no idea who TRINITY was.

"It's Pierre LaVerdere," the voice said. "LouLou gave me your number. I hope you don't mind. Or at least I hope you're willing to talk to me."

Trinity. Well, here was another bomb about to be dropped. He'd learned from the master, so better to beat him to the punch. "Listen," he said. "You were very important to me at Bailey. I appreciate what you did, teaching us how to think and how to express ourselves. But you and LouLou? It puts me in an uncomfortable position."

"I understand," LaVerdere said, and Ben remembered that his former teacher had been good at listening sympathetically—sometimes silently, gaining credibility by refraining from offering advice. He could hear music in the background, maybe TV.

"Where are you?" Ben asked.

"The Spotted Rick."

"You are fucking not," he said. "You came here?"

"It would mean a lot to me if you'd join me at the bar."

Disarming. A straight shooter. Except that LaVerdere never thought a straight line was the shortest distance between two points. LaVerdere got what he wanted by throwing curveballs. It was no coincidence that he'd found Rick's, the only bar Ben ever went to. He must have heard about it from LouLou, even if she'd mentioned it only in passing. LaVerdere had a good memory for detail. Ben very much wanted to be able to go back to Rick's without associating it with LaVerdere.

"Come here instead," he said, trying not to sound rattled. "Do you already know my address?"

"No," LaVerdere answered.

He told him the name of the road and explained how to get to his house: Look for a big spherical bush with red berries. If he didn't see that at the base of the driveway, he was in the wrong place. His neighbor was tired of having to redirect people. There: a significant detail for someone who loved details.

He went into the kitchen to see if there was enough ground coffee (yes). He put the magazines scattered across the table in a pile, placing *The New Yorker* on top. The cover was stained from where he'd put down his coffee mugs. The overlapping circles made it look like someone with bad aim had gone at it with a cookie cutter. He opened the refrigerator and was reassured to see milk. Coffee was what he'd offer; he had no intention of sitting around drinking with LaVerdere. He didn't appreciate LouLou's giving out his number, but if she had, shouldn't she at least have given him a heads-up? Or maybe it had been Rick. He didn't know exactly how he'd gotten in touch. Whatever LaVerdere wanted, it didn't mean Ben had to listen for long. He'd lie about a previous obligation, so he'd have an excuse to walk out of his own house after half an hour. He turned on music—whatever was on the radio. Jazz. Jazz was making a comeback, if it had ever left. It sounded like Miles Davis, but he often made the mistake of thinking Miles was playing when he wasn't. The kitchen table was a mess from breakfast. It didn't matter. Men made a mess.

He looked out the window, then moved away. Pathetic. If it had been December, he could have hung his stocking by the fireplace and gone to bed, waiting to hear reindeer landing on the roof. Really—what was LaVerdere doing? Of course he'd had an eye for pretty women. Or was he also thinking about fathering Hailey's child? Or Aqua's?

LaVerdere's hairline was receding. He wore his hair longer, Ben saw, as LaVerdere swung his legs out of the car and stood gazing at the house. An *establishing shot,* in the movies. What the hell are you doing, Ben asked himself. Why would you invite him here? His lie was going to be that he had a doctor's appointment—no; that sounded weak—he had an appointment with his lawyer.

"Forgive me, *I get it,*" LaVerdere said, hands raised in surrender as Ben opened the door before LaVerdere knocked. What a weak chin he had, though with his strong nose and blazing eyes he was still conventionally handsome. LaVerdere was wearing a jacket too thin for the day. He'd remained fit. He wore scuffed Nikes. That had been part of the reverse snobbery at Bailey; though there were no uniforms, the students had been forbidden to wear running shoes except when running. Faculty, therefore, wore them all the time, their footsteps muffled while the students clomped, snow seeping through their soles. Mud, in mud season.

LaVerdere had been in Key West? Walking around in Bermuda shorts? Tevas and tank tops? A Speedo, maybe? A backward baseball cap. Or full Parrot Head regalia. Then back to a job teaching philosophy in New York. Sure, once around the Earth like Puck, a stop here, a stop there—but funny how many times you ended up in the company of your former students.

In the story Daphne described, the townie had simply opened the car door and run. At the gas station on the way to Vermont, he and LouLou had made it a point to keep it together, not to run, though it had been their bad luck that the crazy guy had come back out while they were still standing by the gas pumps. And Tory: the way she punctuated whatever criticism she was delivering to him just as she turned in to a space in the parking lot, so she could get out and slam the door as a grand finale.

"So I just hear from you when LouLou decides to give me an earful? It's good to see you," he said, grudgingly. He shook LaVerdere's hand. "Where are you living, Pierre?" It sounded strange to use LaVerdere's first name, as if he were greeting him in ironic quotation marks.

"Riverside Drive. I left two years after your class graduated. The house is yours, Ben? What a wonderful place. I can't stand soulless contemporary architecture, either. Is it a good thing, living out of the city?"

For LaVerdere, this was nervous blithering. Buckshot.

"Why are you here?" Ben asked.

"Any chance of a drink?"

He thought about pretending he didn't have anything, but that seemed foolish. "Scotch or bourbon?" he asked.

"Scotch."

He felt ashamed when he turned toward the cabinet. He'd caved right away, but he'd also been more unfriendly than he'd intended. That remark about his house, though: It was obvious that these houses announced that their occupants had chosen not to keep up with the times; they were modest old houses that modest, increasingly old people had died in or been forced to leave, but unlike Ben's aged neighbors, anyone who bought them recently had *chosen* to live outside the mainstream. That, or they'd manhandled the old structures into the present, hauling in granite and heavy brass light fixtures, like Steve, who'd wished he could afford Westport. The outside world came in, changed, polished, an expensive price tag on all of it. All the so-called natural materials were meant to represent power, as reflected in hard, polished surfaces. His father had died—that was how Ben had had the money to buy it. His father would have approved of his not paying too much for a house. The old man had let his summer house sit on the market for two years before he made an offer, waiting until the price was rock-bottom. But Ben wasn't going to say anything about what had gone into his decision to buy his house to LaVerdere.

"Ice?"

"Splash of water," LaVerdere said, taking the glass. He went to the sink, added a trickle of water, stirred with his finger.

"Living room?" Ben said, extending his hand. He remembered Kayla, gesturing the minute he started to sit: better in the living room ("If it wouldn't seem too controlling"). . . . In some odd way, he felt detached from the house. It had stopped feeling like his. Or it seemed like his house in a dream, only resembling the original.

"Sure," LaVerdere said, looking around. "Very nice furniture. Much homier than Bailey Academy, which was dependent on the hand-me-downs of benefactors in the process of redecorating. One person tried to get the school to accept an aviary. That's true.

Not that he had one, but he thought he'd have one built on the grounds so Bailey could care for his daughter's canaries after she went to college. I had to sit through an interminable meeting about that the year I was hired. The meeting might have been longer, but he didn't find it funny when I suggested he get a cat instead."

"People gave the school their furniture? Are you kidding?"

"They did, if we couldn't persuade them otherwise: too magnanimous; oh, simply couldn't; better to donate to charity; already full up; couldn't divert our school from its mission in order to properly take care of a tank of guppies in the best possible way— that sort of thing."

"You really said that about the cat?"

"Yes. It came to me in the moment, as a solution to terminal boredom. A. E. Housman, whose work I spared you, used to think up insults in advance, to have them ready to add a name to, when the right wrong person came along. Nothing reprehensible about that, I suppose. At least, the pros and cons might have been a good thing to debate."

Was Housman a poet or a Hollywood director? He didn't want to ask.

"A couple of things here were left by the previous owner. There's a consignment store in town"—there had been, before Daphne decided the real money was in vintage clothing—"I got the andirons and the fireplace screen there."

"Very nice," LaVerdere said. "When I sold my house—you came there, didn't you? No? You'd only been to the apartment? Well, when it sold, the contents went with it. But a turtle doesn't do well without a shell. I should have thought forward." (*Thought forward;* yes, that had been a favorite expression of LaVerdere's.

Politicians were so often guilty of not thinking forward. Nixon, taping everything. Bill Clinton, having sex with Monica Lewinsky.)

"Riverside Drive. High ceilings? Gargoyles perched above the entrance, I'm imagining."

"Yes. If they don't catch on that I'm a sublet and throw me out. I went to Florida to work on a book. I left Bailey to write it. This your chair, or is that not an operative concept here?"

"Sit anywhere you like."

LaVerdere sat in Ben's chair. "Every self-styled philosopher's sure he has a great book in him, right? I found it a humbling experience. Have you kept after your own writing?"

He'd intended to remain standing, shitty as that was. Worse, how transparent, his bid to retain control.

"You remember wrong," Ben said, sitting in LouLou's favorite chair. "I wasn't a writer."

"You did write, Big Ben! In that spiral notebook. You passed it off as notes about chess, but when Tessie found it and gave it to me to return to you, I confess I flipped through."

"Juvenalia."

He hadn't known that Tessie had ever had it, let alone that she'd given it to LaVerdere. It had disappeared, then miraculously reappeared on his dresser. Tessie must have thought LaVerdere's name scratched in tiny cross-hatches on the front cover, elaborately doodled during a particularly boring class on Shakespeare, meant that the notebook belonged to him.

"I was happy to see it. I worried that I discouraged students from the arts, I spent so much time emphasizing science and talking about the techniques of debate. Well, none of us mistook Bailey for an art school, the parents least of all."

"I take it you're happy to be out of there."

"Yes, yes. Terrible winters. I sold the house, though I should have hung on to it. Another mistake, acting too rashly. Florida's not a real place. Ever been to Key West? You can stand at what's called the Southernmost Point and gaze in the direction of Cuba. It's a photo op, as so many things are. I suppose it was more romantic when it wasn't as easy to get there. Or you can walk down Dick Dock—not named by me, but it does convey—and see the ocean from another perspective, the fishing boats off on the horizon line, WaveRunners with some of our brightest minds aboard."

"You won't be surprised that I find it a little hard to imagine you in a place like Key West, from what I've heard of it," Ben said.

LaVerdere nodded. "I had a drink one night with a woman who worked on a boat that took people snorkeling on the reef. She said that two or three times a week, she'd find out that somebody all suited, ready to go over the side, didn't know how to swim. They'd never considered it might be necessary. I really did assume I had a book in me, but then I thought: Why think in those terms? You wouldn't want to have a tumor; it wouldn't be pleasant to have a bump on your back that was the remains of the twin you'd absorbed in utero. So what's so great about an imaginary, internal book? Writing a book seems, oddly, to be something our culture believes in—that everyone 'has one in them.'"

"LaVerdere, you could do stand-up."

"I knew Spalding Gray. We were once rather close. One doesn't want to name-drop, especially when your friend drowns himself."

"I didn't know you knew him."

"None of those Virginia Woolf rocks in the pocket. Anyway, I got myself to Key West in a car that died on a key called Sugarloaf. It had to be towed. I used your preferred mode of travel after that. I hitched. Once you're in Key West you don't need a car, so I suppose it all worked out. I flew back after I'd failed completely. I was lucky enough to get an offer to teach a philosophy course at The New School. Remember Akemi? She's married to the head of the department. Older guy. Calls herself Alexandra Howe. She's a resident at Bellevue. So there I went, back to winter, tail between my legs, tales unwritten."

No one else talked like LaVerdere. Ben felt a surge of fondness.

"I've let you down," LaVerdere said.

"You haven't done anything to me. You do seem to have orbited me pretty effectively, though. Elin. Now LouLou."

"I'm a mere mortal. Not part of the solar system," LaVerdere said. "Which, by your analogy, would make you the sun."

"Yeah. Maybe it's Freudian. *Sun* being a pretty conspicuous pun."

"Good one."

"Tell me, Pierre. Why, in a world full of people, did you have to get it on with my friends and family?"

"I can't say I might not think the same, if the situation were reversed."

LaVerdere hadn't touched his drink. "Your father," he went on. "He and I invested in a real estate venture. If word had gotten out, certain people would definitely have tried to stop us. They would have made trouble—that most usual of human instincts. Your father was concerned about some investments that hadn't worked out and had affected his credit rating. When we decided to work together, I was the front man. We bought an empty mill. You never knew about that? We were going to divide it into condos, allocate the required number of units for so-called affordable housing in order to get a tax break. I'm sure you remember that

Locke talked not about the pursuit of happiness—that was the notion of a man infatuated with the purported superiority of the French, Thomas Jefferson. Locke's assertion called for ordinary citizens—though we know there's no such thing as 'ordinary'—to be guaranteed 'Life, liberty, and the pursuit of *property*.' The two of us formed a corporation. Then, like everyone else who does that, we left Mr. Locke and his ideas behind in the dirt."

"And you were having an affair with Elin at the same time."

"No," he said. "Later."

"When did you get to know my father so well?"

"He and I started talking at some start-of-the-year mixer at Bailey. It turned out he was looking for an investor, though we didn't touch on that initially. He'd been worried about your not having any idea what you'd concentrate on, in your studies. It's always affecting when someone who has real problems is still worried about his son. I told him not to worry because you were observant, you took time to reach decisions. That all things eventually got sorted out. Why would you want your son to believe that he could predict his future? The person who hits through the ball succeeds."

"This comes as a surprise. But how do we get from tennis to Elin?"

"When I heard about his medical problem, I advised him to get treatment at Sloan Kettering, but he'd done his research and he'd set his sights on staying close to home, going to Dana-Farber. By then, of course, he felt a little guilty that our affairs were somewhat entangled. He wished Elin accompanied him more places, but you'd know better than I what sort of an understanding they had. We had a drink one night at my sister's."

"LaVerdere," Ben said, but the story continued.

"Your father joked afterward that I'd taken him to a petting zoo. I'd had no plan except to make a family visit when coincidence brought us near. He thought—your father thought—my relatives had an enviable life. He'd gotten worse news than I knew. We talked about things. Had coffee at some late-night diner. He spoke wistfully about my sister and her husband. He asked me to look out for Elin. Your father and Elin knew so few people."

"They didn't have friends?"

"As it was presented to me, no."

"And by 'look out for,' you assumed he meant—"

"Both of us should have known better. She doesn't have many fond thoughts about me." He stirred his drink again with his finger. "I wasn't him. She loved your father. You knew she disliked your sister."

"Sure. You're the one who told me to trust my intuition."

LaVerdere nodded. "My own sister and I aren't much alike," he said. "She had such a well-kept farm—I agree with your father's perception, there—and the two of them were making cheese with milk their partners supplied, with more requests from food co-ops than they could fulfill. Then she started taking acting lessons. She told us about it. She was interested in doing stand-up. It's interesting that when you were putting me down, you came up with the same idea."

"I thought the point of the Honor Society was that everyone was particularly bright."

"Ben. It's true I'd like to deflect your anger, but I'm trying to be honest." He looked past Ben, into the distance. He said, "You don't light the fire?"

"It pulls heat out of the room."

"Good to be a person who anticipates problems."

"Sarcasm isn't becoming, Pierre. You're the one who taught me that."

"I didn't intend it that way. I was thinking aloud."

"So you thought you'd drive here and go to the bar where I hang out and you'd look me up and discuss your relationship with Elin? I really don't want details about what went wrong, by the way. It would never have occurred to me that you two would be a good match."

"I'm not your father," LaVerdere said, taking a sip of scotch.

"And LouLou. She just laid out her plans, and you thought, Sure, what the hell."

"She and I weren't long into having a drink together when she brought up the situation, and what she was thinking about. It did flatter my ego. But I should never have said to her that if that was what she wanted, I didn't see why we wouldn't just get into bed and do it the usual way. I suppose that was offensive. Most of all, to her partner."

"What do you think it is about you, Pierre?" He'd begun to warm to using his first name. "Why do these things happen?"

"I'm not sure. The request certainly took me aback. Her being gay surprised me more. I didn't know that before we met up at the Knickerbocker. At school, it was obvious she had a crush on you. Undoubtedly, she did. In any case, she's an intelligent—"

"Yeah, and she's attractive, too."

"She is. And I'm happy she lives a life she feels comfortable in. The whole idea's over. I trust she told you that. I don't know what I was thinking. Vanity. Hubris. I embarrass myself."

Why *didn't* he burn logs in his fireplace? Because it would be too sad to sit alone in the cozy room?

"There's one more thing," LaVerdere said.

"Fine, but in about five minutes I've got to leave for an appointment."

"I would also want to brush me off. I understand."

He thought about lying. Even about calling him Pierre again. Instead, he said nothing. He should have had a drink with the man. Where did he get off, being such a prig, when someone had tried to be open?

"You and Elin get along, right?" LaVerdere said. "You've gone there for Christmas?"

"Sometimes." He made a mental note that he should make a kind overture to Elin. His father had set her up. It was stupid, but he'd probably had good intentions. In any case, she wasn't to blame for living her life.

"I did a little exploring when I left Bailey," LaVerdere said. "Key West can be rather disorienting, in that it's land's end. We don't just project metaphors. We also internalize them. In Key West you can actually run out of space. You get to the tippy tip only to find there's no more there there, to invoke a current cliché. You can go only so far, then there's water. It has a disquieting effect. It makes you feel like a narcissist always drifting toward a mirror. The sun on the water provides a mirrorlike effect. And across the distance—what is it, ninety miles?—Cuba. If you look across the water long enough, things you used to believe take off like a swarm of butterflies. But back to what I came to say: Lou-Lou and I met a couple of times while I was thinking things over. Once with Dale. I hadn't read the book, but I have now. It reinforces my belief that experiencing real adversity separates the weak from the strong. Dale told me some stories she left out of the book. A rather lame, passive-aggressive ploy to retain power by letting me know what a victim she already was. She was trying to provoke me. She didn't chip in on the check, which really makes you feel sorry that she thought that sort of protest meant anything. I went with LouLou to the doctor the next day. I had some blood work done. When the results came back, I found out I was HIV-positive. Well, worse than that. It had passed that stage. Sort of like trying to enlist in the military and finding out you're color-blind. That broke the heart of a friend of mine. Couldn't distinguish the sky from the water."

The man was full of surprises, some more awful than others. Why was he pretending to drop this into conversation as if it hardly mattered? When someone told you this, what were you supposed to say? That you were sorry? Might that be all he wanted to hear, then he'd go away?

"These days, as you know, it's not the end of the world. I take medicine. I jog around the reservoir. Make my weekly pilgrimages to Strawberry Fields. Down in the Keys, I'd started fishing and found it quite gratifying. But returning and getting the results of the blood test—it was quite a blow, let me tell you. Put quite a different perspective on my lack of energy. The night sweats. I've slept only with women, and for a long, long time—embarrassing as it is to admit—they've been married. The only drug I ever used was back in my own school days, smoking pot."

"Jesus."

"I've actually been able to keep it together pretty well, but it's a mystery where I got this. I don't need to tell you how depressed this made me. I met my classes, but otherwise I just withdrew."

"Uh-huh."

"Now, you can say no to this," LaVerdere said. "I completely understand that you've got your life here, you're under no obligation, even though you're skeptical about what I've said. About how oblivious I was. I do understand how much LouLou's situation involved you, simply because our dear friends' lives do overlap with ours. Much more's invested in being someone's close friend than in having a one-night stand. So I apologize for even considering sleeping with LouLou, for nearly deluding myself into thinking I might be doing something useful, when I wasn't really thinking at all. But I'm not here to talk about that. You know what I'm going to ask, don't you?"

"No."

"Well—Elin. I've got to tell her. And I don't have the courage to do it alone."

"Elin," he repeated grimly. Of course. Elin.

"I'm sorry to dump this on you. You have every right to tell me to deal with my own problems."

"I guess AIDS is the Lady *and* the Tiger."

LaVerdere ducked his chin slightly to the side. "Very astute," he said. "Maybe better to leave both doors closed rather than risk anything more, hmm?"

"Sorry. In fact, I'm really very sorry. I can't remember the last time I was this sorry. I mean it."

"Thanks, Ben. When you interact with good people, you always get back way more than you put in."

"Oh, man, I really didn't expect to hear anything like this," Ben said.

"Nor did I."

"LouLou knows? That's why she gave you my number?"

"I told you I was a coward. Thank god there was a blood test. Thank god we didn't do anything."

"Right," he said. "But with Elin . . . what do you think is the best way to handle this?"

"Courage fails me in the same way I've failed my body. Can you imagine Elin picking up the phone and learning this?"

"You know, I think I need a breather," Ben said. "Is that okay?"

"It's always best to say what you want."

"Then could I also say that I like you, but I regret getting together? Some things are best left the way they were. I don't know anybody who didn't appreciate all you did for us. But I'm thinking that maybe when you're not fucking former students or people's wives, you should just stay The Teacher."

"I understand that reaction."

"I know. You understand everything, but that doesn't mean people understand you."

"You're angry."

"Since I already look like an idiot who has no idea what's going on with some of the most important people in his life."

"If I had it to do over again, I'd do it differently."

"Well, Pierre, you've got to congratulate yourself that you're a guy who's open to many possibilities."

"When I came here today—" He rubbed his cheek. "No. What I was going to say goes back to the same topic," LaVerdere said. "I should leave." He downed his drink.

"What about Elin? She's got to be checked."

"I'll call her when I get home."

"You will?"

"I shouldn't have put this on you. It's my problem to face up to what I've done. Please don't hate me. I'm mortal. I messed up bigtime. My ego got the best of me. I've obviously failed to figure out even the most basic things."

He stood. Though Ben wished he could look elsewhere, his eyes were riveted. There was more white in LaVerdere's hair than he'd first noticed. What was he doing, being so unkind? Like La-Verdere shouldn't have sex with anybody, like he was obliged to be pure, like Mommy and Daddy? The man had HIV! What the *hell*.

He said, "What was I doing at Bailey Academy? I get why Lou-Lou was there. She was flunking out of public school and constantly running away. And Hailey was obsessed with that musician she had a kid by. Jasper's father totally overreacted to the barn fire, though I personally believe it was an accident Jasper decided to put a spin on and take credit for." Once out of his mouth, the last statement sounded exactly like the lie it was. The fire had been no accident. Every medicine Jasper took, he'd needed. It was clear why Jasper had been sent to Bailey.

"Ironic. His son burns the barn to the ground. Then the father dies when the World Trade Center goes up in flames. Do you talk to Jasper? He's okay?"

"Yeah, we're still friends. I spoke to him a while ago. Since you're straight, I guess I don't have to worry about your looking him up to fuck him."

"I hate to leave when you're still so angry."

"Then answer."

"Anyone whose son or daughter passed the interview and paid the tuition could attend the school, Ben."

"But those other kids really had bad stuff happen to them. Hailey spent the summer before she came at McLean. And she still cried and pulled out her hair. I look back, and I realize Darius was bulimic. They knew, right? That he barfed into the toilet every time he ate?"

"He was seeing a psychiatrist. He wrote stories about it that were published in the literary magazine. I hope he's feeling better now than he did at school."

"Your concern for Darius is very moving."

"How would I know why your father enrolled you? It was a country club of schools."

"LaVerdere," he said. "My father's dead, so I can't ask *him*."

"You're presenting this as a situation that made you unhappy. You were popular, Big Ben. You weren't like Jasper, always having separation anxiety from his mother. You made friends. You've made a life for yourself. I don't think your father was very good at parenting, as it's now called. Kids get shipped off all the time to far worse places. Did you hear that Ha just missed getting a Nobel? He left the same time I did, for Caltech. Word is, he'll get it next time around."

"You're trying to change the subject."

"A fight you had with your sister that particularly upset your father. I didn't personally read applications, you know—though they never minded calling me in to hear about absurd architectural plans for birdhouses. One guy wanted to donate his lariat collection and add a room to the gallery to house it! I'm surprised nobody wanted to donate a roller coaster. If Michael Jackson had known about us, we might have gotten Bubbles as a bequest. I don't remember the details. Maybe he was impulsive in sending you to Bailey. I don't know."

"He said I had a fight with *Brenda*?"

"In the basement? You were dancing, I think. I try to clear this shit out of my mind, too, you know. Some deep-seated resentment about your mother's death that caused the two of you to fight? What does it matter why he did it? You got an excellent education. You fit in. I can name several girls who had a crush on you, even if Jasper seems to have been the one who was always fucking them in the potting shed. You got a scholarship to Cornell."

So, in his father's version, the fight had been between him and Brenda. He and his sister—who was gone from the house at that point—turned into the ones who'd rolled on the basement floor.

"I don't know, LaVerdere. You've got the academic credentials you have, and you're impressed with Cornell? I find that hard to believe. I'm preoccupied with somebody else's wife, but if she were available, I don't know that I'd take up with her," he found himself saying. "To our mutual dismay, LouLou's gay. She's in a relationship. To tell you the truth, Jasper and I never seem to talk. Nobody around here's a real friend. A woman I used to be involved with called it 'life on the lam as a reverse-snobbery style statement.' Maybe I'm like you. I should have stayed in New York, but I lack courage."

"I hope not. It's an hamartia."

"What does that mean?"

"A fatal flaw. Don't you remember our discussions of Shakespeare? Back in those days when it was so exhilarating to believe in predestination. In spite of that, or maybe in a constant attempt to escape that, our friend could circle the globe in forty minutes. Robin Goodfellow would have been wise enough to be in orbit when the towers fell."

"LaVerdere"—It felt much better to call him that than Pierre—"man, what are you going to do about this bad situation you're in?"

"I'm going to call Elin. It's clarified my thoughts just to discuss this with you. Thanks for being willing to listen. Okay. I'm on my way."

"Take care," he said. Since LaVerdere's departure was what he'd most hoped for, he didn't know why he felt defeated. He'd meant to project his voice, but it hadn't worked.

Near the kitchen door, LaVerdere turned back. It was such a predictable gesture, such a bad-movie gesture, Ben wasn't expecting it. "We dissolved the business before your father died. Another company bought the mill from us before the work was completed. Bank loans were tight and we hadn't counted on the expense of removing asbestos. In retrospect, we sold too cheap, too fast. He got fifty percent of what we cleared, absolutely. Elin was there when the lawyer did the paperwork."

"It never occurred to me that you screwed him."

"Thank you. Then maybe I can forgive myself for trying to."

"You're such a mindfuck! Now you're telling me you tried to steal money? Think about this, man: You'll do whatever it takes to keep me off balance. What's going on?"

LaVerdere walked back to the table, picked up the glass, and hurled it against the door. He said, "That's what I feel like inside. That's my final apology."

"Fuckin' *hell*," Ben said. "You think this is some Edward Albee play?"

LaVerdere walked out. How many drinks might he have had at the bar before calling? LaVerdere's slumped shoulders under his jacket's thin material made him look his age. Shattered glass. What a pointless, adolescent thing to do. Walking behind him, Ben wished to be a human broom, more eager to sweep the man out the door than the glass.

Another simultaneous but conflicting thought also occurred to him, along the lines of wishing for the worst to happen, because then it would be over. What if the two of them did continue talking? If he agreed to go to Rick's with LaVerdere, he'd no doubt find out more. Maybe he could listen and not get caught up in the other person's problems. He could pretend he was someone else—one who drank, say, a martini, his father's favorite drink, titrating the vermouth he'd requested be served on the side, or prosecco with half a strawberry bobbing to the surface of the narrow flute.

His intuition told him that LaVerdere would be headed to Rick's. The thought of a simple drink with his old teacher suddenly took hold; certainly it wasn't impossible that whatever further time they spent together could turn out better than he expected. What if he was wrong? Arly thought he was wrong about everything. Steve thought he was so cynical he couldn't think straight. If anyone had intentionally broken a glass at Steve's, Steve would have followed them outside to slug them. Drama concluded, he and LaVerdere could be just two guys spreading their legs on bar stools after the unhappiness ended: Occam's razor; remember not to neglect the simplest explanation, though make sure—LaVerdere had stressed this—that you have all the facts. Maybe a drink would reveal a few more so-called facts. Was certain information somehow exempt from interpretation? But how could you be sure what things meant, how things were, when facts were spun into fiction, and vice versa? You couldn't have two people who were skeptical of each other walking the edge of a razor at the same time, the way angels danced on the head of a pin. That might be downright dangerous.

But actually, that might not be a problem because he and his teacher were both ultimately pretty dumb. Thinking didn't necessarily get you anywhere other than lost in thought. Women were crazy—what could you do? Your buddy was dying—why not honor his last request? Your smart, pretty former student selects you, out of all the world, as the perfect father for her child? If it was true, as LaVerdere liked to say, that everyone had to invent his or her own life, you should certainly give yourself every advantage.

His father had lied. Because he was embarrassed, or, worse, because the confusion really existed in his mind. Because he could handle the idea of a fight between his children better than he could justify tackling his son? Was that one just too fucked-up psychologically?

He thought he'd wait five minutes, then drive to The Spotted Rick. But as he picked up his jacket and opened the door, he realized he'd run out of optimism. His great idea dissipated almost as fast as it popped into his mind. Alcohol wasn't an equalizer; it was kerosene for the fire. It was the missile that whizzed over the peasants, who raised their hands in surrender. "Of course, if these peasants had lived in one of our inner cities, they'd have been immediately shot in the back," as LaVerdere had once written, to Ben's amazement, on the margin of one of LouLou's response papers. Men's actions had little to do with language and metaphor, and everything to do with testosterone and cortisol. Imagine a man as a transparent test tube holding those ingredients, and shake.

Elin had offered an educated guess when he'd pressed her, but she didn't know why he'd gone to Bailey. He'd been sent there because of the dance, the humiliating dance he'd done in the basement, the day he'd discovered a box of photographs of his mother as a young woman. It was one of those mistakes after which you didn't get a second chance, like setting a cat on fire. He'd found his mother's high school graduation picture and been mesmerized; she'd looked like Brenda, but the brows were his, the eyes. He'd held up the photograph like a hand mirror and pretended she was his dance partner—a stupid adolescent moment. They'd swirled across the linoleum floor as jazz played on the radio upstairs. How could he have known that his father kept his secret liquor supply down there, or that he'd descended the stairs in his socks and pajamas to refill his glass? He'd seen Ben doing his best Fred Astaire imitation, dipping and swooping, eyes locked with eyes that looked back from the photograph. Who knows how long he'd watched, standing in the dark, before turning on the overhead light, too astonished even to hide his drink. He'd walked forward— if he'd found Ben masturbating, that would have been better; looking at pornography, even better. When he'd realized exactly what his son had been enchanted with, he'd not only destroyed the photograph, his thick fingers still precise enough to shred it into bits, he'd tackled Ben, the glass breaking as they fell, liquor dousing their clothes. Both had been cut. And then, ashamed by what he'd done, his father had gone upstairs and banished him as soon as he could. Elin had been home. She'd turned on the radio, having no idea what her soundtrack would accompany. Or had she turned it on to block the noise? Was it really possible she'd heard nothing? *Once,* as he now knew, his father had hit Elin.

He couldn't remember how he and his father had risen from the floor, nor where they'd gone or what they'd done afterward. He'd toured Bailey with his father with six stitches taken belatedly on his thumb where the cut kept reopening.

He went to the window. He wondered if deer were outside. Of course they would be. If he took a walk he'd see them or he'd be startled by their shadows, by blackness shivving night's grayness, by the sound of snapped twigs, crunching leaves, branches susurrating in the breeze. If Ginny left Steve—if she sent him off to Texas alone—if she confessed her undying love, was she really the one? She thought his fascination with deer, who carried ticks and ate gardens, made no sense. She liked big TVs and expensive clothes; she was the one who'd had their house all but bulldozed, the renovations had been so extreme. A California girl in the wrong place, probably in the wrong marriage. She was doing her best. He doubted that he and she would be soul mates, either.

He opened the closet, still thinking he might put on his jacket and follow LaVerdere. He picked up a baseball cap that had fallen and tossed it up on the shelf where Jasper's father's beret still lay. The Man. His silly hat made of soft wool. It had been there a long time. It was as if he could fool himself into thinking Mr. C. was still alive, because he had this tiny part of him. Ben corrected himself: this souvenir. More bluntly, this *hat*. That was a conventional move of debating: to send something up, then—when it was so much larger than life that it seemed ridiculous—to deflate the exaggeration, as if it were the thing itself.

The Man's beret. The Man was dead—which was the real reason he rarely called Jasper; what to say or, worse, whatever he said, there'd always be his parents' deaths left out. Jasper had once shown him a photograph of his mother's healing incision. The photograph had notes and numbering on the bottom; it was obviously not a regular photograph. Operating room as war zone. All those battles fought with the sharpest knife blades opening the body, leaving behind red, welted roads.

Twenty-two

I've been to his apartment twice and taped notes inside by the mailboxes. He doesn't pick up his phone. He hasn't been back to The New School. I went there before his class was supposed to start, but somebody else was using the room. He's gone."

No doubt without telling Elin, Ben thought. So how long should he wait before calling? Why had this become his problem?

"Dale's worried he's killed himself. She thought I should tell you we understand why you equate us with bringing trouble into your life, but she wants you to remember how much we both care for you. She wrote you a note and tore it up. Do you hate me?"

"No. But I don't want to continue talking about this. Not your private life, not his visit, not where he is or isn't. I don't care. He can continue being LaVerdere. People who want the world to take notice don't rush to kill themselves. Have a good weekend, LouLou."

"Please don't blow me off with clichés."

"Break a leg. Today is the first day of the rest of your life. Do unto others."

"You're furious. I don't know what to do."

"I've got to get going."

"I understand," she said, after a pause. "You let it all build up because you feel like there aren't words anymore for what you need to say."

That was insightful. He disconnected without saying goodbye. Then, before he lost courage, he called Elin. She picked up on the second ring.

"Elin," he said. "What's new?"

He felt like someone trying to sound casual while questioning god: Okay, so you just created the world?

"I've ordered tulip bulbs from a new place in the Midwest. I'm going to expand the garden. I made a drawing of plants that will fan out from the birdbath and bloom in sequential stages."

Obviously, she didn't know. Elin, who'd taught him how to sniff a wine cork. Who'd explained that hats were necessary because body heat was lost through the head. She'd been a regular Miss Manners, minus irony—that is, unless she'd always known what happened between him and his father in the basement. Quite possibly, she'd been the one who'd suggested he go away to school. Not many women wanted to live with somebody else's teenage son. How should he phrase it? Should he say, "When you fucked LaVerdere," or "When you and LaVerdere slept together"?

"Do you know about White Flower Farm?" she said. "I've ordered jasmine from them so I can inhale spring before it arrives. It's a little extravagant, but not as expensive as good perfume. I probably should leave things the way they are, but a beautiful garden is always a selling point. Ben, I've been thinking of putting your dad's place on the market. It's a lot to keep up, and all I really need are some houseplants. Well, you can tell I haven't worked this out yet. I'm getting older. The house is filled with memories of him. If I listed it, would that break your heart?"

His father had bought the house as a retreat, then done nothing but worry about its upkeep—so much so that he'd ended up finding excuses not to go there. His sister had liked being there more than he had—though of course, he'd had his tree house, and his books. He'd liked the obvious: being high up. Water was more important to Brenda. She'd enjoyed her solitary rowing. She'd trained her binoculars on the birds, and researched their names and their habits. Elin had never made the slightest attempt to get to know Brenda, which made him sadder now than he'd been at the time.

"Elin, I'm totally behind anything you want to do."

"I'm flattered you've called. I've heard so little from you lately—which I don't mean as a reproach. I just love to be in touch."

"Elin. Did my father have financial problems I didn't know about?"

"Everyone has money troubles from time to time. Let's not talk about that. You're the one who doesn't like to talk about money."

"Please answer me."

"He had some cash flow problems for a while when you were at school."

Cash flow problems. That euphemism replaced what word?

"When was it, exactly, that you slept with LaVerdere?" he asked.

"Excuse me?"

"He was here yesterday. At my house. He told me."

"He did?" she said, after a pause. "Well, I guess he did. That's why you're calling. It's why you're angry."

"I appreciate the fact that when I ask you something, you're honest. But you have to answer."

"I do?" She sounded confused.

He waited.

"When your father was in the hospital in Boston," she said finally. "He came to see me."

"Routine visit, to check in and see how a former student's stepmother was doing, when he hardly knew you."

"I should have come to Bailey more often. I know it. I felt so out of place with those other mothers. And the teachers—to be honest, some of them intimidated me."

"Something had to have happened before my father died between you and LaVerdere, who apparently intimidated the rest of the world, but not you. Something happened, even if it was a drink."

"That's really all it was. He visited your father in the hospital. I called when he was there—I knew who he was, of course, but I'd met him only once. Twice. And your father sent him over to the house. He wanted to hear the truth about how I was doing. I mean, I think he wanted Pierre to bring word back about what shape I was really in. He didn't call. He drove over. We had a glass of wine. Nothing happened."

"I'm sorry I felt I had to ask," he said. "Believe me, though, it wasn't simple curiosity."

"Why would you call wanting to talk about such things?" she said, her voice faint.

"Don't cry until you hear the worst of it," he said. "Elin, he's tested positive for HIV. Go to the doctor. Okay?"

"What?"

"Do you think I find this easy? Do you think I want to know any of this? I'll spare you the rest. He came and said what he had to say, and now he's gone off to continue his life of self-righteousness and cowardice."

"What do you mean?" she said, quietly. "He's in my living room."

"Tell me he is not in your fucking living room," he said. "Tell me he's not there to get you into bed again, without even telling you what's happened."

There was a long pause. In his house, a cricket began to chirp. From where? Where was the fucking thing? How could they be that loud, but stay hidden?

"Elin, for god's sake! He tells me, but not you? He blows off his teaching job and won't return calls? Go ask him. For all I know he lied. And that's the best scenario."

"I can't believe what you said. It's like a bad dream."

"Elin!"

"What should I do?"

"I told you. And whatever the truth is, I'm very sorry. I'm sorry. I could rename myself Very Sorry."

"I'm so embarrassed."

"Don't feel that way. But go talk to him, right now."

"This can't be true."

"He's so crazy, it's not impossible he lied to me," he said. "Good luck."

"Oh, please don't say 'Good luck' like that. You've always meant so much to me."

He hung up. It was like talking to LouLou: Say it this way, don't say it that way. Take cues from me, don't think for yourself.

Let me intimidate you with my neediness, if being aggressive fails. Or, in Arly's case, let me manipulate you, let me make it seem like you're the one who's aggressive.

The cricket was near the stove. Live and let live. He took out his phone. He turned it on, intending to call LouLou. Instead, he found himself scrolling through photographs. There was a whole series of Maude, investigating the tree, reared back in her mother's arms, tickling Ginny with a stick topped by a monarch butterfly made out of netting. That was his favorite, the sunlight illuminating both mother and child. LaVerdere had long ago insisted, until Ben and his friends came to believe it, that there was no best, definitive moment of anything, except as time seemed to stop for someone already predisposed to love what he or she saw.

He looked at the photograph approvingly. Then, after not having returned his calls for quite a while, he forwarded the picture, without comment, to Steve.

Twenty-three

He'd been thinking about his old school notebook, and trying not to, ever since LaVerdere's visit. It lay on the shelf of the hall closet, along with The Man's beret—a shelf he never reached up to because he kept his favorite baseball caps on hooks near the back door. The notebook had been fouled once he found out LaVerdere had opened it years before. It was as if the pages had been undeveloped film, and exposing it to light had obliterated the images. Stupid even to have kept it; he shouldn't romanticize what had never been intended as anything but a sort of diary, or stories that never materialized. Some days Ben had only made a notation about the weather, or about a bird he'd seen that he couldn't name.

He lifted the notebook down. Something like this, as his friend Daphne would say, might do very well on eBay. It would be listed in the "Ephemera" category (a notion that had much amused him). When he'd dropped by her store recently, she'd been on the site, scrolling through junk from people's attics, photographs of cousins they'd never met who'd been killed in the war; sailboat after sailboat, drawn badly on graph paper; a year's utility bills; someone's love letters, missing the replies. She'd shaken her head as she zoomed in on matchbooks, postcards of grim highway motels, flimsy pamphlets offering suggestions about what to prepare on your new griddle.

He went into the living room to flip through, finding himself stopping in the middle of a story he'd written at Bailey in response to LaVerdere's assignment to inhabit the mind of another character. He flipped back, now; his own handwriting was nearly unrecognizable. Predictably, he saw, he'd invented someone larger than life, rather than—say—trying to understand Jasper. Or Brenda. He remembered how happy it had made LaVerdere to pretend not to know how to distinguish fact from fiction. The way novels had begun to change had of course been an easy pitch right into LaVerdere's outstretched glove. If so-called real historical figures appeared in the text, did that make it nonfiction? If a fictional character was recognizable—if a writer admitted using someone he or she knew as a main character—did that alone mean that you were reading nonfiction? Fiction writing, like poetry, was for girls; he wouldn't have tried it at all, except that LaVerdere had intentionally mystified the genres, rather than drawing any lines. Maybe this was the assignment that had gotten LouLou in trouble when the head she decided to get inside belonged to her married lover. At least she hadn't used his real name, so he couldn't be tracked down. Boston was a big city. If some of her friends had heard her say that she was having an affair with a married man, did that make it *this* married man? LaVerdere hadn't been the one to blow her cover, and Ben still wasn't sure who had, though at the time it had been rumored to be Eleanor Rule. La-Verdere had became LouLou's defender; of course she'd expected him to back her up about the "fiction" she was writing.

Ben opened his notebook and flipped to a random page. It was a rough draft of a paper for LaVerdere, discussing simile. Not only was his handwriting very different now, he'd even drawn numerals in a different way. He turned a few pages, looking for something more interesting.

. . . *whether LaVerdere had been humoring Bob Cabot or not about the necessity of getting clarity by taking decisive action, he'd not only agreed (after three Guinnesses and a shot of Jameson), but been truly thankful when LaVerdere produced his own cell so he could call his brother in New York and see if they could talk.*

Now, reading his schoolboy attempt to channel The Man, something stopped Ben. He turned the notebook sideways. Written vertically, in the margin, printed in caps, was: V. REALISTIC. DAD NEVER GOT IT THAT YOU HAD TO ACTUALLY CHARGE YOUR PHONE.

After his arrival, Mr. C. had at long last CLICHÉ *decided to listen to his brother's advice about uncomplicating his life. Also, he'd listened seriously to his new friend Pierre's good counsel. He'd needed to hear LaVerdere tell him Jasper was doing fine, that the divorce wouldn't scar the boy for life. He hadn't taken to LaVerdere when they first met, but he'd disliked the other person at Jasper's admissions interview even more—an Asian man who obviously wanted to be elsewhere, who said nothing.* YOUR INTERVIEW NOT MINE. HA PRETENDED HE WANTED TO BE MY CHESS BUDDY SUCKING UP TO THE MAN.

Bob Cabot had been wrong about LaVerdere. The guy was hardly French aristocracy: he'd been fathered by a Quebecois traveling salesman who'd spent most of his life, after leaving Montreal, in Ames, Iowa, with his Prom

Queen wife. Pierre had left the Midwest as a fellowship student to attend the one Ivy League university that offered him a financial aid package, Colum-bia. BEN, GATSBY'S BEEN WRITTEN. *Once there, his father had taken the train into New York to introduce Pierre to his half sister, the spawn* FISH? *of his father's long affair with a woman in Hell's Kitchen. She was six weeks older than Pierre. She was not his twin.* YOU MADE THIS WEIRD SHIT UP? *Everybody had a complicated life, everybody. At some point, you had to accept the way things were and move on. He hadn't caused his wife's cancer, and furthermore, she might beat it. She was determined, and tough, and she'd also had more than her share of luck with other things, including the bets she placed on the horses.* GREYHOUNDS NOT HORSES DICKWAD. *As LaVerdere had pointed out over drinks, optimists often forgot to factor in luck. So they'd toasted luck.*

Mr. C. stood on the corner, annoyed when a cab driver was too lazy to cut across from the other side. The Man got into another taxi and headed downtown.

Ben flipped back toward the beginning, to a page unmarked by Jasper's commentary: *Orange juice squeezed by Tessie.*

Another page:

Notes from the Underground *by Fyodor Dostoyevsky:* "Our roman-tic is a man of great breadth of vision and the most consummate rascal of all our rascals. I assure you—from experience. That, of course, is all true if our romantic is intelligent. Good Lord, what am I saying? The romantic is al-ways intelligent. I only mean to observe that if there were fools among our romantics, they need not be taken into account for the simple reason that they had transformed themselves into Germans when still in their prime and, to preserve that pristine jewel-like purity of theirs, gone and settled somewhere abroad, preferably in Weimar or Black Forest."

Ben flipped back again and found it as he turned the page: *9/11.*

Next [a ripped-out page tucked back in]:

*Jasper fucked Aqua. Tessie saw them doing it in the laundry room. A.
cried. Jasper talked Tessie out of telling Ha, who was supposed to be chap-
erone, which would have been talking to a statue anyway. Darius found out
and put tacks in Jasper's bed and walked up to A. in the cafeteria and gave
her wrist an Indian rope burn. I think he loves her. If A. ever tells about the
tree up past the jogging trail where Ray stashes Jasper's weed, J. will get
exiled to the Black Forest whether he wants to be deported or not. Then look
out. He can burn down the forest too.*

Ben turned back to his attempt at a short story. There was the
graffiti: Jasper's big block-letter printing in his never-finished
story—yet another set of comments by someone who'd invaded
his privacy. Maybe the nature of the prank had been that Jasper
had intended for the comments to be found later, though the kids
at Bailey didn't tend to play jokes that took time to pay off. He
might have assumed the obvious and thought Ben would see them
immediately, though apparently—what a geek he'd been!—he'd
kept writing, without looking back. The drafts of his writing as-
signments had stopped sometime before graduation. What the
hell. Arly had opened his mail, indulging her paranoia, throwing
letters on the floor after she'd scrutinized them: Elin's banal good
wishes, mixed up with his underwear and dirty socks.

He put the notebook aside, picked up his cell, and dialed.
"Hey," he said, when his friend got it on the first ring. "I'm not
calling too early?"

"No, no. I'm up. Everything good?"

He'd thought he was calling for a simple reason, but Jasper's
voice confused him; he didn't know where to begin. By blurting
out disingenuously that he would have taken the bus with him
years before to see his mother? How could he have gone with
someone who didn't tell you he was leaving? Jasper had always

been a loner. Ben's mother had died even younger than Jasper's had. But they'd grown up, they'd lived through those years, Jasper would be marrying the woman he lived with.

"Ben? You there?" Jasper said.

"Yeah. I don't know why I'm only telling you this now, because it's not like I forgot about it, but all this time, the thing is, I've had your father's hat."

"Excuse me?"

"The beret? Remember? LaVerdere was right about his being in the middle of a breakdown. He dropped it and I picked it up. I still have it."

"Oh. Is this some AA apology, or something?"

"No. Definitely not. I wanted to know if you'd like me to mail it to you."

"Just toss it," Jasper said.

Well—he'd asked Elin for none of his father's things. He could understand not getting sentimental.

"Ben, hey, it's not a great time. The coffeemaker just fucked up and I'm running late. Listen, let's talk again, okay?"

Only then did he realize that he'd wanted to tell Jasper about LaVerdere's visit, what he'd found out about why he'd been sent to Bailey, maybe even let him know about LouLou and Dale's request. He heard a woman's voice in the background.

"Anytime, man. Give a call," Ben said.

"Okay, later," Jasper said.

Ben went into the hallway. He looked at the beret on the hall table. How truly strange for Mr. C. to have shown up at Bailey looking like an expat on the lam from Les Deux Magots. Adults were so weird. Adults had no idea how to be a lot of the time. He picked it up—even touching it saddened him—and swirled it on one finger like pizza dough. Then he dropped it in the trash. It could sit there until he emptied the baskets into a big plastic bag he carried through the rooms every Sunday, gathering up things for Monday pickup. He shook his head at his notebook and tossed that in as well.

What if he died (Elin's rationale for buying new underwear before every long car trip) and someone found such juvenile posturing? He wondered if Arly thought about some of the things she'd left behind, including the porn magazines hidden in a pillowcase. Who but Arly would buy actual magazines? Where had he put those? They might have to wait to be discarded in the following week's trash. When Steve still lived next door—*that* departure had been as quick as an arsonist running from a lit fire—and he'd gone to help uncrate the TV, he hadn't thought Steve was lying about watching porn, just that he'd spontaneously told the truth. A private company removed his trash, as they still removed the trash next door, where a single mother now lived with her teenage daughter; she'd moved in one day after Steve, Gin, and Maude vacated the house. She had a dog that could only be distinguished from a football by its pointy ears.

Jesus. He supposed he was now living in suburbia.

He put on his jacket and went out past the nonexistent meadow to the shed, where there was still a small pile of firewood remaining from the half-cord he'd bought from Steve's guy last year. He'd make a fire, even if it did draw warm air out of the house. Had he really said that, had he really been such an asshole that he'd given that explanation—even if it was true—to LaVerdere? He picked up a few logs, looking around for something to carry them in, but he didn't see anything. A rag, or something, on the dirt floor. He pushed it with the toe of his shoe. It turned out to be a small felt toy with cross-stitched eyes that must have belonged to Maude. To his surprise, tears welled up in his eyes. Steve had given him—in what was one of Steve's favorite expressions—a "heads-up" about moving to take a better job that he had to say yes or no to immediately ("heads-up," in Ben's experience, synonymous with This News Will Really Give You a Headache), but since Steve seemed so unfazed by the possibility of leaving, Ben had put it out of his mind until Gin appeared, crying. Full circle: She'd come alone the first time he met her, and eventually them; she'd come alone to burst into tears and announce their departure.

A wheelbarrow with a deflated tire sat in the corner, another pile of wood inside it, along with dried leaves and a cluster of branches. He picked up the top two logs because they looked particularly dry, exactly the right length and width. He left, the smell of earth and mold stinging his nose, kicking the door closed behind him, pieces of bark falling, as well as some big bug that startled him as it jumped. Maybe the thing had been a frog. Well—it was all ridiculous. LaVerdere couldn't have been serious about how nice the house was. Key West and Riverside Drive both sounded pretty good, and if you said the names of those places, people wouldn't cock their heads in confusion. LouLou bringing her box of orchids! Those were certainly gone—as was LouLou, but he didn't want to think about that. He'd become sentimental, like an old person who couldn't relinquish anything—unless it was a few crappy juice glasses left behind, or a busted chair too heavy to get out the door. All these years he'd kept the beret, but good for him, for tossing it. The notebook, too, deserved singling out; that, he thought, he'd pull out of the trash because its pages could be used to light the fire.

Twenty-four

H e left his job when the company in D.C., which seemed to think he was only a human calculator who loved to live in the realm of speculation, pulled itself out of a downward spiral and expanded west instead of south, where it had intended to go. He'd have to relocate to Seattle to stay in the game. Steve's father had taken a trip to see a favorite cousin out there shortly before he died. Ben had been able to draw up papers with projected scenarios for the next five years, and the old man had picked the options he thought best, so that was taken care of by the time he'd died. All the bequests were in order: The Guggenheim Foundation was certainly pleased. Steve had recently sent, snail mail, an article about the CEO of a nonprofit his father had also favored, ripped out of *Town & Country*—good guess that Ben wouldn't have stumbled on that, though he supposed he might have in the waiting room of the new, young female dentist in town who specialized in cosmetic dentistry. Steve had also included a beautifully designed brochure advertising townhouses in a gated community not far from where he and Gin lived that he hinted Ben might be interested in. Without the benefit of seeing Steve's face, it could be very difficult to know when Steve was kidding. He'd included a photograph of Maude, wearing a necklace that might have been pearls—hard to say, but he hoped not. Had they moved to Texas and thrown up their hands right away, as Gin had worried they might? She hadn't worried about their parenting so much as she'd worried that in such a big place, they'd fade into anonymity—that they'd kick back and stay where they'd landed, far away from woodland walks. No one could replace their friend Ben (as she'd said, pointedly).

After he'd severed his connection to his old employer in D.C. (why were they so outraged, when every other student who graduated from college now could code?), he started working at a business in town, a job he'd at first felt defensive about because it was such a step down financially, but which he now viewed as providing something for the community, as fighting the good fight. Daphne Randolph's fiancé, Ned, bought and expanded Ash Street's failing greasy spoon, transforming it with his architect father's help into a popular bookstore/café. Ned worked there on weekends, because that seemed to be when the interesting customers came in. It was closed Sundays and Mondays. Ben worked the other three days a week. On a recent Wednesday, William Kennedy's wife had been pointed out to him, shopping with a young woman who might have been one of the Kennedy children. Ben had met Russell Banks, who said he had a place in the Adirondacks, and bought several hardbacks. The owner had gone off for a beer with Banks. A *Vogue* editor shopped in the store. A reality-show actress with a cult following. She'd sold her hair trimmings on eBay, Daphne told him, for a lot of money.

His dog, Batman, had been abandoned outside the bookstore café. He'd started hanging around near the back door, tucking his too-long tail down low if you approached, as if you meant to kick him or worse. Not a good feeling, when the dog did his skittish, scared dance. The barista started giving him food. The dog had been calmed down and won over by a few scones. But the situation was dire (Mimi the barista was never optimistic). The dog had been taken to the crowded animal shelter, which could no longer be depended on not to euthanize animals. At Mimi's urging, Ben had gone to get him "just for a while." "I know you're right for each other, I know it, I'm totally sure," she'd said. She was kindhearted, an animal lover. Still—and he might agree with her—she'd felt he hadn't put enough thought into the dog's name. All those superheroes were already dismissed, in Mimi's opinion; they didn't need to be further trivialized by people naming their dogs after them. Who *had* all those comic-book heroes and TV superheroes been that had lingered through his youth? A lot of them were people who'd died young, like Christopher Reeve, entirely mortal except for his embarrassingly bad body suit. In the early days, their costumes had been stretched over their unconditioned bodies. They'd had no alternative to speaking bad dialogue with a straight face. An earlier Superman, George Reeves, his father's Superman, had killed himself. Maybe that was (thank you, LaVerdere) the *hamartia:* put on a costume that bad, and you're dead.

He and Mimi had fooled around. They'd had sex twice, though once it had just been at work, after hours, on the chaise Ned stretched out on if he had a migraine. To make up for that hurried moment, the other time they'd stayed at a hotel, and room service had delivered dinner and wine. He'd still been in the phase when he wanted to please her when she'd decided to call it quits. She'd been too young, but she was legal. In their late-night conversations, mostly over the phone, he was never sure if she was asking him to decode the world or code it. He'd told her a little about Cornell and nothing about Bailey.

He checked his phone for messages while he toed the dog's fur. Dogs were great, the way they farted and looked up, so confused. In their sleep they ran like Mercury (at the bidding of Zeus, so that analogy worked out flatteringly). Doggie dreams: their squeaked-out ecstasy as they ran through fields. Meadows. Memories of long-ago meadows.

What kind of people dumped a dog? Ben and Batman at first had had an uneasy relationship before they'd bonded. Rawhide bones were the dog's caduceus. But he was also a humble fellow, he wasn't just about his magic. The dog liked tuna fish. A lot. A sleek coat soon replaced the colorless undercoat Ben combed out, using a brush down back and belly. Batman slept beside Ben's bed. So, to his way of thinking, Ben had morphed into a typical, middle-class guy with a few friends—maybe he was more like his father than he realized. He retained a love for tennis. (Not so, golf; that had been Steve's thing. He played, but his long-ago lie to Steve about having injured his foot, in the months before they moved, turned out to be prophetic. Some days he had to stop playing with the manager of the new, huge grocery store mid-game.) At least he'd figured out early on that the quality of life meant more than slavishly following the money.

He'd rummaged around before trash day and retrieved The Man's beret. It was fine, unstained by anything that had been tossed on top of it, hardly wrinkled. After a brief steaming as the kettle whistled, followed by a night drying on the kitchen counter, he'd taken it to work. "Cool!" Mimi said. "Totally! Thanks, Ben!" Like all girls wearing berets, she looked jaunty and flirty.

One briefly glimpsed piece of paper tucked into his notebook, lit to become a torch poked under the logs, had been from Hailey (they'd made out a few times at Bailey): a nasty note, asking how he felt about being The Boy Who Left Girls. Prescient, as he'd now become The Man Who Left Women, those times they didn't walk first. Hailey was one of the few classmates he'd seen in recent years. Instead of the eye patch, she now had an artificial eye. She'd married a scientist who worked at MIT, but the marriage hadn't worked out. She'd told Ben that a lot of the girls at Bailey had expected that eventually he'd marry LouLou.

He'd been startled, but he said nothing. He'd come to see Lou-Lou so differently. She'd been self-involved, sometimes manic, always high-maintenance. She'd certainly taken up a lot of space. What amazed him most, though, was how withholding she could be even when she was telling the wildest stories, making the most extravagant plans.

He and Hailey had been walking through the Met when she started talking about the past. They'd wandered into the Egyptian rooms, where the mummies' silence was so profound, it had seemed oddly conducive to talking. When she told him what the girls had thought, he'd assumed she was flirting. He'd put his arm around her to give her shoulder a light squeeze. She'd stiffened and looked away, about as happy as someone getting a flu shot. That had been that. He had certainly withheld from her the information that LouLou had left Dale for another woman, moving to

Amsterdam to live with her new love on a houseboat. Baby—what baby? Dale—who's Dale?

There was no one else after Mimi made it clear she preferred men her own age who had what she called "sensitivity" (one had a MOM tattoo, the other a yin/yang symbol on his thick neck; those were the sensitive jerks she considered superior to him). At Amy's salon, Mimi had heard from Amy, or Kayla had been there, that— this was the way she put it, when she told him—he'd brought Kayla's son a tacky present, then flirted with the babysitter. The *babysitter*? If you were a single man in a small town, you didn't escape being talked about in ridiculous ways, because every woman you didn't want to sleep with found it easier to think they had good reason to reject you—unless, of course, you were gay.

He sometimes saw women for coffee, including those he got together with from OkCupid, but of course he couldn't meet them where he worked—that would have seemed too public, as well as making Mimi think he was pathetic. They did sometimes go to Rick's (under new ownership, as Rick's Parkinson's progressed), and afterward, those times he'd talked about it to Daphne, asking her if coffee killed brain cells, if that was why he had no interest in talking to any of the women for more than three minutes, he'd endured Daphne's kidding about his inflated sense of himself. She only half listened; all she really wanted to know were the ages of the various women. He wished he could still shoot the shit with Rick, but Rick had only been able to speak in a whisper after his last setback.

Every now and then he browsed the internet, looking at eBay (Daphne had gotten him addicted) and other sites for old postcards of his town and the area nearby, which continued to fill up with summer people, or couples who wanted weekend places. Wealthy people who bought up farmland, then paved the dirt roads leading to the houses. If Dennis Tito—god! He remembered the guy's name; he remembered because the famous dictator had had the same last name . . . if *Dennis Tito* were still alive, now an even richer old man, he might be the next person to show up in town. There was already a performance artist and an Italian who was a prince in his country, who'd opened a shop that specialized in Tuscan olive oil. Once or twice (meaning at least a dozen times) he'd shaken a few drops on Batman's dry food. Daugherty's Dairy was for sale for $2.2 million. The Time Warner guy's place had already changed hands; bought, renovated (including an infinity pool), but never moved into. It was fitted out with Corinthian columns and a wraparound porch—nice touch—back on the market, with a higher asking price. An area of the front lawn had been made into an ice skating rink, though it became an empty frame when winter ended.

When the newest supermarket opened across the town line, he and Mimi had wandered through at midnight, happy to have the store to themselves to laugh at somebody's idea of what people who *weren't* stoned wanted late at night. Every now and then he got some communication from a realtor asking if he wanted to sell his property. At first, these postcards featured postage-stamp-size photos of houses, red lines slashed through them on the diagonal, saying SOLD. Soon, the photographs tended not to be of the house itself. They'd show the pool, or the rolling lawn, an idealized depiction of rosebushes in bloom or lambs cavorting on Thalo green grass, the realtor's picture a godlike cameo on the upper right.

Twenty-five

He felt bad for Dale, whose relationship with her new girlfriend had lasted only a few months (he'd gotten a picture of them on Valentine's Day, right after they'd first met, huddled in matching bomber jackets, sitting on the side of an outdoor fountain that sent up a jet of pink-tinted water, wearing pink socks patterned with red hearts, pant legs raised). Dale had given up the lease on her Upper West Side two-bedroom to move in with the woman in Washington Heights. She'd no sooner relocated than the girlfriend had had a change of heart. Dale decamped to a friend's fold-out before finding an Airbnb above a coffee shop, with an air mattress and a bamboo curtain in what had been the dining alcove. Dale had sent a selfie of her stunned face against the bamboo backdrop, one hand holding up a little glass vase with green bamboo sprouting delicately from it, as part of a group email telling her friends where she was.

He'd emailed her a day or so before to see if she'd like to go with him to an evening at the Brooklyn Botanic Garden—a fundraiser to benefit a physical-rehab center that worked with Darius Beltz's daughter. Every spring Ben bought tickets, though he'd never gone.

"Thanks. Let me think about it. Not that I wouldn't love to see you, but it might feel strange, being together without LouLou. It might make me sad, or seeing me might bring you down."

"Offer stands," he wrote back. "I invited you because I'd love to see you."

He really hoped Dale had moved on with her life in spite of losing someone she cared about, followed by a disappointing experience with her second book. When he contacted her, she'd written back that she had a new email address, since she'd soon be changing jobs. What exactly had her job been? He'd never been clear on that. Everything had always been about LouLou. Maybe Dale regretted having given notice (she'd sounded nervous when she said, "changing jobs"). That was another downside to having LouLou around; she had a way of spreading discontent. He hoped the change Dale was making would be an improvement. She was the real thing—a person who'd been through a rough time but had emerged okay.

The next day she'd texted MEET U THERE! Of course she wasn't the kind of person who'd expect to be picked up. Of course no woman in New York would expect such a thing. Elin had told him to walk on the outside when he was walking on a sidewalk alongside a woman. Which side should you be on when you were on a path in the woods? Outside, in case deer (which Ginny would have found an annoyance) streaked by? Inside, to protect your companion from low-hanging branches? Elin had insisted that he hold open a door for anyone if he reached the door first, male or female. He had no way of knowing whether his own mother would have gotten around to giving him so much instruction, though he doubted it. His father's long-ago talks with him about sex had been restricted to anatomy lessons, the two of them huddling in a corner, his father pointing at drawings in a medical book with a finger that touched the very edge of the page to turn it. He still sometimes had to shake those illustrations out of his mind when he saw a woman undress. Now that Daphne was engaged, who would that be?

He told Dale he'd pick her up. He lied, saying that he had an errand that would put him in her neighborhood anyway. The longer he stayed out of the city, the less attraction it held. That was either defensive, or the simple truth. How could you tell, or why would you bother to distinguish, whether a somatic reaction meant you yearned for New York or feared being there? Weren't yearning and fear pretty indistinguishable? A question worthy of LaVerdere.

His suit fit, and he wore it with a shirt he'd bought at Daphne's for ten bucks. At the last minute he folded a tie (an Alexander Julian eighties monstrosity that reminded him, weirdly, of the insane rug at Bailey) in his pocket. There was no dress code—of course not, if they already had your money. Dale hadn't asked whether the occasion was formal. She wore only black, like so many New Yorkers. Daphne *would* have liked to go to such an event. She missed life in the city, and she wasn't intimidated by crowds ("Energizing"). Elin, because of her love of flowers, would of course have loved being at such an event, but she'd married and moved to Chicago.

As he got near Dale's apartment, he started looking for numbers, reassured that they were going up instead of down. It was clear that you were an ex–New Yorker when you forgot to ask the name of the cross street.

Then he saw Dale, outside the building, as she'd insisted she'd be, looking for his car. When he pulled to the curb and she jumped in, she leaned over to give him a hug. *A nose ring.* A metallic substance protruding from her nostril brushed his cheek. She wore black pants with an extreme crease and a black leather jacket. The shirt underneath was also black, with a few splashes of color meant to look like bullet holes. He had to admit the color contrast brought more attention to her eyes. He was gratified by how relieved he felt to see her. Her low black boots must have been brand new.

"LouLou, LouLou, LouLou, LouLou," she said. "There. Now it's over. We don't have to mention her again. Ever."

"I wasn't even thinking of her," he said. "You look great, Dale. I'm glad you decided to come."

"Somebody picks me up and takes me to a party? Sure."

"Things are good?"

"Good enough," she said. "You?"

"I'm fine. Putting in too many hours at the bookstore, but business keeps picking up, and my former company's crashing and burning, so I guess I got out just in time."

"Didn't you own stock?" she asked.

"Good memory. I did, but I ditched it at Christmas, which turns out to have been a good move." (In one of their infrequent phone calls, Steve had quickly assessed the situation and told him to sell his stock immediately.) "My significant other is my dog, by the way. Great dog. Named for one of our most important American heroes."

"Woody Guthrie?"

"Nope. Think: Lives in a cave. Wears a cape."

"Some guy you picked up at a sex club?" she deadpanned.

While they were idling at the light, a quick drug deal took place between the car to his right and a guy on a moped: a real sleight of hand, with the bicyclist seeming only to fumble his helmet. A cop car pulled up alongside him at the next red light. A young cop looked out his side window, then looked straight ahead. Whatever had caught the cop's eye, it hadn't been Ben. The light was a quick one. It turned green.

"I've been over the flu for a month now, or three weeks, anyway. I lost seven pounds when I was hospitalized. Dehydrated."

"That's awful. Did you get your flu shot?"

"Everybody asks that. Didn't you hear that they got it wrong this year?"

"I did know that, I guess." Mimi had the flu. He'd taken a lot of teasing because he'd been too afraid to go near her, so he'd ordered her a gift basket of food from Amazon Prime. They'd had to hire a temp and had been lucky someone's high-school-dropout son was willing to step in. The only difficult thing had been telling the kid that as good as he was, he'd have to be laid off when Mimi recovered. This, he'd been delegated to do by Ned. Ben had felt so bad, he'd hired the kid to move some rocks and to paint his bedroom—tasks he'd also done perfectly. Hanging out with him, he'd learned about vampire movies, Australian music, string theory (apparently, it was running into trouble), and unheralded Swiss chess masters. The kid had beaten him every game. When his time at the café ended, he'd taken a bus to Indiana to be with his girlfriend. For some reason, the kid's father barely spoke to Ben, and the mother stopped coming in entirely.

"I hadn't been in the hospital since I was ten," she said. "Nobody could visit. I mean, maybe if I had immediate family and they put on a mask—but in my case, who'd want immediate family?"

"That must have been unpleasant."

"It isn't working," she said.

"What isn't?"

"The LouLou exorcism. Maybe you've got to do it, too."

"Really, Dale, I'm not sitting here thinking about her."

Some idiot threw a skateboard into traffic and rode for a while, causing a taxi driver to almost swerve into a bag lady crossing mid-block. He leaned on his horn.

"I'm really trying to move on," she said. "So far, that consists of having found a new agent, and giving notice at my job. I've met a few people, but who can you expect to meet in bars except drunks, right? Have you met anybody?"

"No. But I've had a few too many coffees lately. Maybe drinks would help."

"You miss that woman who moved, right? Your neighbor?"

"I do. I miss all three of them. He and I talk, from time to time." Two calls—one, an unexpected, booze-fueled, late-night Christmas Eve conversation about people's desires, displaced onto Santa, and Steve's dislike of symbolic occasions, in general, along with a second phone call about the stock market—weren't exactly "time to time," he supposed. "In any case, they're in Texas now."

"That's rad," she said. "I've got to say, they didn't strike me as Texans."

"He shoots armadillos in his yard."

"He took me aside and asked me straight out if you were having an affair with his wife."

"You've got to be kidding."

"Why would I make that up? He ran into me at the health food store when I was buying peanut butter. You never had anything ordinary to eat."

"We never touched each other."

"I told him he'd have to ask you. I was a little ticked off to be put on the spot."

"*That's ridiculous,*" he said.

"I'm sorry I brought it up. But now there's no secrets between us. It's better that way."

"Well, that's for sure," he said. Steve? He'd asked Dale that?

"Tell me one very true thing," Ginny had said to him not long before they moved, stopping on the path. She could be a little precious in her attempts to relate meaningfully—as Arly had pointed out. Still, the question had taken him aback. He'd asked if she felt what he'd been saying was somehow inadequate. But that wasn't what she'd meant: She wanted to know what the first thing was that had popped into his head. Leave it to Gin to think that you could backtrack to immediacy. She didn't want him to say something disarming or provocative or to confess some dark secret. Like everybody else, she just wanted to know she was at the forefront of his thoughts. He'd been holding Maude, who'd protested their stopping by kicking his hips. "Bye-bye, Mommy," he'd said, waving Maude's little wrist like a ventriloquist. "Every day I'm growing up and moving farther and farther away."

"You're informing me that my daughter's growing up and will leave me? That's the one true thing you want to say?"

"When they grow up, everybody leaves everybody," he'd said. "It's all about leaving."

The cars were moving fast on the West Side Highway. Once you knew how to drive in New York, your instincts never failed you. But you couldn't hesitate, once you pulled out; you never signaled, and when you shot into the next lane, you had to keep accelerating. Steve had asked Dale that? Hadn't he worried that Dale would tell him?

But she hadn't. It was weird, how many things you never knew, though there were more ways to impart information every day. Maybe somebody would invent a What You Don't Know app. La-Verdere had always said that the difficult thing was to know enough to ask the right question. Ben had found out later that this wasn't an observation LaVerdere had originated; it had been accepted wisdom at Bailey.

The day had been warm before turning suddenly chilly. Fog hung over the Hudson River, though there was okay visibility on the highway. From somewhere inside the mottled whiteness he saw a bird flying. How he wished Dale hadn't made her incantatory remarks about LouLou. To name a thing did indeed invoke its presence—perhaps more so, if you knew it was nowhere near. LouLou, in Amsterdam. LouLou was always on the run. She was her own, personal triathlon. How long did she stick with anything? A week? A month? A year?

A silver SUV passed, going at great speed, cutting in so sharply he had to check his reflex to brake. The car streaked out of sight like a stick of chalk coming to the edge of a blackboard (so old-school; they'd had blackboards at Bailey). They continued downtown—a word that had become, in his lifetime, synonymous with what wasn't there. They could build all the new buildings and parks and memorials they wanted, but downtown would always be the absence of what used to exist.

He'd never touched Ginny. He wouldn't have fathered Lou-Lou's child, either artificially or in the conventional way. Wherever she was tonight, someone was no doubt taking LouLou's side at this very moment, against him, against Dale, against the world: Better to be disliked by people who didn't know you than by people who did, he thought.

The fog was thick enough to be a special effect arranged for the appearance of the devil. There were so many devils, though—who'd get cast as the lead? LaVerdere, with his Machiavellian maneuvering. But he wasn't the devil, just a sad approximation. A devil in a diorama, instead of a potent force in the real world. Look at the easy prey he'd settled for: a scared, middle-aged woman on the verge of becoming a widow. Then, later, LouLou. He had no better prospect than a troubled former student? The thirty-year-old married man in Boston she'd seen at Bailey could have been jailed for statutory rape if he'd been caught. And those other losers: drunken Masters of the Universe and random blowhards. What a relief when she came up with Dale. What a huge, fucking relief. They'd envisioned a future, Dale and LouLou, LouLou, LouLou, LouLou, who floated in his mind as delicately as ash, and sank in his heart as heavily as a stone, though finally her selfishness demystified her. She was no longer an enigma, she was only hard, hard and self-protective. Her spell had been broken when she'd gone too far. When she mistook him for somebody she could manipulate, knowing all along she had her fail-safe lined up. She was betting that if LaVerdere turned her down, Ben would reconsider, out of jealousy.

Which he might possibly have done, there might have been one chance in a hundred, if LaVerdere hadn't come to his house and exposed her, making obvious her habitual pattern of jerking people around. Ginny had also miscalculated, thinking that if he adored

Maude, he'd adore her, by extension. Like any California girl, she expected to be adored, even if—maybe because—adoration went nowhere. It was difficult to imagine Ginny in Dallas. The land of big hair and breast implants, as well as an omnipresent awareness that kept everyone in a time warp, shocked, shocked, at who shot J.R. The place was an urban wasteland, anchored by oil and the banking industry, malls, and of course the earlier, real-life shooting from the window of the Texas School Book Depository.

Dale's hand lay on top of her little black bag plunked in the space between seats. No New York City gel manicure with squared-off nails. That's not who she was. She had stubby fingers, unadorned with rings. Her nails had been chewed to the quick; her cuticles were ragged. It was a hand that someone who loved her would want to hold in order to hide it, to protect her from what she unintentionally revealed. He wasn't that person, but as they sped downtown he felt the urge to grab her hand, to interrupt her thoughts. He could hear LouLou's name going through her mind repeatedly, and that was painful. If he'd still been an awkward teenager he could have slid his fingers slowly over hers, but he'd scare her; she'd misunderstand if he did such a thing. She'd had enough surprises; her life had been nothing but surprises, whether they came disguised as elephants or giraffes, lions or tigers. Her mother had embodied the enemy, then revealed that enemy to be tortured, mournful, weak. As he kept his eyes on the road and forced himself not to be distracted by the fog Rothko'd over the water, as he kept pace with the traffic and drove like a maniac, he couldn't touch her, for every obvious reason.